CUTTING REMARKS

CUTTING REMARKS

A Melanie Bass Mystery

CHRISTINE FALCONE

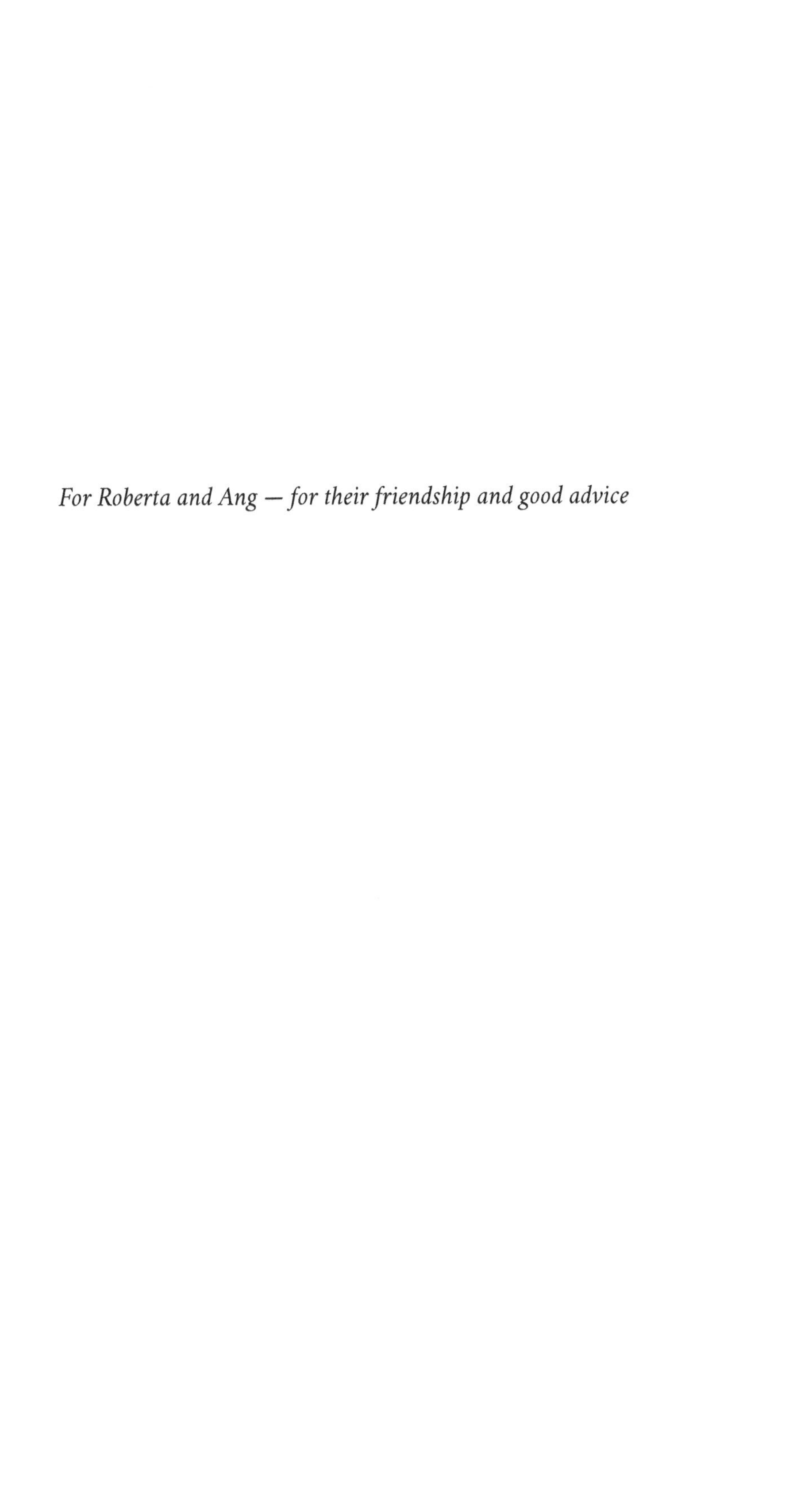

For Roberta and Ang — for their friendship and good advice

Chapter One

I could barely keep my eyes open as I drove through the April snow squall. True to its reputation, the Connecticut weather had changed from sixty-degree weather to another taste of winter. On top of the crazy weather, it had been a grueling week at work. I couldn't say "no" to Judy, my supervisor, at Coretrack Homecare, when she pleaded with me to pick up a couple of extra shifts. I was looking forward to finally having the weekend off.

As soon as I pulled into my driveway, my cell phone rang. My friend Lynn's voice was apologetic, "I know it's short notice, and you probably have plans for Sunday, but would you and Justin be able to attend brunch at Mrs. Drover's house? She called to say two of her nieces and their husbands are in town for the weekend, and she wants to introduce me to them. She asked me to invite you and Justin since you will be my maid of honor. Alex's cousin Ben will be coming also, so this is a chance for you to meet the best man."

My first response was an inward groan. I had planned to do nothing but relax on Sunday. But then again, I'd heard so much about Lynn's fiancé, Alex's mother, most of it not very good, that I was curious to meet her in person.Ummm. Sure. I'll call Justin and see if he's free to come with me."

"Thank you. I'll be glad to have backup when I meet more of Alex's family, though Alex assures me I'll get along fine with his cousins." She gave me the address of Mrs. Drover's house in Westport and said she would meet us there at 11 AM.

Lynn's relationship with her future mother-in-law had a rocky start. Mrs. Drover hired a private investigator to check on Lynn as soon as she saw her son was getting serious about her. Understandably, Lynn had not reacted well when she found out. Even before that, however, Lynn had gotten the feeling that her fiancé's mother did not approve of her, and she was struggling to form a bond with Mrs. Drover.

I called my boyfriend, Justin, as soon as I got off the phone with Lynn. He was as curious as I was to see if she was really the dragon lady Lynn made her out to be.

"I would love to be there, but I promised to cover the weekend for Pat Stuart at his small animal practice in Branford," Justin said. "I'll be over Sunday evening, though, to get your take on Alex's mother."

"All right, wish me luck. I'll give you a full report on how things went." I was disappointed he couldn't come with me, but at least I would be there should Lynn need my support.

On Sunday morning, I checked my closet for something appropriate to wear to brunch at the home of someone prominent in the Fairfield County social scene. Unfortunately, my wardrobe tipped toward long on comfortable and woefully short on chic. I settled on a navy-blue textured dress I'd worn to a Community Nursing Banquet, paired with my favorite black flats. Lucky for me, the return to winter had been fleeting, and Sunday was a cool but sunny spring day.

As I drove up Mrs. Drover's long drive, my thoughts were on Lynn and how she was fairing being surrounded by Alex's family. There were already several cars parked in the circular drive, as well as a van bearing the logo of Le Petit Gourmet. I stopped to admire the exterior of the house and surrounding property, thinking that it was certainly large for one person. I remembered, though, that Lynn had mentioned that Alex's family also owned a cottage on the Madison shoreline and that his mother usually spent much of the summer there.

After I rang the bell, the door was answered by a young lady dressed in black slacks and shirt, her hair held back in a tight bun. My assumption that she was hired to help at the brunch was confirmed when she said, "May I take your coat? Mrs. Drover and the other guests are in the sitting room to your left." She ushered me toward a room where I could hear the murmur of voices.

As I entered, I saw Lynn seated on a large sectional sofa next to an attractive brunette who appeared to be in her early thirties. It looked as if they had been engaged in a conversation, but as I entered, Lynn excused herself and came to greet me.

She whispered, "Thank heaven you're here," to me before guiding me toward a woman seated in a floral print easy chair, set apart from the rest of the guests.

"Diana, this is Melanie."

The woman had her blonde hair cut in a stylish bob, her unlined face bore very little make-up, and my first thought was that she certainly looked at least twenty years younger than what I knew her actual age must be. It was her eyes that I found most arresting, however. When I was ten years old, my parents took me to The Beardsley Zoo. Diana Drover had the same cold, assessing look I had seen on the tiger, as if deciding whether to pounce or walk away.

Diana held out her hand. I took it, and for one crazy moment, wasn't sure if she wanted me to kiss it or shake it. Instead, she gave my hand a firm squeeze, "So glad to finally meet you."

"Nice to meet you also," I said.

I was saved from having to make any small talk with her by one of the waitpersons entering and announcing that brunch was ready to be served.

Once seated, Lynn introduced me to the rest of the guests and explained I would be serving as her maid of honor. I tried to be as inconspicuous as possible as I studied the people gathered around the table. Alex's cousins, Jill and Olivia, and their husbands seemed laid back and appeared to really like Lynn. Alex's cousin Ben didn't join in the easy teasing between his sisters, but when asked why he was so quiet, he apologized and said he'd had a busy week at work and was still recovering. I also noted that he was the only one at the table to down three Bloody Marys. All in all, though, the brunch seemed to be going well.

We had nearly finished eating, and the catering staff was pouring second cups of coffee, when the doorbell rang. I noticed when we were first seated that there was one empty chair at the table next to me, but I assumed it had been meant for Justin.

A woman's voice came from the foyer, "I remember the way, thanks!"

I was sitting across from Alex and Lynn, and as soon as the woman spoke, I saw Alex stiffen slightly, a confused look on his face.

"Hi all!" The woman who appeared in the doorway was stunning. Her pale blonde hair was pulled back into a loose bun, and her turquoise blouse brought out the unusual blue-green of her eyes. She gave off the air of someone who was used to making an entrance.

Diana stood and held out her arms. "Celia! So glad you could make it!" They exchanged air kisses, and as Celia turned to smile at the group, Diana said, "You all remember Celia Pound, she and Alex were inseparable growing up!" There were some murmurs of "hello" and "nice to see you" around the table. Diana turned to the woman, "I was so thrilled to hear that you were back in town. Do sit down." She motioned to the only available seat, next to me and across from Alex.

Judging by the uncomfortable looks on his cousins' faces and the terrified look on Alex's, I had a sneaking suspicion that Alex and Celia had been more than childhood friends at some point. This was confirmed when Celia flounced over to where Alex was rooted to his seat. She bent to give him a noisy kiss and said, "Oh, I'm so glad to see you, darling!"

I glanced across the table at Lynn. I could see the color starting to rise on Lynn's face, and her jaw was firmly set. I could tell she was trying to hide her reaction to what Celi had just done.

"You're looking wonderful 'Zander! I guess you're thriving now that you are rid of that harpy, Astrid. Now that you are free, we have to go out and tear up the town again for old times' sake." She seemed to notice Lynn for the first time then and held out her hand to Lynn, "Hi. You are?"

Alex suddenly jolted out of his daze. "Oh, I'd like you to meet my fiancé, Lynn. Lynn, my friend Celia."

Celia quickly looked toward the head of the table where Diana was seated, a puzzled look on her face. "Oh, congratulations. Lynn, please don't take offense at what I said, I like to tease Alex." I thought her apology sounded sincere.

All talking at the table had stopped briefly while Celia made her grand entrance, but now Alex's cousin Jill leaned over to whisper to Lynn, "Astrid *was* a harpy, though." That broke the ice, and people started up a conversation again.

I introduced myself to Celia and did my best to keep her engaged in conversation and from talking to either Alex or Lynn. I learned she worked for an art gallery in the city, was single, and hadn't seen Alex in a couple of years. She was thrilled to get a call from Diana Drover inviting her to stop over this morning, so glad to see "everyone" again and pleased to hear Alex was remarrying. I noticed a definite lack of conviction in that last part.

Just when it seemed that brunch would end without any further unpleasant surprises, Diana cleared her throat and said, "Celia, how was your buying trip in Milan? Did you find what you were hoping to obtain for the gallery?"

Celia smiled and said, "I found one piece I think will be worth the trip. I'll show you a photo of it later."

"Lynn, tell Celia what it is you do. You dabble a bit with painting, don't you? She might be able to give you some advice on how fine art is done." The malice in Diana's voice was unmistakable.

I could see the color rise in Lynn's face again. Before she could respond, however, Alex said, "Mother! Lynn does more than dabble, and you know it!"

Diana's voice was syrupy as she said, "I'm sorry. I was only trying to help. I thought maybe Celia could..."

Lynn jumped up and threw her napkin onto the table, and said, "Excuse me a moment, please." I got up to follow her as she ran out of the room.

I could hear Alex saying something to his mother as I steered Lynn toward the sofa in the sitting room. "Sit a minute and just breathe. What Mrs. Drover did was meant to upset you. Don't let it. Her words were mean-spirited and obviously untrue." I could see now that Diana Drover was indeed a dragon lady.

"I can't believe she invited that woman. I know exactly what she's trying to do. She wants to make sure that Alex and I never get married." She wiped the tears that had started to drip down her cheeks and, raising her voice, said, "Well, Alex and I *will* get married even if it is over her dead body!"

Alex's cousin Olivia was just coming into the room and hesitated briefly at Lynn's outburst. "Uh…I just wanted to make sure you are all right. Can I get you anything?"

Lynn gave her a weak smile, "No, thank you. I'll be okay."

Olivia nodded and then said, "Don't pay any attention to my aunt. We all know she is a difficult woman to be around." She patted Lynn's shoulder before she left the room.

"What can I do?" I asked Lynn. "Shall I get Alex?"

I had just finished speaking when Alex strode into the room. "Lynn, I don't think my mother meant to offend you." He sat down on the other side of her and put his arm around her shoulders, kissing her gently on the temple. "Don't let what happened ruin our day. Come say goodbye, and then we can leave."

I took that as my cue to leave also, but said to Lynn as I stood up, "Will you be all right?"

"Yes, thank you."

I sincerely doubted what Mrs. Drover did and said was meant innocently, and I couldn't believe Alex thought that either.

As I left the sitting room, I passed Celia standing outside, just to the side of the doorway, an unreadable look on her face. The word 'lurking' came to mind, but then maybe I was projecting my ire at Mrs. Drover onto Celia.

The party was clearly over now as Alex's cousins were retrieving their coats and bidding each other goodbye.

As Jill's husband helped her into her coat, she said, "Please tell Lynn we said goodbye. It was wonderful to meet her."

"Yes, and tell her we are looking forward to the wedding, and if there is anything she needs help with to please let me know," Olivia said. The sisters and their spouses walked out together.

Before I left, I glanced into the dining room again to see Alex's cousin Ben talking to his aunt. I couldn't hear what he was saying, but from the way he was gesturing, then standing with his arms crossed shaking his head, he was obviously upset. I hoped he was telling her how inappropriate her behavior was. She seemed not to be fazed by whatever he was saying and flicked her hand as if shooing a fly before turning and walking away.

I grabbed my coat and left. It had certainly turned out to be a memorable brunch. I was glad I had been there for Lynn but realized she had not been exaggerating the effort it would take to get along with her future mother-in-law. I was afraid I did not foresee a good outcome.

Chapter Two

The following day, Lynn's issues with Mrs. Drover were still very much on my mind. I had to put my concerns aside for now however, as our agency was still very busy, and I had patients to see.

At lunch time I stopped in at the office to pick up a few supplies before my afternoon appointments. A woman I had never seen before was talking to my supervisor, Judy.

"Melanie! I'm glad you're here. I want to introduce you to somebody. This is Nora Stevens; she is thinking about coming to work with us. She recently moved to the area and says she has heard good things about Coretrack. She has four years of experience working as a nurse in home healthcare. I've told her we'd love to have her join our agency."

Nora looked to be in her late twenties, just a few years younger than me, but there seemed to be an aura of self-containment about her that I usually associated with someone much older.

"I'm Melanie Bass. Welcome." I smiled and gave her a quick wave, and she nodded in return.

Judy cleared her throat, "I've given her the basic low down on how we operate at Coretrack, but I was wondering, could you let her shadow you this afternoon on your patient visits?" Judy gave me a pleading look.

I felt like I'd been ambushed. I was usually happy to help orient new nurses to our organization, but I had planned on trying to squeak in a couple of quick errands before I saw my first patient of the afternoon. I absolutely *had* to get to the grocery store, and if I didn't get to the pet supply store, my little terrier, Bruno, was going to give me his sad-eyed look when I had no more doggie treats for him. There was no way I could opt out of doing it, though. Judy had always been accommodating when I needed time off for personal reasons or to switch a day off. I'd have to try and do my errands after work.

"Sure. I'll call Mrs. Paine and see if it's okay if I get to her house a bit early. She's very sweet but tends to be chatty, and that way, I can stay on schedule without stressing about being late for the next patient." I suggested to Nora that we take my car and I drop her off at the agency after I finished seeing the patients on my schedule for the afternoon.

"Certainly." She gathered up her bag and jacket from the chair where she had left them and followed me to my Subaru.

Neither one of us said much as I headed toward Mrs. Paine's house. My mind kept drifting to the way the previous day's brunch had ended at Mrs. Drover's. However, after a while, I felt the silence was becoming uncomfortable and decided to ask Nora a bit about herself. "So, are you from Connecticut?"

"Uh. No. Why?" When I glanced over at her, she looked like I'd asked her for her bank account number.

"I didn't know if you were familiar with this area. Are you from somewhere else in New England?"

I could have sworn I saw her visibly relax. "No, I've not been to this part of the country before. I came from Arizona."

"Really! Where in Arizona? I have a friend who is from the Phoenix area."

"Oh, well, I'm not actually *from* Arizona. I was just working there for a while, in a really small county tucked up in the northwest corner. Your friend probably never heard of it. I never even got to visit Phoenix while I was there." She let out a nervous laugh.

Too bad, I thought. It would have been nice to establish a connection through Lynn.

I tried again. "Are you married? I'm divorced. Well, I was, but my ex-husband was murdered, so I'm not sure what that makes me now." She was making me feel awkward, and I'm prone to babbling when I'm uncomfortable.

"No. Not married."

"Have you always worked in home care? I worked in med-surg before I started at Coretrack."

"No."

I waited for her to elaborate, but she said nothing more. It was like prying gum off the sidewalk to get information out of Nora. Luckily, we were almost at Mrs. Paine's house, so I decided to stop asking questions which she didn't seem too enthused to answer. I just hoped she would exhibit a bit more willingness to interact with the patients.

I needn't have worried. I introduced her to Mrs. Paine, who was eighty-four and being monitored for congestive heart failure. I explained that Nora was considering joining our agency, and Mrs. Paine took it from there.

"Oh, I hope you do decide to work for Coretrack." Mrs. Paine took my hand in one of hers and grabbed Nora's with the other. "Melanie is wonderful! All the nurses there are wonderful! I have had such a good experience with that agency. Over the years, that has not always been the case with some of the homecare places I've had to deal with." She dropped both our hands and looked up into Nora's eyes, and said, "Do join their forces!"

Nora smiled at her. "Well, if all their patients are as lovely as you, I just might."

After having to refuse her offer of tea and cookies three times, I assured Mrs. Paine she was doing a very good job in following her medication and diet regime and checked to make sure she had her next doctor's appointment made and had no questions for me. We left with just enough time to make my next appointment.

The next visit went well also, and I noticed Nora seemed comfortable with my routine and even made a bit of small talk with Mr. and Mrs. Everton. Mostly just comparing the weather in New England versus the Southwest, but it was at least something.

As we left the Evertons' house, I said, "We have been really busy lately, but I have an unusually light afternoon today, so that is everyone I have scheduled. Are there any questions about the agency I can answer for you?"

"No. Thank you for taking me along today."

"Well, I hope it helped you make your decision about coming to work at

Coretrack." Something about her made me unsure of what I hoped that decision would be.

I dropped her off at her car. It was easy to spot as it was the only one in the lot with Arizona plates. I would have to mention her to Lynn. Though, come to think of it, Nora never told me the name of the town she worked in, or even where she was before that. I knew that Judy would want a report on how it went with Nora. I decided I would tell her I found her quiet but willing to engage with patients and that she seemed to be familiar with some of our usual patient care. I would leave it at that, however, since I would feel petty telling her that I couldn't help but find something strange about the woman.

Chapter Three

After I finished writing my nursing notes on my patients, I finally had time to catch up on my errands. I not only stocked up on groceries and dog treats but bought a new squeaky toy I knew Bruno would love.

I planned to call Lynn after dinner. I wanted to find out if there had been any more drama after I left Sunday morning, and to see if Alex had told her more about his past relationship with Celia Pound. Before I got a chance to call her, however, I looked out the front window to see Lynn's car pulling into my driveway.

After she greeted Bruno with a pat on the head and a scratch under the chin, Lynn looked at me and raised her eyebrows. "Quite the morning yesterday, wasn't it? Thank you again for being there. I don't know how I would have coped with Diana if I hadn't had your support."

"Were there any more issues after I left?"

"No. I didn't know how I was going to face Diana again, but as it turned out, I never even had to see her to say goodbye. *Celia* evidently wanted to show her some photos or something, so they went off together to Diana's study. Alex whisked me out of there right after you left."

"What do you think possessed Mrs. Drover to invite Celia to stop over on Sunday?" I asked, even though I was pretty sure I knew the answer.

"To provoke me, of course." Lynn went over to the sink to fill a glass with water, then sat at the kitchen table. "Alex and I had a ...discussion...last evening. I let him know I was still livid about his mother's insults and the fact that she had invited one of his former girlfriends to come to the house while we were having a pre-wedding get-together. Alex said I had no reason to be upset, he and Celia were over a long time ago, and that I should ignore his mother's comments."

"What did you say?" I thought Alex was being insensitive to think that what his mother said and did could be so easily brushed off.

"I told him it wasn't that easy. His mother's behavior really hurt me. I told him he was blind if he didn't see that she was trying to get us to call off the wedding. He denied it, of course. He said, 'that's just the way she is' and that she had no objection to the wedding."

"Oh boy."

"Oh boy, is right. But like I said, I refuse to let her get in the way of our marriage."

I knew it would take a lot of patience and forgiveness on Lynn's part, but if she truly loved Alex and was sure she wanted to marry him, I believed she would succeed. "Alex's cousins seemed nice, at least."

"Yes, they seemed genuinely happy for us and made me feel comfortable right away. Alex said the four of them were close when they were kids. He said for years, he and his cousins and their parents would all spend a month or so together at the cottage in Madison and that it was always the best time of the summer."

"That's wonderful! It is obvious that they still maintain a bond." I couldn't help wondering, though, if Alex's mother had always been difficult and how that had affected their vacations. It sounded like whatever happened then; he only remembered it as a good time. "Has Alex ever taken you to see the cottage?"

"Not yet. He's told me about it, though. He said that it was built after the First World War by his great-grandfather as a family vacation home. According to him, there is some kind of complicated stipulation as to who actually inherits it, but that it has always been for the use of whoever in his family wants to spend time there. Even though I haven't seen it in person yet, I have seen pictures taken there when Alex and his cousins were young. I don't think either you or I would consider it a cottage, though. From what I understand, it has six or seven bedrooms, two living rooms, and a boathouse.

Alex said there was some updating done in the eighties and the early 2000s, but in general, the house is much the same as when his great-grandfather had it built."

"Wow! That sounds amazing. I would love to see the place myself."

Lynn laughed, "Well, you just might be able to wangle an invitation soon. I have an in with a member of the family."

Lynn stifled a yawn. "I think it's time I headed home. I didn't sleep well last night after what happened at Diana Drover's and then the argument with Alex. Thank you for listening to my woes again."

"I was glad to do it. Try to focus on the happy aspects of your upcoming wedding. You can't control how Mrs. Drover acts, but you can control how you act in response."

Lynn nodded and said, "Good advice, but that woman knows just how to push my buttons so I respond in the worst possible way."

Chapter Four

I received a call from Judy at Coretrack Homecare on Wednesday. She called to let me know that Nora Stevens had been hired and would start the following day.

"I'm hoping she won't require a long orientation before we can let her take patients of her own. You said she seemed familiar with a lot of our practices and procedures, right?"

"Well, I only had the one afternoon we spent together, so I can't tell if she'll be able to jump right in or if she needs to work with someone else before she's ready to see patients on her own." I certainly didn't feel comfortable vouching for Nora's ability based on the short time I spent with her. "I think..."

"That's why I want you to be the one to work with her. You can get a better idea about her and make sure she is giving safe care." I could hear the strain in Judy's voice. "You'll do it, won't you?"

I couldn't get rid of the unease I felt in agreeing to do what Judy was asking. I'd never felt this way before, and I couldn't put my finger on what was different this time. "All right. I'll work with her, but if I feel she's not right for the agency, I'm going to let you know right away."

Judy let out a sigh of relief. "Thank you."

I had just gotten off the phone with Judy and was about to take Bruno for a walk when I got another call.

Lynn was talking so fast I couldn't understand her at first. "...dead. They found her this afternoon. Alex called..."

"Who's dead?" I got a chill up my spine as I anticipated her answer.

"Diana Drover. Alex called me a few minutes ago. He wanted me to hear it from him before it was all over the news. She was found at the cottage in Madison. Alex said he has no idea what she was doing there. It's early in the season for her to want to spend any time there. The groundskeeper found her when he came to do his scheduled maintenance. Alex was so distraught I didn't get much more information from him."

I had no warm feelings toward Mrs. Drover, but I still felt shocked and saddened to hear she was dead. "That's horrible! Do you know what happened? Why she died?"

I could hear Lynn take a shuddering breath, "Alex used the word 'killed.' That makes it seem like it wasn't natural causes. I don't know if it was an accident or…do you think someone could have murdered her?'

From what I had heard about her and, given what I witnessed with my own eyes, that was a good possibility. "I don't know, but certainly, the police will be looking to rule that out."

"Melanie—I was there yesterday! What if she was already dead, or what if she was murdered and whoever killed her was still there when I was?"

"You were at the cottage? What time? Was Alex with you?"

Lynn hesitated a moment before replying. "I went on my own after one of my afternoon classes. I remembered the address, and since we were just discussing it on Monday, I got curious about the house. I decided to go and take a quick look, maybe peer in the windows, to see what the inside looks like. I know how creepy that sounds, but I figured it wouldn't hurt anything. I thought I might do a painting of the house as a surprise for Alex. I was going to ask him to give me the grand tour this weekend. But now…."

It sounded like she was beginning to hyperventilate. "Lynn. Listen to me. Take a deep breath. We don't even know for sure she was murdered. Did you notice anyone else there? Maybe see a car parked in the driveway or nearby?"

"No. I don't remember if I even saw Mrs. Drover's car there. I don't know, I can't remember. The driveway is long, and there are trees and brush shielding it from the main road. There is a garage—I think. When I got there, I was focusing on the house itself. It is beautiful. Big and rustic, I thought it was very welcoming looking. I could see some of the neighboring houses along the shore, but it didn't look like anyone else was around. At least I didn't think so at first."

"What do you mean? Did you see someone else?"

"While I was there, I had a little accident." She took a deep breath and said, "I was going up the steps to the wrap-around porch, and I thought I heard a noise, a soft thump, or a bang or something. It sounded like it was coming from somewhere on the property. When I turned around to look, I scraped my hand on something sticking out of the railing. Whatever it was gave me a nice gouge on the back of my hand. I was so startled, I dropped my keys and then bumped my nose when I bent to pick them up."

"Oh, dear. Are you all right?"

"Yes, fine now, but when it happened, there was blood everywhere. I grabbed some tissues from my purse, but by then between my hand and my nose, my jacket was totally ruined. I was standing on the porch, thinking about what a mess I was, when I heard someone calling to me. It was a woman, a neighbor, I guess. She wanted to know why I was there and what had happened to me. She sounded very unfriendly and seemed to insinuate that I was trespassing. I was so flustered, I suddenly felt like an intruder. Instead of telling her who I was and why I was there I just said everything was fine and I must have the wrong address. Then I just left."

"The woman who spoke to you, do you remember what she looked like? Did she call to you from her yard or did she come over to you?"

"She just called me from her property. I only have a vague memory of what she looked like. Older, thin. Strong voice, though."

"Try to remember all you can about what you saw and heard while you were there. What was the noise you heard? Were there any sounds coming from the house? It'll be important if they confirm Mrs. Drover didn't die due to an accident."

"I realize I need to try to remember everything I noticed, but right now, I can't help thinking about anything but poor Alex. He sounded devastated when he called me."

"Where is Alex now?"

"He went to talk to the police and to identify her body." She sounded as if she was about to burst into tears. "I offered to go with him, but he said he wanted to go alone. He said he would call me after he was through with the formalities."

I gave Bruno the command to sit and grabbed his leash off the hook by the front door. "Why don't you put the kettle on for tea? Bruno and I are coming over to sit with you while you wait to hear from Alex."

"All right." I could hear her stifle a sob. "I admit I wanted Alex's mother to butt out of our lives, but not like this!"

On the way to Lynn's condo, I thought about what Mrs. Drover's death would mean for Lynn and Alex's wedding. They were due to be married in four months, and I couldn't imagine that it wouldn't throw a pall over the celebration. I did feel very bad for Alex; it was shocking to lose his mother that way. I imagined that Lynn must feel a little guilty, too, given how she had felt about Mrs. Drover. It was often easier to forget the wrongs someone did to you when they were no longer around.

I was glad I took Bruno with me, not only because I owed him an outing since he never got his walk, but once I got to Lynn's, I realized how comforting it was to have him along. Bruno was his usual rambunctious self and showed Lynn how glad he was to see her. She immediately picked him up and kissed and cuddled him. I could see that she had been crying before we got there.

I reached out to hug her. "I'm sorry."

She took a deep breath, then said, "I don't deserve your sympathy right now. I'm not crying over Diama's death. I'm ashamed because a part of me is relieved that I won't have to deal with her in the future. That's terrible, isn't it?"

The same thought had also passed through my mind, and I had felt a bit guilty about it, also. "No. I mean, it is awful the woman is dead. But I can see how you would feel that way. Or at least have conflicted feelings about her death."

Lynn nodded. "I knew you'd understand. But I would never want Alex to know I feel like that."

As I looked around her living room, I noticed a few boxes sitting near her painting supplies. "What's all this?"

She followed my gaze and said, "Oh. I thought it was time I got a more professional space for my painting. I found a little place where I can work downtown. I was getting ready to move my things there when I heard about Diana."

"Do you have any more information on what happened? Has Alex called you yet?"

"No. Not yet."

Just then, Lynn's phone rang.

Her conversation with Alex was brief. I heard her gasp at one point and say, "Oh, no! That's horrible. So, there is no doubt, then. Why don't I come to your….okay, please be careful, and call me later."

Lynn ended the call, a stricken look on her face. "It looks like Diana died of a stab wound. Her neck. The police are still searching for the murder weapon. They say it was a long, thin blade." She had lost what little color she had left and looked like she was about to be sick.

"Do you need to go to Alex? I can give you a ride if you are feeling shaky," I said.

"No. Alex said his cousin Ben was with him. He said Ben was taking him for a drink…or two. He'll call me later when he is back at his place."

Both Lynn and I sat quietly for a few minutes. Even though I knew it was a possibility, it still came as a shock to me that Mrs. Drover was murdered. Both Lynn and I had experienced the killing of someone close to us before when Artie Krapaneck was killed. But it never loses its impact when someone you know is murdered.

"Who would want to kill Mrs. Drover?" I said. Lynn looked up suddenly, and the look she gave me made me realize how silly that question was. "I mean, who would actually go through with it?"

Lynn said, "I suppose it could have been an intruder. From what Alex told me it was unusual for anyone to be at the house this time of year. Maybe someone thought the house was empty and was looking for valuables; though I have no idea what was kept there that was valuable."

"Was the door unlocked the day you went there?"

Lynn shook her head. "I never got as far as trying the door. The neighbor stopped me before I was close enough to look in the windows or anything."

"You said the groundskeeper found her? She was inside the house, though?"

Lynn nodded. "That's what Alex said."

"I wonder what made the groundskeeper check the house. Did he routinely go inside when he came to do his work? I'm sure the police will question him if they haven't done so already." I suddenly thought of Sunny Cody. She had investigated Artie's death, and after I had helped her with a case last fall, we had become friends. Sort of. I wondered if she would share any information she received with me now. Just as quickly, I realized it wasn't likely. Unless Lynn and I found something that would help her with her investigation.

Lynn was apparently thinking along similar lines. "Do you think Detective Cody will be investigating Di... the murder?"

"I don't know. I think so, though I know there is also a new detective working at the department now."

The alarm on Lynn's watch went off. "Shoot. I have an art class to teach at the community center in forty-five minutes. I better wash my face and get ready."

"Will you be all right to do your class? I'm sure if you explain the circumstances, it will be fine if you cancel."

She gave me a weak smile. "No. I feel less shaky now, and besides, it will give me something to concentrate on besides what happened and waiting for Alex's call."

"Okay, then. Bruno and I will let you get ready. Be sure to call if you find out anything else, or you need anything." We gave each other a parting hug, and she reached down to stroke Bruno once more.

"Thank you for coming over. I'll let you know what I find out from Alex."

Chapter Five

When I got home, I called Justin to let him know what had happened to Mrs. Drover. He was just as shocked as I had been.

"She was *murdered?* Do the police have any suspects yet?"

"I really don't know anything more."

"How is Lynn taking it? She and Mrs. Drover weren't exactly close, were they?"

I suddenly felt protective of Lynn. "That's true, but she is still very upset over what happened!"

"Sorry, of course she would be." He was quiet for a few seconds, "The police will be all over this, though. Right?"

I knew what he was hinting at. "I'm sure they will. But I can't deny I'm anxious to know who did it."

The moment of silence at his end of the call told me he knew what I was thinking. "Well, I hope the police make an arrest quickly, you know, so there is no need for you to be snooping around."

"I hope so, too. Not that it will take away the pain I'm sure Alex feels at the death of his mother, but at least it may offer him some closure." I purposely avoided responding to the second part of what he'd said.

* * *

I was a little worried when I didn't hear from Lynn that evening, but then I thought maybe Alex did have a few more drinks than planned with his cousin and didn't call her until late. It was also possible that she had gone to his house when he got home, and they needed to spend some time alone together dealing with the death of his mother.

As I drove to work the next day, I knew I wouldn't have much time to mull over who could have killed Mrs. Drover. I had promised Judy I would act as a preceptor for Nora Stevens, evaluating her care and helping her settle in at Coretrack. Nora hadn't been particularly sociable on the day I first met her, but I thought maybe it was because she was unsure if she would accept the nursing position Judy offered her. She might have been so closemouthed because she felt she wouldn't have any dealings with me ever again. In any case, I just needed to make sure she gave appropriate and safe nursing care; we didn't need to become best friends.

Nora was waiting for me when I got to the office. Judy said that all the paperwork was completed, and Nora was ready to accompany me on my patient visits.

As we got in my car, I said, "So. Judy said you have had several years' experience doing homecare. Is that right?"

She glanced at me and said, "Yes. That's right."

"You said you last worked in Arizona; did you always work there? Is that where you are from?"

"No."

I was getting a bit impatient with Nora's reluctance to share information. She suddenly gave me a weak smile and said, "Colorado. I'm from Colorado."

"Okay. Thanks. I'd love to hear about it sometime. I've always wanted to visit the Rocky Mountains." I didn't think it would be any use to grill her any further, and we were almost at our first patient's house, anyway.

As we pulled into Mr. Ryan's driveway, I said, "I'll introduce you and explain that you are new to the agency. Mr. Ryan is seventy-eight years old and on anticoagulants for a heart arrhythmia. He had a stroke two months ago. He is doing well now, but his physician still wants us to monitor his progress, and I want to see how his wife is doing. She was glad when he was discharged home from the rehab facility, but a bit nervous also. She's particularly concerned about whether he will be able to manage getting in and out of chairs and bed on his own. Why don't you examine him and check that he is taking his meds? If you have any questions or need help with anything, I'll be glad to back you up. Is that all right?"

"Of course." She grabbed her work bag from the rear seat and was out of the car and halfway to the front door before I caught up with her.

Nora became a different person once she started Mr. Ryan's care. She immediately set him at ease with a gently joking manner, and she was very efficient in checking his vitals and in doing a physical assessment. I found I had nothing to do but stand there and smile and make small talk with Mrs. Ryan. It was a good start to the day.

Our next stop was with Mrs. Paine, who took full credit for convincing Nora to come to work at Coretrack Homecare. Like the first visit, I found Nora was competent to handle all the care on her own. As the day wore on, I had to do very little in the way of instructing Nora on caring for our patients. I was relieved that it appeared she would not need a long orientation period after all. I couldn't say her social skills outside the patient environment were good, but she had good communication skills while giving care.

I dropped Nora off at the office after we were through for the day and after all the charting was done. I was going back to my car, when I ran into my friend and colleague, Debbie.

After we caught up on what was happening in our lives, Debbie said, "I hear you are orienting the new nurse, Nora." She smirked at me, "I spoke to her the other day. Or I should say, I spoke, and she dodged every effort at pleasant conversation."

"She is different with the patients, though. I was impressed by her level of care." I hesitated, "But..."

"I know. There's something odd about her, like there's a puzzle piece missing somewhere."

I nodded. "My feelings exactly."

Debbie patted my arm, "Well, good luck."

I felt a bit guilty after speaking to Debbie. Just because Nora was stingy in sharing personal info it was not right to label her as odd. I had to agree with Debbie, though, in spite of her nursing abilities, something about Nora still made me feel uncomfortable.

As I drove home, my thoughts quickly shifted to the murder of Lynn's future mother-in-law. As I expected, Diana Drover's death had made all the news feeds, but very little had been released about the specifics of her murder or any potential suspects. All the stories focused on Mrs. Drover's prominent position in local society and her reputation as a champion fundraiser for several charities. By listening to the media reports, you would certainly think Diana Drover had been a pillar of the community. There was no denying that she was involved in good works, but I couldn't imagine that Mrs. Drover had a habit of only offending those close to her. In her dealings with those working on those committees and fund-raising events, she must have ruffled a few feathers at least.

I still hadn't heard from Lynn by that evening, so after Bruno and I took our after-dinner walk, I decided to call her. I wondered if she had gotten any more information on what the police think happened, or if Alex had any thoughts on why his mother was at the cottage or who could have killed her.

Lynn answered her phone right away. "Hi. Are you at home, or are you at Alex's house?"

"I'm home. I spoke to Alex late last night, and I went to see him this afternoon. He's trying hard to keep it together, but I think he's still in shock. He hasn't gotten much information from the police on anything yet. They did tell him that he will have to wait for the results of the autopsy before the body can be released for burial."

"How about you? Are you holding up okay?" I said.

Lynn sighed, "I'm doing okay. I'm just upset for Alex. He asked me if I would help him pick out burial clothes and with the arrangements for the funeral. I said I would, but suggested his cousins, Jill and Olivia, also help. I don't want full responsibility for arranging Diana's last 'event.' I have visions of her rising up from the dead and berating me for what I chose to bury her in and the selection of music at her service!"

"I'm sure you'll do fine," I said. "Do you have any thoughts on who could have murdered her? Did Alex ever mention her having any enemies?"

"He never mentioned her having any rivals or anything. But then Alex never really discussed much about his mother with me, other than relaying her strong suggestions for every aspect of our wedding." Lynn paused for a moment, "I do remember overhearing her once ranting on about a woman named Wendy Reich. She called her a sanctimonious bitch and said that she couldn't understand why people didn't see her for what she was. I have no idea who she is or what Diana was so upset about."

I jotted down the name "Wendy Reichs," followed by a question mark. "I'll see if I can find out who she is and if the dislike was mutual."

"Wait. I want to know who killed her also, but shouldn't we leave it up to the police to investigate?"

"Of course, but I thought…"

Lynn didn't let me finish, "But I suppose if we check a few things out ourselves and are careful…"

"I agree. If we find out anything, we can let the police know and they could take it from there." I swore to myself that was exactly what we would do.

The following morning, I googled Wendy Reichs. I found out she was a long-time member of the Norwalk Hospital Women's Auxiliary, head of the Westport Clothes for Kids Drive, and the founder and president of an organization called We Are Here To Help. I then googled the organization and learned they had received a Community Star award for their work in aiding recent immigrants get settled in their new communities in the surrounding towns. It sounded like something Diana Drover would have supported, so I wondered why she would not have had an alliance with Mrs. Reichs. As I searched further, however, I found a small article written the previous fall. It hinted at discord in We Are Here To Help. It said that Diana Drover, well known for her many charitable works, charged financial irregularities in the management of WAHTH. Those allegations eventually proved to be unfounded, but due to the questions Mrs. Drover raised the organization lost one of its "most powerful backers". That would certainly be a reason for Wendy Reichs to have a grudge against Mrs. Drover.

I printed out the information, and the next day, I decided to go to see Lynn and let her know what I had found out. I could also see if she had heard any more about when Mrs. Drover's services could be held.

As I put on my jacket to leave, I glanced over to find Bruno sitting calmly, staring at me.

"Okay, you can come. Let's take a ride to see Auntie Lynn again."

As I pulled into a visitor parking space at Lynn's condo complex, I saw a familiar figure getting out of her car. Detective Sunny Cody turned as I called out to her. "Hi. I'd ask what you are doing here, but I assume it has to do with the murder of Lynn's future mother-in-law."

Sunny gave me a strained smile. "Yes, I need to get a statement from Mrs. Duncan. Why are you here?" I saw Sunny glance down at Bruno, and her expression softened.

"Lynn's been pretty rattled by what happened to Mrs. Drover. I'm here to see how she is doing today." I didn't add that we were trying to get a lot of the same information she was.

We approached the door together, and when it opened Lynn looked at Sunny Cody and then raised her eyebrows at me. "Please. Come in." She stooped down to pet Bruno and murmur to him briefly.

I gave Lynn a quick hug and said, "I came to see how you are doing. I met Detective Cody on the way in."

Sunny motioned to the living room area. "I'd like to ask you a few questions, Mrs. Duncan." She looked at me, "I can ask Ms. Bass to wait outside, if you like."

I felt a sense of alarm at her formality.

"No, of course not. I'd like Melanie to stay." Lynn suddenly sounded a bit strained, and I thought she might be starting to feel the same sense of apprehension I felt. She motioned us to sit and pulled Bruno up into her lap. "How can I help you? I was shocked at Mrs. Drover's death," her voice wobbled a little, "and my fiancé is, understandably, not taking it well either, I'm afraid."

Sunny looked down at a small pad she held in her hands. "I'll get right to the point. We have a witness who described seeing a car parked at the cottage on the day of Mrs. Drover's death. She was able to describe the car and get a partial plate number. It was your car."

I made a mental note, so they did think Diana had been killed on the day

Lynn was there.

Lynn took a deep breath, "Yes, I'm sorry. I guess I should have come in before this to let you know. I went there to look at the house. I planned to do a painting of it for my fiancé. A woman, I think it was a neighbor, startled me before I could see much of it, however. I left right after she accosted me. Was she the one who reported seeing me?"

Detective Cody didn't answer her question. "So, you didn't go into the house? You didn't see or speak to Mrs. Drover?"

"No! I had no idea she was even there. When do they think …she was killed?"

Again, Sunny didn't answer Lynn. I was beginning to get a bad feeling. I saw her look at the dressing on Lynn's left hand. "How did you injure your hand?"

"I…there must have been a nail or a piece of metal sticking out near the railing. I cut my hand when I was going up the stairs." It seemed Lynn suddenly got the implication of what Sunny was asking. Bruno must have picked up on Lynn's tension, because he leapt from her lap and came to rest by my feet. I was surprised he didn't sense my own unease.

"There was blood on the front porch and the stairs leading from it. The woman who saw you said your jacket was covered in blood."

"I was startled when I cut my hand and dropped my keys. When I bent to pick them up, I banged my nose, and it started to bleed." She sounded very flustered. "The blood on my jacket was from my nose. I guess it dripped onto the floor of the porch, also."

Sunny jotted something in her little notebook. "Where is that jacket now?"

"I…threw it away. I couldn't get the blood stains out." There were tears in Lynn's eyes now.

I started to interrupt and remind Sunny how silly it was for her to be suspicious of Lynn, but before I could say anything, she continued. "Mrs. Duncan, we have heard from two witnesses that you threatened Mrs. Drover. That you said you would marry Dr. Drover, and I quote, 'even if it is over her dead body.'"

Lynn turned the color of uncooked dough. "I never meant it literally. I would never actually hurt her!"

I couldn't hold my tongue any longer. "This is ridiculous! People make silly threats all the time. Sun…, Detective Cody you know darn well Lynn didn't kill Mrs. Drover, I can't believe you are even following this line of investigation!" I jumped up and rushed to stand by Lynn, placing my hand on her shoulder. Bruno jumped back onto the couch and nestled against Lynn's hip in what I took to be a show of solidarity.

Sunny didn't respond but stood up and went over to where Lynn had her easel and paints set up. She looked around briefly, then, donning a latex glove, picked up Lynn's palette knife. It was blunt-tipped, and from what I could see, pretty flexible. I couldn't imagine it being used as a murder weapon, but Sunny turned to Lynn and said, "I'm going to need to take this."

I jumped up. "Really, Sunny…"

Lynn said, "Take it. The only thing you'll find on it is crimson paint." She waved toward the painting of a field of poppies she had been working on.

Sunny ignored both of us, took out an evidence bag, and dropped the palette knife into it. Taking off her glove and shoving the kit back into her pocket, Sunny said, "We'll be speaking to you again, Mrs. Duncan. You'll need to remain in the area." With that, she turned and left.

"Stay Bruno!" I rushed out after her, jogging to keep up. "Come on, Sunny, you can't be serious! You know Lynn, she didn't do this. Violence is not in her nature."

Sunny stopped and turned to me, "Look, I came to do this interview as a favor to you and to her. This is Detective Crane's case. He wanted to question her down at the station. I had to ask, no, beg, to be the one to question her and to do a preliminary interview here. He's going to want to question her again himself, and when he does, it's going to be on his turf. This is just a taste of what's in store for her. Her history of discord with the victim is not going to work in her favor."

"In spite of her good works, Diana Drover was not a nice woman. I'm sure you'll find that there probably is more than one person who threatened her. From what I found out…" I saw the look on Sunny's face and cut off what I was about to say.

"No. No. You are not to start your own inquiry into this. I know you have helped me in the past, but as I said, this is not my investigation. Support your friend the best you can but leave the detective work to the police department." She opened the door to her car, and, before she got in, said, "I know you think Lynn isn't capable of killing someone, but you never really know how a person will act when under stress."

I began to walk back toward Lynn's door, thinking that Lynn had once said the same thing to me.

Chapter Six

I let myself back into Lynn's condo and found her sitting on her little painting stool in front of a blank canvas she had set up in the corner of her living room. Bruno was lying on the floor beside her. She didn't turn around, but said, "What do I do now? They think I killed her."

The despair in her voice was heartbreaking. I went to stand beside her. "I'm sure at this stage, the police have to question everyone connected to Mrs. Drover. If they question you again, just tell them what happened. You had nothing to do with Mrs. Drover's death, so regardless of what Sunny Cody said, you have nothing to worry about." I kept telling myself that that was true.

"What will Alex say when he hears I'm under suspicion? How will I be able to face him?"

"He'll tell the police the same thing we did. That it's ridiculous." I took her hands and led her toward her kitchen. "Let's make tea. Then we'll brainstorm and figure out who could really be responsible for killing Mrs. Drover." I snatched a piece of paper from a pad she kept on her counter. "I found something on Wendy Reichs, the woman you heard her criticizing. It looks like there was bad blood between the two of them. I'm sure if we dig deeper, we'll find more women who had no love for Diana Drover, too." I wrote down Wendy Reichs. "What about the staff she employed? Who is the caretaker who found her? I'm sure the police have interviewed him already, but I wonder what he had to say." I wrote "caretaker—name?" on my list. "I'm guessing she had to have either full-time or part-time house staff. I'd love to know how…"

I was interrupted when the door burst open, and Alex Drover rushed in. He strode over to Lynn and took her into his arms. "Are you okay?"

"The police were here, they think…"

"I know." His voice went from soothing to angry. "I told them it wasn't you. They were asking all sorts of ridiculous questions about how you and my mother got along and if I had ever heard you make any threats against her. I told them they should be out there trying to find who actually killed her, not harassing you."

I was very relieved to see that Alex was supportive of her. Though I didn't want Lynn to know, I was unsure how he would react to the police accusing her. "Detective Cody said that Detective Crane would be in charge of the case. Is he the officer who spoke to you?"

Alex turned to me, "Maybe. I've spoken to so many police officers in the past couple of days that I can't remember them all."

I hadn't had a chance before to offer Alex my condolences. "I'm so sorry for the loss of your mother. Please let me know if there is anything I can do to help."

"Thank you. Just knowing Lynn can rely on a friend like you makes me feel better."

We went to sit in the living room. Lynn and Alex seemed to support each other on the sofa.

I cleared my throat, "I'm sure this has all been a terrible shock for you." I paused, "Can you think of anyone who had a grudge against your mother, someone who would resort to violence?" He sat quietly for a few moments. "I know the police have asked you the same questions, but maybe you have new thoughts about who would want to hurt her."

He shook his head, "You probably already know my mother was not always easy to get along with; she had strong opinions and wasn't always subtle in expressing them. But I don't know of anyone she upset enough to want to kill her."

"How did she get on with the house staff? Did the caretaker at the Madison cottage have any issues with her? He was the one who found her, could he…?"

"Edgar? No! He's been employed by the family to take care of the place since I was a boy. He knew to let my mother's complaints and comments roll off his back. As far as the cleaning and cooking staff...well, I have to say there was a lot of turnover. However, when my mother got to be too much, the staff usually just quit."

"How about family?" I saw him tense up as soon as I asked. "Did your mother get along well with most of the family?"

He smiled, though it looked like a nervous smile, "Does everyone in your family get along? There were always spats with someone, but quickly forgotten, or moved past." I could tell the subject was closed, as far as he was concerned. "The police have asked all these questions. I appreciate you trying to help, but I'm not sure it's a good idea for you to be involved." He took Lynn's hand.

"Have the police gotten back to you to let you know how the investigation is going? Other than letting you know they were questioning Lynn?" I said.

"No. I have heard from the funeral home, though, and they say we can begin to plan the service." He looked at Lynn, "When I go to speak with them, you'll go with me, won't you? I could call Olivia or Jill to help us if you want me to."

I remembered that Detective Cody said they had two witnesses who swore Lynn had threatened Diana Drover. I guessed that one must be Celia Pound. She had a very smug look on her face as I passed her, lurking outside the doorway after Lynn had made her supposed threat, but the other had to be Alex's cousin Olivia. She had walked into the room right as Lynn blurted the words. If she was one of the people who had accused Lynn, I thought that would be a very uncomfortable collaboration.

Lynn looked over at me, and I could tell she had come to the same conclusion. "No. I think we can manage ourselves, don't you?"

Alex put his arm around her, "Yes, of course."

I sensed that Lynn and Alex needed a bit of time alone together, so I decided Bruno and I should take our leave for now. "I'll check in with you tomorrow, Lynn. Call me if either of you need anything in the meanwhile." I grabbed the list of possible suspects I had started from the counter before I left.

When Bruno and I got home, I felt a sudden surge of fatigue as the strong emotions the day had held drained from my body. Justin and I had plans for later, however. We were taking his grandfather out to dinner for his birthday. I looked at the time and decided I had an hour to take a quick rest before I had to feed and take out Bruno and then get ready before Justin was due to pick me up. I snuggled down on the sofa, Bruno by my side, but I found I couldn't sleep. I turned the events of the day over and over in my mind.

I held off telling Justin in the car that Lynn was under suspicion for Mrs. Drover's murder. I wanted to tell him and Charlie at the same time. Charlie Duggan had started out as a patient, but we had since become friends, and he had helped me as I got involved in a couple of sticky situations in the past. Not to mention, he was Justin's grandfather and had been involved in my meeting Justin. I really wanted Charlie's input on the police questioning Lynn, and I didn't want to have to tell the story twice.

I went with Justin to ring Charlie's bell and was thrilled when he opened the door.

"Oh, my word! I will be the envy of every woman in the restaurant, being escorted by two such handsome men." I gave Charlie a kiss on the cheek. "Happy Birthday."

Charlie smoothed the front of his shirt and said, "Not many people I'd wear a tie for. As it was, I had to dig this one out of the back of the closet."

Justin offered his grandfather his arm as we went down the front steps, but Charlie waved it away. "I can walk almost as good on the fake leg now as I did on the real one."

When we entered the restaurant, I could see Charlie's eyes light up, "Very nice. Hope the food is as good as it smells."

I waited until we were seated before I told them the news about Lynn.

Justin said, "You have got to be kidding. That's ridiculous!"

I shook my head no.

"That the friend you are always telling me about? The artist?" Charlie said.

"Yes. You may remember I told you her future mother-in-law, and Lynn did not always get along. Mrs. Drover was very critical of Lynn, and she felt that she did not want Alex to marry her. Unfortunately, it turns out Lynn was at the cottage in Madison the day Mrs. Drover was killed." I explained what Lynn had said about having the mishap that left her bloody and the neighbor seeing her and approaching her.

"Sorry, but I got to say, I'm not surprised the police are looking hard at your friend." Charlie must have seen the worried look on my face, because he said, "I believe you when you say she didn't do it, just saying you look at the facts, and she was worth questioning."

The waitperson came to take our orders, so we paused our conversation for a moment.

Justin had a worried look on his face now. "Now that I've heard the whole story, I have to agree with my grandfather." I was ready to argue with him, but he continued, "However, I know Lynn, and I don't believe she could ever do something like that."

I leaned over to give him a quick peck on the cheek. "Thanks."

"That Drover woman's murder was on the local news. Said she was some kind of big-shot society woman or something. Not that I ever traveled in those sorts of circles, but I figure no matter your social status, the more people you know, the greater the chance that you're likely to piss off a few. From what you're telling me, this lady had no qualms about pissing people off."

"That's what I thought, also. I started making a list of people the police might want to question." Justin was seated to my left, and I could hear him take a deep breath. I placed my hand over his and said, "But that is as far as I've gone."

Charlie gave Justin a quick sidelong glance, then said, "My friend Bill was always talking about how his wife is into that charity work and stuff. I could ask him if she ever worked with the Drover woman. See if she knows anything about who would have a grudge against her."

I smiled at him, "Thanks, Charlie." Once again, Charlie's vast network of connections might come in handy.

Our food arrived then, and while we ate the conversation turned to how good the food was, and Charlie told funny stories about Justin as a little boy.

The issue of just how involved I planned to get in finding Diana Drover's killer was dropped. For the time being.

Later, in the car, after we dropped Charlie off at his house, I said, "Your grandfather seemed to have a good time tonight. I'm so glad you suggested we take him out for his birthday."

Justin smiled, "Yes, it was great to see him enjoying himself." He was quiet for a few moments, then said, "I was thinking. Jim Peters, the canine officer with the police department, is due to bring in Pegasus, the department's dog, for his annual physical. I could see if I can get information out of him about what he knows regarding the Drover investigation." He glanced over at me.

I was dumbstruck for a moment. "You mean you will help find out who might have killed Mrs. Drover?"

"I'll see if I can find out if they have any information that might point to someone other than Lynn. I'm not promising anything. I'm not even sure I can get him to talk about it." He looked over at me again, "I just want to put your mind at ease so you don't feel you need to get further involved."

I smiled, "Okay." Even if Justin wasn't able to get much information, I was encouraged by the fact he agreed to get involved.

Chapter Seven

My first appointment the following day was with Ralph Tabor. He had had a particularly nasty accident with an ax that left him with a wound requiring a surgical repair. The repair site on his right leg looked very painful, but I was glad to see it had started to heal and showed no signs of infection. His wife stood by, shaking her head as I did the dressing change.

"Thinks he's Paul Bunyan. I tried to tell him to wait for our son Kyle to come with his chainsaw to cut up that fallen tree. But no." She reached over to give his shoulder a gentle shove.

Mr. Tabor drew his breath in sharply as I placed a square of gauze as gently as I could over the wound.

"Sorry. I'm almost done," I said.

Mr. Tabor said, "No. You're fine. You are much more gentle than the nurse who came the first day." He turned to his wife, "What did she say her name was?"

"Nora. I think," she said.

"That's right. Very businesslike, got right to work. Just ripped that old dressing right off, though she did apologize when I let out a yelp."

"Oh, no! I'm so sorry that happened. I'm sure she didn't realize how rough she was being." I knew no such thing, but I did believe Nora probably hadn't intended to hurt the man. I told Judy that Nora seemed competent and that she didn't need to have me tag along after her anymore. I hoped I hadn't been premature in my assessment.

"You're probably right. Other than that, she was nice." Mrs. Tabor looked to her husband for confirmation.

He nodded. "Yes, didn't seem like she wanted to engage in any chit-chat or anything, though. I tried to get her talking to take my mind off the fact the dressing change hurt like the dickens. At first, she just gave me some one-word answers, but then she opened up a little once I got out of her that she was from Spokane. I was stationed near there at Fairchild Air Force Base when I was in the military. We talked about the area for a while."

I paused in putting my supplies back in my bag. "Hunh. I didn't realize Nora was from Washington." I swore she told me she was from Colorado.

"Yeah, funny the connections you discover you have with people. Anyway, you have a much gentler touch than her. Don't tell her I said that, though." Mr. Tabor said.

This was the first thing I had heard about Nora or how she was doing at Coretrack since I finished her orientation. I assumed she had settled in okay. I made a mental note to ask Judy, when I got a chance, what information she had on her, or at least the details she could share.

* * *

The days were starting to get longer, and it was beginning to feel more like spring now, so I was eager to take Bruno for a walk after dinner. We were just approaching our house after the walk when I saw Lynn's car pull up in front.

"Thank heaven you're home! I need a glass of wine. Do you have any? If not, I'll settle for tea, but brew it strong!" Lynn fell into step with Bruno and me.

As we went into the house, I said, "I have wine. What happened?" I unhooked Bruno's leash and said, "Let's go sit in the kitchen."

I grabbed a bottle of Pino Grigio from the refrigerator and poured a generous glass for Lynn and a half glass for myself.

"I just came from the police station. Detective Crane called me and said he wanted me to come in and 'review the information' I gave Detective Cody. I was scared, and I asked him if I should contact a lawyer. He said no, not yet.

He said, '*Not yet.*'" I could see her hand trembling a little as she raised her glass to take a sip. "That made me even more nervous."

"What did he ask? How did he seem?"

"He tried to come across as friendly and non-threatening, but I felt it was an act." She took another sip of wine. "He read back what Detective Cody wrote down the other day and asked if I still wanted to stand by my statement or did I want to add anything. I told him no. That was what happened and that I knew nothing about Mrs. Drover's death; that I didn't even know she was dead until Alex told me."

I nodded, "Okay."

"He kept circling back to how I got the blood on my jacket, though, and asking me why I destroyed it. I told him I didn't destroy it, I discarded it because it was ruined, that at that point I didn't know of a reason why I shouldn't."

"What did he say to that? Did he ask you about anything else?" Just as Charlie and Justin pointed out, her actions could sound suspicious, so I understood why she felt so nervous. "Didn't you say that some of your blood dripped onto the porch? Did you wipe that up?"

She shook her head, "No. I was too busy trying to clean myself up, and then when the neighbor yelled over to me to question my right to be there, I just left."

"Okay, good. When they analyze that blood, it will prove to be yours."

"That's true." She paused and said, "But there is something else, some information I think he wasn't giving me."

"What do you mean?"

"He asked several times if I went into the house, and I kept telling him I hadn't. I don't know if they could have found something they are trying to link to my blood on the porch, or if it was something else they found inside. Anyway, after I went over what happened again, he finally said I could go, but he might have some further questions later." Lynn looked totally drained now.

"I think that's a good sign. If they had any actual evidence to link you to the murder, I'm pretty sure he wouldn't have let you go." I took a sip of wine.

"I know they won't find any, but I still feel nervous. I know it's silly, but when I was talking to Detective Crane, I felt as if I really was guilty of something."

I could empathize with how she felt. I had had a similar experience when dealing with the police. "That's not that unusual, but don't let being questioned by the police intimidate you."

"I'm trying not to. But..." She sighed, then drank the rest of her wine. "When I told Alex that the police wanted me to come down to the station for more questioning, he wanted to know why. He wanted to know if they had found more evidence and if I'd told him everything about what happened that day." She paused as if to keep control of her emotions. "I told him of course I had, that I didn't know why they wanted to question me again. I asked him if he believed me, and he said of course he did. But he didn't sound totally convincing this time."

"Oh, Lynn." I silently cursed Alex, but said, "Of course he believes you about what happened, but the whole situation of his mother being murdered and you being questioned by the police may be causing him to have all kinds of confusing thoughts. It's a terrible strain on both of you."

"Maybe you're right, and that's all it is. I hope so. How could he possibly think I would do such a horrible thing?"

How, indeed, I thought. I suddenly realized what time it was when Bruno came over to me, gently nudging my leg. I got up to refill his water bowl and feed him. I asked Lynn, "Would you like to stay for dinner? I've got leftover mac and cheese I was going to heat up, and I could throw together a salad to go with it."

She smiled and said, "Okay. Sounds lovely. I'll make the salad while you heat up the mac and cheese."

By the time we had finished dinner, I was glad to see that Lynn seemed to have calmed down a bit. As soon as we cleaned up, however, she said, "Thank you for feeding me, but I think I'd better go now. Alex and I have an early meeting with the funeral home director tomorrow to make the arrangements." She took a deep breath, "Wish me luck."

"It will go fine. I'm sure Alex will be glad that you'll be there to support him. And the funeral director will likely have a few suggestions if you are unsure of what to do."

After she left, I had a sudden flashback to the day I met Lynn at Artie's funeral the previous summer. Not only had I met Lynn there, but it turned out that Artie's murderer had also made an appearance. It occurred to me that there would be a lot of people who had been connected to Mrs. Drover at her service. It would be a good opportunity to talk to some of them and find out who might have had a very good reason to want her dead.

Chapter Eight

I called Lynn the next evening to find out how the meeting with the funeral director went and to see if everything was in place now for the service. She said that she thought the meeting went well. Mr. Halprin did indeed have some suggestions based on his experience with other well-known local "celebrities," and Alex seemed to feel satisfied with the planned ceremony. She said the funeral was to be held in two days at Christ and Holy Trinity Episcopal Church in Westport.

Justin asked if I wanted him to go with me, but I said it wasn't necessary. He'd never even met Mrs. Drover, and he and Dr. Reddy had a full schedule at their veterinary practice on the day of the funeral. I assured him Lynn would understand.

* * *

I planned to arrive early for the funeral service. I soon realized it was a good thing I had, or I might not have been able to find a seat in the church. I entered a pew on the same side of the church as Lynn and Alex but sat several rows behind them. I wanted to be able to look around as the service proceeded so I could gauge peoples' expressions and reactions. I was hoping to see someone acting guilty or suspiciously. I wasn't sure what that would look like, but felt I would know when I saw it. It was a foolish plan. It was almost impossible to even move, as mourners were packed into the pews shoulder to shoulder, and there was standing room only at the back of the church.

I wondered how many people actually knew Mrs. Drover or the family, and how many came at the prospect of being at the funeral of someone whose murder had been big news. I overheard several comments from those around me as we waited for the service to begin. There were expressions of "she was such a master at getting causes funded" and "I loved her blog on how the food at that new restaurant, Che Dupre, was worth every penny." But there seemed to be even more comments around me in the "I hate to speak ill of the dead…," and "too bad she's gone" vein where the speaker was clearly not very sorry at all. I didn't hear any remarks that gave me a clue as to who might have killed her, however.

I watched the mourners in the row behind Lynn and Alex. His cousins, Olivia and Jill, were seated side by side. Next to Jill was a woman who bore a strong resemblance to Mrs. Drover. I assumed she was their mother, Alex's Aunt Eleanor. Lynn told me that despite Alex's claim that there were no lingering disputes in the family, for the past several years, Mrs. Drover and her sister rarely spoke to each other. Alex said they had a falling out at some point, though he didn't know what caused it. I saw the three women lean forward a few times to whisper to Alex and pat his back or put a hand on his shoulder; no one seemed to be trying to reassure or comfort Lynn. I wished I had chosen a seat closer to her so I could have at least given her an occasional supportive look as she turned to scan the church. I couldn't hazard a guess as to who the four other people in the row were, I assumed other family members. Then the woman seated next to Aunt Eleanor turned and leaned in to say something to Jill, and I realized it was Celia Pound. Mrs. Drover had said that she and Alex had been childhood friends, but I hadn't realized Celia had been that close to his family, also.

Lynn's worries about the service not being as impressive as Mrs. Drover would have wanted were unwarranted. Alex's cousin, Ben, and Olivia and Jill's husbands were three of the pallbearers. The hymns and readings were beautiful, and the eulogies were touching. I hardly knew the woman and did not like what I did know of her, but I had tears in my eyes.

After the service was finished and the family exited the church, I tried to make my way as quickly as possible outside to speak to Lynn. Once I'd made it to the steps of the church, I scanned the crowd and saw a group of people gathered around Alex to express their condolences, but I didn't see Lynn with him. I finally spied her, standing off to the side, by herself.

I walked up to her and gave her a hug and a big smile. "You did a wonderful job with the funeral service. Mrs. Drover would have had nothing to complain about."

"Thank you. I didn't really do much, however. Mr. Halprin, the funeral director, came up with most of it." She tipped her chin toward Alex's cousins, who were standing by his side, their backs to us. "And Jill and Olivia called Alex to make some suggestions on the scripture readings and music. I didn't dare contradict their choices, and besides, they were good ones." I thought I detected a slight tremor in her voice.

"Have you spoken to Alex's family since his mother's death?"

"His cousin Ben gave me a brief hug before we got into the limo to come here. His aunt and cousins said hello when they arrived at the church but didn't meet my eyes when they spoke to me. All in all, I get a feeling they're uncomfortable around me."

"Why? Do you think Olivia may be feeling guilty about talking to the police? They certainly can't really believe you were involved in Mrs. Drover's death."

"I'm not sure what is going on."

"Still, shouldn't you be by Alex's side? You are his fiancé."

Just then, I picked out another person standing near to Alex. Celia. She seemed to know many of the people who were coming up to Alex and greeted them warmly. I grabbed Lynn's arm. "Come on, his family can just get over it—you are going to stand by Alex's side."

I started to lead her through the crowd when Alex suddenly looked over and saw her.

"Lynn! There you are. Come on, we're about to head to the cemetery." He reached out to pull her alongside him.

Lynn turned to me and mouthed, "Please come."

This time, at the graveside service, I tried to worm my way as close to where Lynn stood as I could. I saw her glance quickly in my direction and give me a grateful look. Lynn stood to one side of Alex, and his Aunt Eleanor stood to his other side. I noticed she wept quietly as the priest recited the final prayer. I could only imagine that no matter what had happened between her and her sister, she regretted the lost time now. Once again, I tried to watch the reactions of the people surrounding the casket as it sat at the graveside. Alex seemed stoic, though I know Lynn had said he had been a wreck the day before. Ben kept looking everywhere but at the casket, his glance frequently going to Alex. I thought he was trying to catch his eye. His sisters, Olivia and Jill, leaned back against their husbands, a solemn look on their faces. I searched the faces of the other mourners, but everyone seemed either respectfully somber, or slightly bored. I noticed Celia Pound had once again found a way to get close to where the family stood. At one point, she leaned to whisper to a woman standing near to her, tipping her head ever so slightly toward Lynn. The woman's mouth tightened, and she shook her head.

Lynn made her way over to me once the graveside service was completed and said, "Family and close friends are invited to come to a gathering at Gabriele's Steakhouse. Meet me there," she lowered her voice, "I overheard something interesting."

Twenty minutes later, when I entered the room Alex had reserved for the after-funeral reception, it was packed. I had to wonder what his definition of close friends and family was. I scanned the crowd and saw Lynn talking to Malcolm Devlin, one of the doctors at High Life Dermatology, where she used to work. Since Lynn looked to be greeting mourners, I went to stand off to the side by the buffet table until I could get her attention and find out what she had heard.

As I was approaching the lavishly laid buffet, I overheard a woman saying, "Oh, please, Mrs. Reichs, go right ahead." I turned to see a tall, middle-aged brunette dressed in a dark blue dress making her way through the crowd toward the food. I followed her and fell in line behind her as she scanned the sumptuous buffet.

"Excuse me, but aren't you Wendy Reichs?" I asked.

She turned briefly toward me, then continued down the line. After placing some avocado toast and sausage frittata on her plate, she turned to me and said, "Yes. I'm sorry, do I know you?"

"No. My name is Melanie Bass. I am a good friend of Alex's fiancé, Lynn. I am going to be the maid of honor at their wedding. I thought I recognized you, and I've heard about your work with the Ladies Auxiliary at Norwalk Hospital. I work in community healthcare, and I've heard good things about the work you do there." I could tell the person behind me was getting impatient with me clogging up the line, so I hurried to fill my plate—it didn't matter with what, it all looked delicious.

"I hear you were instrumental in helping to set up the "Ring for a Ride" program to help the elderly get to their appointments. I'd love to hear more about that." I tried to make my voice as heartfelt as possible. I motioned toward two chairs slightly set apart from the crowd. I hoped what I'd discovered in the bit of research I'd been able to do on her had been accurate.

As we claimed our seats, she gave me a look of obvious pride. "Yes, I'm very proud of that initiative. Though, I must admit I was just a small cog in the mechanism of getting that program set up."

I had to give her points for not grabbing all the glory. I had, in fact, learned from a friend on the committee that while her name was on the proposal, the grunt work had been done by others. "In any case, it was a wonderful idea."

We sat in silence for a few moments, enjoying the food which was every bit as delicious as it looked. Then I motioned to the crowd gathered in the room, "Such a lovely turnout for Mrs. Drover's service. Her death was quite a shock." I tried to gauge her reaction.

She nodded and said, "Yes, how terrible." I couldn't read her expression.

I aimed to sound completely innocent, "Did you know Mrs. Drover through working with her on some of her charities?"

She paused before answering, "Yes, Diana certainly loved being the center of attention. She had quite a habit of making whatever she worked on 'her charities.'" She shook her head slightly, then said, "Sorry. That was catty. It's just that Diana and I didn't always see eye to eye on things, and she could be quite vengeful if she didn't get her way." She narrowed her eyes at me,

"You must wonder what I'm doing here after that. Let's just say, I have my reasons."

Mrs. Reichs drained the Bloody Mary she was holding, stood up then, and said, "Anyway. May she rest in peace. Nice meeting you." With that, I watched as she left the reception.

After Mrs. Reich's exit, I checked the crowd again to see Lynn was now standing next to Alex. I gave her a little wave, and she excused herself and headed toward where I was sitting. "Who was that you were talking to?" she said as she sat down next to me.

"That was Wendy Reichs." I told Lynn about my exchange with her. "She doesn't look like the type to plunge a knife into someone's throat, but what she said certainly doesn't take her off the list of suspects as far as I'm concerned."

"I agree. But why would she be at the cottage with Diana? It doesn't sound like they were likely to spend any time together unless they had to."

She did have a point. "What was it you overheard that you wanted to tell me?"

Lynn scanned the crowd as if looking for someone. "Don't look yet, but over by the vase of lilies in the corner is a gray-haired man in a green shirt with a charcoal grey jacket. That's Edgar Flint, the maintenance man who takes care of the cottage in Madison. Yesterday, while I was at Alex's, he stopped over. Evidently, Alex asked him to come to see him. He thought Edgar was due his wages for the past two weeks, and with his mother gone now, Alex was afraid no one had paid him. They went into Alex's home office, but the door wasn't shut all the way."

Two people stopped to greet each other right in front of us. Lynn waited until they walked away before continuing. I took a quick peek at Edgar. He was still standing in the corner and seemed uncomfortable in the posh crowd.

"Anyway. I overheard Edgar tell Alex that he didn't need to be paid, that Mrs. Drover took care of it before her death. That he had gotten a nice severance package from her. She summoned him to the cottage, and he thought it was about some shrubbery she had mentioned she wanted added to the west side border. But when he arrived, she thanked him for his years of service but said that he was no longer needed. She didn't give him any reason why."

"Did he say when all this happened?" I asked.

"That's just it. He said she asked him to meet her there the day before she was killed, and that's when she told him. He said he didn't know what to make of her firing him like that, so he took the check and left. The next day, after he had had a chance to think about it, he decided to go back and pick up some of the tools that were his own and try to speak to her, find out what he had done wrong that caused her to let him go. That's when he went into the house and found her body."

"Do you think he told the police all this?" I said.

"Alex asked him the same thing. He mumbled something, but I don't think he ever gave Alex a definite answer. I backed away then because they were coming out of the office."

"Wow. Did Alex say anything after he left?"

"I asked him if everything was all right, and he said yes, fine. He didn't go into what Edgar told him, but I could see that it was bothering him."

I searched the crowd once again for Edgar and saw him speaking to Alex. He took Alex's hand and gave what looked like a small bow. It looked to me as if he was about to leave. I turned to Lynn and said, "Wait here." As I made my way toward the doorway, weaving my way through the crowd, I had about thirty seconds to think of a way to approach him.

"Hello. Don't you do the landscape work for Alex's family? I'm a friend of his and I'm looking for someone to do something with my property," I said.

He looked disconcerted at first, but then said, "Yes, I am. What are you looking to do?"

I thought quick. "Oh, we can discuss that another time." I put a hand on his arm. "I'm so sorry. I just realized I heard that it was you that found Mrs. Drover. How horrible!" I took my hand away but gave him a sympathetic look.

He swallowed, "Yes, it was." He patted his pockets, as if looking for something, then said, "I don't have a card on me. When you are ready to have the work done maybe you can get my number from Dr. Drover." He looked as if he was going to walk away.

I shifted a little so he would have to step around me to leave. "I mean, not only was it terrible to find her that way, but I assume that then you had to be questioned by the police. That must have been an ordeal, too."

He looked uneasy, "Yes. I admit it wasn't great. But I just told them what I found when I got there. I was upset, but I told them all I remembered."

"That's good. I'm a friend of Detective Cody. She's one of the officers investigating the crime, and she says that often people hold back on what they tell the police. She says that then when the police find out about it, it always looks bad for the person." I cringed inwardly at what I knew Sunny would think of my tactics, but judging by his reaction, it was working.

He shifted his weight and then said, "Look, I..."

I continued, "Alex told me his mother let you go shortly before she was killed, and so I wondered why you were there at the house that day. Was this something you told the police?"

He looked startled. He grabbed my arm and pulled me out of the room toward the entryway of the restaurant. "I don't know who you are, but..." He was breathing rapidly now, taking shallow breaths. I was afraid he was going to hyperventilate and pass out. "I didn't mention the getting let go part, or why I went back that afternoon because... well, I got in trouble with the police a while ago. I was charged with assault after a bar fight. I was worried that when Mrs. Drover found out I would lose my job, but she gave me a second chance. I've never been in any trouble since, but I was worried if the cops found out that, it would look bad."

I didn't want to tell him that in all probability, the police already knew if they searched for any records on him. "So, you have no idea who killed Mrs. Drover?"

He looked a little sick now. "No. I swear."

I nodded. "And there is nothing else you noticed or heard that could help find the murderer.?"

He hesitated a moment before answering. "No. Nothing."

Something about the way he said it made me wonder if that was true and why he was reluctant to mention it.

I nodded, "All right. Thank you for talking to me."

As I turned to go, he said, "So you'll call me about that work you want done, right?"

"Sure." It looked like I was going to have to add some shrubbery to the west side of my driveway.

Chapter Nine

I found Lynn sitting where I'd left her. As I approached her, I saw Alex's cousins Olivia and Jill walking toward her, also. I hung back a bit, pretending to be looking at my phone, but close enough so I could still hear what was said.

Olivia scooted into the chair next to Lynn, and Jill took the seat next to her sister. Olivia spoke first. "I just want to tell you I feel terrible about telling the police what I overheard you say to Aunt Diana. I had no choice, though. The police said that someone had come forward to say that they heard you make a threat against her that day and that I could confirm it."

I heard Lynn say, "I was upset. Of course I didn't mean it."

"I tried to tell the detective that, but he said that C…the other person was adamant that she felt you were serious about what you said. That you would do anything to make sure Aunt Diana didn't find a way to prevent Alex from marrying you."

This, of course, confirmed the suspicion both Lynn and I had about it being Celia who was the one to report Lynn to the police.

"No matter how his mother and I got along, I would never do anything like that, especially because it is causing Alex so much pain."

Both women were silent for a moment, but then stood up, and Jill said, "In any case, we decided that we should hold off making any judgments until the police actually arrest whoever killed Aunt Diana." They both gave her a weak smile, patted her on the arm, and walked away.

Lynn stood and came over to where I was eavesdropping. "Did you hear that? What did you make of it?"

"I wouldn't exactly say that they are convinced of your innocence, but at least they aren't pointing you out as the guilty party, either. At least not yet," I said.

"Even though they tried not to use her name, they admitted it was Celia who went to the police first. You saw how she was looking at Alex when she burst into brunch that day. Do you think she is trying to get Alex to suspect me so she could move in on him?"

"Maybe," I said. "She did seem confused when she found out Alex was engaged to you. It was as if she had come with expectations of striking up a relationship with him again." And I thought I knew who would have been behind those expectations. "Or maybe she is just one of those people who wants to be at the forefront of helping in any police investigation." I felt a little pang of guilt since I understood that urge.

"I suppose that could be true. What did you find out from Edgar?"

I motioned her to the chairs we had been sitting in before. "You were right to suspect he hadn't told the police everything about what had transpired the day Mrs. Drover was killed. He said he was nervous because he had been arrested for assault in the past and was afraid of how that would look." I saw Lynn's eyebrows go up at that.

I continued, "I don't think he killed her though. He seemed bewildered by being let go, but not angry with Mrs. Drover. I think he saw something or heard something that day that he isn't admitting to, however."

"Why do you think he would do that?"

"That's what I would like to know," I said. I looked up to see that the room was beginning to empty out. Alex's aunt and cousins took turns hugging him, and it looked as if they were preparing to leave. Jill's husband appeared to be supporting his mother-in-law as they headed toward the door. Alex looked drained.

Lynn got up and said, "I'll call you," as she went over to help him say goodbye to the last of the mourners.

I once again gave my condolences to Alex and prepared to leave, also. I looked around the room one more time and was glad to see that, thankfully, Celia Pound had left. For someone who had apparently not been in touch with Alex or his family for a while, she seemed to suddenly want to slip back into a familiar role. On the way out, I was thinking about the conversations I'd had with Wendy Reichs and Edgar when I was jarred by the sight of Celia Pound and Alex's cousin Ben in close conversation at the bar.

Chapter Ten

When I got home from the funeral, Bruno greeted me like I had been away on a week-long cruise. He alternated between profuse licking of my hands and running around me in circles, his whole back end wagging. I felt guilty as I realized that ever since Mrs. Drover's murder, I had been neglecting to spend the usual amount of time playing with him.

"Okay, buddy, let me change my clothes, and we'll go for a walk." As if he understood, he made one final hop and then followed me to my room.

It was a beautiful day, the weather warmer than usual for the third week of April. A fact I had failed to really appreciate until I put Bruno into the car for a trip to walk on the bike path at Hammonasset Beach State Park. Suddenly, my spirits lifted.

The park was busy with other people walking their dogs, people flying kites in the field, and some eager sun worshipers clad in light jackets but with bare feet lounging in chairs on the beach. Today, despite the ban on dogs on the beach itself, I let Bruno join the other dogs whose parents were ignoring the rules and let him scamper along the waterline chasing the waves as they lapped the shore. It soon became obvious he was going to need a bath when we got home after a particularly vigorous digging session in the soft sand. For a while, I was able to put any thoughts about who could be responsible for Diana Drover's murder from my mind and concentrate on the whooshing sound of the waves and the feel of the sun on my face. I only wished Justin and his dog, Jasper, could be walking with us. I resolved to call him and ask if we could go for a walk this weekend, provided, of course, he wasn't on call at the vet's office. Despite my plan to concentrate on the walk itself, I found my mind drifting to what I had learned from the two people I had spoken to already about Diana Drover. I wanted his take on the information I had gotten. I wondered also if he had seen the police dog, Pegasus, yet, and if he had been able to get any information out of his handler.

I called his office as soon as we got home, hoping he was not with a patient and had a few minutes to talk. I told him about Lynn being questioned at the police station and the conversations with Wendy Reichs and Edgar Flint.

"Now I wish I had taken the day off to go to the funeral with you. It still makes me uncomfortable that you're questioning potential murders on your own."

"You needn't worry. I was in a very public place," I said.

"But you'll share what you learned with the police, right? That way, they can take it from there." I could hear the tension in his voice.

"Yes, of course." I didn't add that I still wanted to get just a bit more information, before I went to speak to them, however. "Speaking of police, were you able to find out anything from Officer Peters?"

He grunted, "No. We were chatting about what a great dog Pegasus is, and he mentioned how the department was gearing up for the influx of summer people, and I thought I was pretty slick in trying to turn the conversation to the Drover case. He apparently saw right through me and instead wanted to know what I'd heard and how well I knew Alex Drover's fiancé." He chuckled. "Obviously, I'm not as good at getting people to talk as you are."

"It was a long shot anyway. Thank you for trying."

I could hear one of the vet techs calling him. "I have to go now, but remember, if you are going to get involved in this case, I want to continue to help you."

* * *

By the following day, I had decided it might be worth it to follow up with Wendy Reichs concerning Mrs. Drover's murder. She had been a bit cryptic about her reasons for being at the funeral of a woman she did not like. I didn't get the feeling it was to gloat over her death, and if she didn't kill Diana Drover herself, maybe she had some idea of who might have had a reason and the ability to do it.

I would have to wait until my next day off, however, before I could go to speak to her, since I had a full schedule today.

This was my first time seeing Gina Baker. I was covering for Nora Stevens, who had requested the day off. I read Mrs. Baker's chart before I arrived at her house. She was a forty-two-year-old woman who had sustained a back injury in a motor vehicle accident three years previously. She had undergone medical treatment for her injury without significant relief, so had had surgery one week prior and was discharged from the hospital three days ago. Nora saw her the day after discharge and recorded that she was doing well and that she had no concerns about Mrs. Baker's pain or wound. I was seeing her to make sure all was still going well.

The man who met me at the door was pale, sporting what looked like a three-day growth of beard, and was dressed in a wrinkled dress shirt and jeans.

"Mr. Baker? I'm…"

"Yes, yes, come in." He stepped back and motioned me into the house. "I'm Ron. Gina is in there." He motioned to a room to his right.

I could hear a soft moaning coming from what turned out to be the living room. Gina was seated in an armchair, her feet on a small stool and a pillow propped behind her back. Her head was thrown back, and her eyes were closed.

"Hello, Mrs. Baker, my name is Melanie Bass. I'm covering for Nora, the nurse who saw you the other day."

She cracked her eyes open but didn't say anything.

"I guess I don't have to ask how your pain level is. I can see that you are in a lot of pain, and…"

She let out a sound between a laugh and a sob, "It's a freakin twelve if you want to know! I can't, I just can't anymore!" She began to sob in earnest then.

Mr. Baker rushed to kneel beside her chair and grab her hand. He glared up at me, "Do something! Can't you do something to help her?"

I put down my work bag and went over to squat beside her on the other side. After handing her some tissues, I gently massaged her upper back. "It's okay, Gina. Let's see what we can do to help with the pain. When did you last take your pain medicine?"

She took a deep breath, winced, then said, "About forty-five minutes ago." She looked to her husband for confirmation.

He nodded and stood up to stand beside her. "She took them every four hours last night even though the instructions said every six hours. She didn't sleep at all; nothing seemed to help."

Her eyes began to fill up with tears again. "I don't have any more pills left now. I thought the doctor was supposed to give me enough to last at least five days. I called the doctor last evening to see if I could get something stronger for the pain, or even just a refill on this med, but he said I should have had enough to last for several days. He made me feel like a drug addict or something! I'm in pain! I just want it to ease up. I can't get comfortable!"

"I'm going take a look and make sure your incision is healing, and there is no sign of an infection that could be causing you so much pain." I gently guided her to lean forward and checked under her dressing. The incision was slightly reddened but within the limits of what would be expected at this stage after the surgery, and there was no drainage. "Everything looks good back here."

Just then, she let out a moan and began to breathe quickly. Her husband dropped her hand and began to stroke her hair. "Why is she in so much pain, then?"

"I don't understand. When I was in the hospital my pain was under good control, even the first day at home I was okay. Now, nothing seems to work!" She said.

I could see that she was indeed in a lot of pain, but I also understood her physician's reluctance to prescribe a stronger pain reliever. According to her chart, she was sent home with a prescription for Percocet/acetaminophen. Her doctor was right; she should have had enough to last her for several days. I wondered if she had taken even more medication than she admitted. "I'll call Dr. Jordan now and let him know that you are in this much pain. Maybe he'll give you just a day or two worth of something stronger."

I was able to get in touch with Dr. Jordan's nurse, and I explained that somehow, Mrs. Baker was indeed out of her pain meds and needed something to tide her over until she saw the doctor. After being on hold for a few minutes, she came back on the line to say the doctor was going to call in a prescription for just enough medication to last until the following day. He wanted to see her in his office and then assess her himself.

Mr. Baker immediately grabbed his jacket as if to go out to the pharmacy.

I said, "Give Dr. Jordan a few minutes to send in the new prescription before you go." I was curious about just how much extra pain medication Gina had taken, so I added, "Could you get me the vial the medication came in? I just want to check how many pills it says it contains. Sometimes, the pharmacy may not have enough to fill the prescription completely and will just dispense what they have and fill the rest as soon as they get it." He nodded and went to retrieve the vial.

I rubbed Gina's back again and said, "Meanwhile, let's practice some breathing exercises to help until the medication you took kicks in."

As Ron handed me the empty vial, he said, "The nurse that came the other day counted them, and she said we should be fine to last until Gina's next appointment."

"I know I should have more left, but I just wanted to feel some relief." Gina looked as if she was going to cry again.

The number of pills printed on the medication label matched the number prescribed. She should not have run out unless she took much more than directed. Even accounting for her taking a couple of extra doses, Mrs. Baker was missing five pills. I didn't like one thought that occurred to me. "You said Nora, the nurse who came to visit you the first day, counted out your pills? Did she say why she wanted to do that?"

"She said it was protocol that she check them. I don't know if she actually counted them or not, though. Gina had to go to the bathroom and the nurse asked me if I could help her walk there while she packed up her bag to go,"

Ron said.

I tried to come up with a plausible explanation. I tried to banish the bad feeling I was getting about what could have happened. I had to ask myself why I was so suspicious of Nora. I reasoned that a recent experience I'd had made me more sensitive than usual to the use of narcotics. It would be a very serious charge to suggest that Nora had taken narcotics from Gina Baker's supply and one I couldn't prove. "I'm not sure what happened, but we will do all we can to straighten it out."

Ron grabbed his coat again, "I'll just wait for the med if the pharmacy doesn't have it ready yet. Maybe if I explain how much pain my wife is in, they can hurry up."

I waited with Gina after her husband left. She seemed more comfortable as the pain reliever began to kick in. After a few minutes, she smiled at me and said, "I can't thank you enough for your help. I know you have other appointments. Ron will be back soon. I'll be fine until he gets home."

I felt bad leaving her, but she was right, I did have other patients to see. "All right. I hope everything goes well at the doctor's tomorrow. If he wants someone from the agency to check on you again, I'll be glad to do it." I didn't know how Nora Stevens was going to react to me taking over the case, but I thought it would be for the best. I didn't want to accuse her of anything until I got her side of the story about what might have happened at the Bakers.

When I got back to the main office at Coretrack, I was glad to see my supervisor, Judy, was still there. I wanted to speak to Nora in person, if possible, when I asked her what happened at the Bakers. I waited for Judy to finish with a phone call she was on and then said, "Hi. I was just wondering if you could give me Nora Stevens's address."

Judy began to pull up information on her computer. "Sure, but why?"

"I've seen a couple of the patients she has also cared for recently, and I wanted to discuss a few things with her." I tried to keep things as vague as possible until I was sure about what happened.

Judy looked up at me over her reading glasses. "Is there something I should know about?"

"No. Not yet, anyway."

Judy gave me a long look, "Okay. But you know I need to be notified immediately if there is reason for concern." She scrolled down the document she had pulled up. "Humm. I only have a P.O. box as an address for Nora. When she first started here she said she was staying in a motel while she looked for a place to live. I guess she forgot to give me her new address."

That did not give me much comfort. Nora was already a bit of a puzzle; no one seemed to know exactly where she moved from or why she chose to move to this area. "How about her cell phone number? You must have that."

Judy gave me the number she had for Nora, but when I tried to reach her at that number, it just rang, and no voice mail picked up. I checked the schedule and found we both were scheduled to work in two days. I would have to wait until then to try to catch her before we both went to our first patient appointments.

Chapter Eleven

I had some time after work the following afternoon, so decided to try to speak to Wendy Reichs again. I had gotten her phone number from a friend who knew her from the Norwalk Hospital Auxiliary. I was just about to call her when I saw a dark-colored vehicle pull into my driveway. Bruno dutifully began barking to alert me of the intruder, but quieted when I told him to. I didn't recognize the man who got out of the car, but my experience with law enforcement told me that he looked like a cop.

Bruno must have gotten the same vibe I did because he retreated to stand behind me as I opened the door.

The officer who approached was pleasant-looking. He looked to be in his early forties, he had a slight build with light colored hair beginning to recede at the hairline. He was waiting at the bottom of the steps and off to the side of the front door but smiled and came up the steps after I opened it. "Good evening, Miss Bass, I'm Detective Zachary Crane." He held up his ID, "I'm investigating the death of Diana Drover. I was wondering if we could speak for a few minutes."

"Of course. Come in." I had no idea why he would want to speak to me, but I was certainly curious. I motioned to a chair in the living room, and we sat opposite each other.

He looked around the room with a look of approval, then he smiled again and said, "I understand that you're a good friend of Lynn Duncan."

I nodded, "Yes. It's terrible what happened to her fiancé's mother. But..."

"See..." he leaned forward, his elbows on his knees, "that's what I wanted to talk to you about. I have heard some talk that you've been asking a few questions of people who knew Mrs. Drover. I assume this is in hopes of helping establish Mrs. Duncan's innocence in the murder." His voice was pleasant, almost cajoling, but there was something not very reassuring at all about the way he said it.

"I was just…"

He leaned back and interrupted me again, "I've spoken to both Detective Cody and Officer Bridges, and they've informed me that you have a remarkable talent for helping to solve crimes. That's very admirable." He stood up, "But in this instance, I must insist that you stay out of our investigation." He smiled again, but there was no warmth in it. He headed for the door, then turned and said, "I mean it. Stand down." He nodded, "Have a good evening."

I watched his car leave, then said to Bruno, "Well. It's not like we haven't heard those words before. He obviously doesn't know us, does he?" For some reason, this time, his warning made me worried, though. Not that I intended to do what he asked. Lynn was one of my closest friends now. There was no way I was going to let her be falsely arrested for Mrs. Drover's death.

I picked up my phone and took a moment to think about how I would approach Wendy Reichs about what she said regarding her reasons for being at Mrs. Drover's funeral. I considered leading with an inquiry into setting up a "Ring for a Ride" in the New Haven area, but instead decided to cut to the real reason for my phone call.

I identified myself when she answered the call and reminded her where we had met. Her initial silence made me think she was just going to hang up, but, after a few moments, she said, "Yes, I remember."

"Forgive me, but I can't help wondering what your relationship with Mrs. Drover was really like. I mean, you said the two of you didn't get along, yet you were among the mourners at her funeral. When you spoke to me, you were quite cryptic about your reasons for being there."

"Is that what this is really about? If you have somehow gotten the idea that I might have had something to do with Diana's death, then I can tell you that that is ridiculous. If thoughts could kill, then yes, I might, in fact, be guilty of murder, but then so would a lot of people."

"So, was your reason for attending her funeral to confirm the end to your rivalry?" I asked.

"No, of course not. Diana and I were not always at odds with each other. I might even have once called us friends. That is, until Diana's ego got in the way of even listening to another's opinion or giving credit where credit was due. However, after she was killed, I did a great deal of thinking about our relationship. The awful thought suddenly occurred to me that maybe I was equally guilty of many of the things I accused her of. That was why I felt it necessary to attend her funeral. Even though it was postmortem, as it were, I thought I owed it to her to admit that I might also have been in the wrong sometimes." She took a deep breath, "And just so you are aware, I have been questioned by the police already and told them the same thing."

Her explanation did sound authentic, much as I would have liked to believe she was involved in the murder. "I owe you an apology for questioning your motive for being at Mrs. Drover's funeral, I'm afraid. I wonder, though, if you know of anyone who would be capable of killing her?"

"No. As I said, I have already spoken to the police about this. I don't know how or why the investigation involves you, but I will be very interested to know who did kill Diana, also."

Before I could say anything else, she ended the call.

* * *

I waited at the Coretrack Homecare office until Nora arrived the following day. After we had both confirmed our patient appointments, I approached her.

"Hi, Nora. If you have a moment, I wanted to talk to you about something."

"Of course." She headed toward two chairs right outside Judy's office.

"No, let's go in here." She gave me a wary look as I motioned to the small conference room to our right.

After we were seated, I took a deep breath and said, "I saw Gina Baker a few days ago. She is a patient you had done a check on after her discharge post spinal surgery."

I saw by the look on Nora's face that she remembered Gina. "Yes, she was doing very well the day I saw her. Did she develop some complications afterward?"

"As a matter of fact, she was having quite a bit of trouble with pain control. She had taken all of the pain medication prescribed, and they should have lasted her at least a few more days."

Nora straightened in her chair, "I was worried about that. I stressed with both her and her husband that they needed to follow the instructions on the medication label, but I got the sense Mrs. Baker has a low pain threshold." Her voice was indignant. "She obviously didn't follow my instructions."

"Gina did admit to taking a couple of extra doses, but even with that, she should have had enough to last longer than they did."

Nora looked surprised. "Are you implying that you think her husband may have taken some of the narcotics?"

"No. I got no indication that he would do that. I'm not sure what happened, but one thing that struck me as odd was that the Bakers said you counted the pills she had been dispensed and said they had the correct amount. They said you told them it was protocol to do so."

Nora suddenly looked closed down. "No, that's wrong. They misheard me. I said they should count the tablets themselves to be sure they had the correct amount. Mrs. Baker was quite sleepy from her medication so she may not remember what happened correctly, and her husband was quite flustered and must not have been paying attention." Nora's voice was firm, but she had been looking down at the table as she spoke, instead of at me. She did look up then, "I hope you were able to reassure them that I knew nothing about the medication shortage. That there was some misunderstanding about what happened."

I noticed she didn't inquire if Mrs. Baker was able to finally get the pain relief she needed. "For now, we were able to solve the problem; she was going to see her physician to be assessed for appropriate pain relief."

"Well, good. What must have happened was Mrs. Baker upped her dose and didn't realize it would cause her to run out, or maybe she dropped a couple of pills and didn't notice." She stood up and said, "Thank you for letting me know about this, but I think I better get going so I'm not late for my first appointment."

I didn't know what to believe. I reasoned that I didn't have any evidence of wrongdoing on anyone's part, only a bad feeling about Nora, and this was mostly based on the mystery that seemed to surround her. I knew that I could be acting overcritical due to this, but I wondered if I should inform our supervisor, Judy Pelzer, about my concerns. After wrestling with my decision for a bit, I decided to wait until I had proof that Nora was guilty of some misconduct.

The rest of my day went without issues, and I put any questions I had about Nora out of my mind.

Lynn called me just as I was about to leave for home.

She sounded tense. "I can't believe this. First, when I got to my studio to do some work on the painting Mrs. Woodworth commissioned, it looked... disturbed. Like someone had been there.

"You mean like someone had broken in or something?"

"I don't know, nothing was missing, and I'm just getting used to the space, so maybe I'm imagining things. I just got a creepy feeling. Anyway, that's the least of it. My car died today on my way home. I had to have it towed. I'm at the garage now, and I just got a call from Detective Crane. He wants me to come down to the station right away. I would have called Alex, but I know he has a full schedule of appointments today. Could you pick me up here and bring me?"

"Of course, but why does Crane want to talk to you again?" I had a feeling that it was more than a worry about interrupting Alex's schedule that had Lynn hesitant to call him.

"I have no idea. I've told him everything that happened the day Mrs. Drover was killed—more than once."

The fact that Detective Crane wanted Lynn to come to the police station again also made me a bit uneasy. I hadn't heard if they had other suspects they were investigating, and Detective Crane seemed to really be focusing on Lynn. I made a mental note to pay a visit to Sunny Cody and see if I could get some information out of her.

Lynn was waiting for me in front of Steve's Auto Shop. As she got into my car she said, "The mechanic said it was a leak in the thing gum bob, I can't remember what it's called. Anyway, it should be ready tomorrow. Unfortunately, it doesn't sound like an inexpensive repair."

I noticed she wasn't focusing on the fact we were headed to the Madison Police Station, where she would no doubt be put through the third degree once again. The haggard look on her face said volumes, however.

As we got closer to the station, she turned to me. "Would you mind coming in with me?"

"Of course not. If they let me."

"I'll tell them I want you there. Unless they are prepared to charge me with something I think I'm allowed to have someone there for emotional support."

I wasn't sure about that, but at least if I was there and thought there was reason for concern, I could call a lawyer on her behalf.

When we got to the station, we were directed to an interrogation room. The young police officer gave me a questioning look, but Lynn grabbed my arm and pulled me along with her.

"Just have a seat. Detective Crane will be with you in a moment." The officer's tone was friendly, but I don't think it did anything to reduce the apprehension Lynn was feeling. I know it didn't do anything to mine.

We both sat in silence, watching the door, as we waited. After several minutes, Detective Crane burst in, carrying something enclosed in a clear bag. Sunny Cody entered right behind him.

"Thank you for coming in, Mrs. Duncan." He looked at me and started to say, "Ms. Bass, I'll have to ask you—"

Lynn interrupted him. "No. I want her to stay."

He looked at Sunny, who nodded. She glared at me, however.

Detective Crane took out a folder containing several sheets of paper. He looked down, referring to one of them. "Mrs. Duncan, when I spoke to you previously, you stated you had not entered the residence at 23 Sea Shell Road on the day of Mrs. Drover's murder."

Lynn nodded, "That's correct. I never went inside."

He placed the small package he had been carrying on the table now. From what I could see, it looked like a cloth covered with rust stains. Stains I recognized as dried blood. "This scarf was found as the team searched the murder scene again for the weapon. The blood matches Mrs. Drover's. The scarf was stuffed in a decorative vase near one of the doors to the front porch. Doctor Drover said he is sure it doesn't belong to his mother. I would like to know if it belongs to you." He pushed the bag across the table to Lynn.

I heard Lynn draw in her breath sharply. "That's not mine." We looked at each other wide-eyed.

It suddenly felt like something was wedged in my throat. "That's my scarf. But...how.... what was it doing where you found it?"

Detective Crane looked sharply at me. Sunny Cody looked stunned.

"Are you sure that you found that at the murder scene? I have never even been to the cottage in Madison. How could it be soaked with Mrs. Drover's blood?" I realized I was babbling, but I was beyond mystified at what could be going on.

Sunny seemed to have recovered her composure. "Melanie, you said that you have never been to 23 Sea Shore Drive?"

I shook my head, "Never."

"Are you sure this is your scarf? Look at it more closely," she said. The look on Detective Crane's face made it plain he didn't appreciate Sunny taking over the interrogation.

I pulled the bag containing the blue and green floral print silk scarf toward me. Justin bought one just like it for me after I admired it in a shop in Guilford. But she was right. It was probably not one of a kind. My heart sank almost immediately, however. I had gotten my scarf snagged on a tack protruding from a chair when Justin and I had been out to dinner one night, and I could see the snag toward one edge. I swallowed before I answered, "I recognize the pull in the fabric toward the bottom of the scarf. I'm pretty sure it is mine. But I have no idea how it ended up at the scene with Diana Drover's body." I looked from Detective Crane to Sunny.

Sunny suddenly stood and motioned to Detective Crane to step outside the room with her. Before they closed the door, I caught a snatch of what Detective Crane said, "...remind you I'm in charge...," then the door banged shut.

After they left the room, Lynn said, "Are you sure that is yours?"

"Yes, I must have lost it, and whoever did kill Mrs. Drover found it." I tried to think of when I had it last, but my mind suddenly froze.

Lynn said, "I don't like what's going on. How could the killer end up with your scarf? That doesn't make sense."

The door burst open again, and Detective Crane and Sunny strode back in. There seemed to be quite a bit of tension between them now. Detective Crane looked at Sunny, then said, "Mrs. Duncan, you can go for now." Lynn didn't move, however. He looked at me. "Ms. Bass, I'd like to review with you your movements on the day of Mrs. Drover's murder."

He took out a clean sheet of paper, informed me he would be recording my statement, and pressed a button on the recorder.

I looked to Sunny and saw her nod almost imperceptibly.

I frantically thought back to that day. The morning would be easy. I had patient appointments until 11:30 AM. The afternoon was a bit more problematic. "Uhm. I reported to the office at Coretrack Healthcare at 8 AM. My supervisor, Judy Pelzer, can verify that. I had patient appointments throughout the morning. I can give you the names of the people I saw if you need it."

He seemed to be making some kind of list or notation on his paper. "And what time did you finish seeing patients?"

I hesitated a moment, "I finished seeing my last patient at 11:30. I scheduled the afternoon off to catch up on some things I needed to do."

Detective Crane fixed his gaze on me, "What was it you needed to do? Can anyone verify where you were between 11:30 and 5 PM?"

That must be the time frame for when Mrs. Drover was killed. Unfortunately, the only witness to where I was was Bruno. I spent the afternoon doing spring cleaning, attacking the house top to bottom. I took a break to play with Bruno in the back yard for a while and then cleaned out some of the flower beds in front of the house. My nosy neighbor Karen and her daughter were away at Disney World for a few days, so she couldn't verify I was where I claimed. "I spent the afternoon cleaning and doing yard work. I didn't see anyone else. Just Bruno, my dog."

I looked to Sunny Cody for encouragement, but her expression was unreadable.

"So, basically, your actions from 11:30 AM until 5 PM are unaccounted for," he said.

"No, I told you…"

Sunny interrupted me, "I am acquainted with Ms. Bass, and while there is a possibility she could have been at the crime scene, I am inclined to believe her account of her actions that day."

Detective Crane glared at her, and Sunny gave him a cold stare back. Then he looked at Lynn as he asked me. "Any possibility your *friend* could have borrowed your scarf, Ms. Bass?"

Lynn quickly said, "No."

I thought a moment. I was sure she hadn't, and added, "No. I must have lost it somewhere." Something was starting to niggle at my brain, though. A memory I couldn't quite grasp.

We went round and round again where he tried to press me to tell him how the scarf ended up where it did, and I kept repeating that I had no idea. After several minutes, Sunny Cody blew out her breath loudly, and said, "Okay, I think we have covered this ground sufficiently."

Detective Crane glared at Sunny again but punched the button to shut off the recorder. "You both can go. For now. If I was you, Ms. Bass, I'd remember what happened to my scarf before we speak again."

Chapter Twelve

Neither one of us said anything until we got into the car. Then Lynn burst out, "OMG! What is going on? How could *you* end up linked to the murder?"

I felt unusually calm, much like I felt when I'd worked on Med/Surg and a patient was crumping before my eyes. This was no time to fall apart. "I don't know. But I keep trying to remember when I last wore that scarf." Suddenly, what I was trying to remember clicked into place. I could see myself walking up the drive to Mrs. Drover's house. It was warmer than I'd expected that day, and while it was a great accent to my dress, I began to feel perspiration break out at my neckline. I took the scarf off as I was shown into the house and shoved it in my coat pocket.

I turned to Lynn. "I was wearing it the day of the brunch at Mrs. Drover's. I took it off and left it in my coat pocket, and I don't remember seeing it after that."

Lynn looked excited, "So it's possible you lost it there. But how did it get to the cottage in Madison?"

I started the car, "Do you know if anyone is still at the Westport house? Any of the staff?"

"I think Alex said the housekeeper is still there. She has a small apartment at the rear of the house. He said he was going to ask her to stay on for a while. At least until after the estate is settled and he decides what to do with everything. Why?"

"Do you mind taking a ride with me? If she is there, I want to see if she found my scarf."

"You don't think she had anything to do with Mrs. Drover's death, do you?"

"I don't know, but as Detective Crane said, it would be in my best interest to prove I had nothing to do with my scarf being soaked with Diana Drover's blood and hidden at the murder scene."

I felt a pang of guilt again as I realized that it was getting late and I should be getting home to take care of Bruno. Karen and Jenny were home from their trip, so I made a quick call to ask Jenny to feed Bruno and take him out again. Then, we headed toward Westport. We were in luck, and traffic was unusually light on I-95, so we made good time in getting there in under the usual fifty minutes. When we got to Mrs. Drover's house, it was just starting to get dark, but I saw there were a few lights on in the front of the house and a car in the driveway.

"Did Alex say he was coming here after work today?" I said.

Lynn shook her head, "No. He said he had a late day and was seeing patients until 8 PM."

We had to wait several minutes after we rang the bell for someone to answer the door. We were just about to go around to the back to try there when the door was eased open.

"Ben! Hi! I didn't expect to find you here," Lynn said.

Alex's cousin looked equally surprised. "Lynn. I didn't expect you either." He stepped back to let us enter. "Is Alex with you?" He looked around as if to see if he was lurking somewhere before he shut the door again.

"Um. No." She motioned to me, "You remember Melanie."

He smiled at me, "Sure. So nice to see you again. I never got a chance to speak to you at my aunt's service and to thank you for coming." He stepped back so we could enter.

"I'm sorry for your loss. Lynn and Alex did a wonderful job at arranging it, don't you agree?" I said.

"Yes, it was very touching."

There was a moment of uncomfortable silence, at least he seemed uncomfortable, before he continued, "So. Why are you here today?"

I spoke up, "I think I may have left something here the day your aunt had us for brunch. A green and blue floral print silk scarf. I was wondering if anyone saw it. It has some sentimental value for me."

He shook his head and shrugged his shoulders slightly. "No. I'm afraid I haven't seen it." He looked from one to the other of us, as if unsure what to do next.

Lynn said, "Is Mrs. Cullen here? Maybe she knows what happened to it."

"Yes. Good idea. I'll go get her." He started to walk away, then turned and said to Lynn, "I wanted you to know that I don't think….you know…you did what they are saying." Without waiting for her reaction, he headed down the hallway toward another part of the house.

I looked at Lynn, "Well. That's one member of the family on your side, at least. Besides Alex, of course."

"Yes. I guess that's something."

"Why do you think he is here?" I asked.

"I don't know."

While we were waiting for Mrs. Cullen to appear, we wandered down the hall into a room with light spilling from the doorway. It looked like it was a combination library and office. There were bookcases lining two walls and a small sitting area with a couple of very comfortable-looking easy chairs grouped together. The final side had a desk placed in front of a window that took up most of the wall. In the fading light I could just make out the garden. I thought the view while sitting at the desk must be beautiful in daylight. There was a computer on the desktop. It looked to be turned off, but next to it was a stack of ruffled-looking papers.

Suddenly, Ben rushed into the room but stopped dead when he saw us in there. "Oh, there you are. Mrs. Cullen will be right with you." He walked to the desk and straightened the papers, then shoved them into the middle drawer of the desk. He turned to look at us again, "It was very nice seeing you both, but I need to be going now." He hesitated, "Unless you need something else."

Lynn answered, "No. We're good."

I had just started to examine the books on one of the bookshelves, when a voice behind me said, "You wanted to see me."

The look on the woman's face was just this side of hostile.

I kept my tone light, "Hello, nice to meet you, Mrs. Cullen. I'm a friend of Lynn's...and Alex's. I was here the day Mrs. Drover had them over for brunch with Alex's cousins. I think I left my scarf behind. It was..."

"I didn't find any scarves." She cut a look at Lynn.

"Actually, I found one, Grandma. It was on the coat room floor." A young woman I recognized as the person who let me in that day and took my coat, had entered the room. "Hi, I'm Muriel Fredricks." She held out her hand to both Lynn and me. "I was helping my grandmother straighten up after the brunch, and I found a green and blue scarf. I showed it to Mrs. Drover. She checked with her nieces and Ms. Pound, and they said they didn't know who it belonged to. She said that she thought it must belong to Ms. Duncan then, and she would take care of returning it." The girl looked at Lynn. "She said she was going to see her son in the next few days to speak to him about something. She said she would bring it to him to give to you."

I felt like a spring had come uncoiled in my chest. "Would you be willing to tell the police what you just said. It doesn't look like Mrs. Drover got a chance to give the scarf to Doctor Drover. It was found at the murder scene, and the police need to know how it got there."

Mrs. Cullen's expression had softened a little, "Of course! We'll do whatever we can to help find the monster who killed Mrs. Drover." She appeared to be looking at Lynn as she spoke.

I took Sunny Cody's business card from my wallet and handed it to Muriel. "If you call this number, Detective Cody can put you in touch with the detective in charge of the investigation. Please just tell them what you told me."

The girl nodded. "And let me give you my contact information, just in case."

I felt ten pounds lighter as we got back into the car. "That explains how the scarf got to the cottage in Madison, at least."

"But it does nothing to help find who really killed her," Lynn said. She was quiet for a bit, then said, "I wonder if Alex knew she was planning on coming to see him that day."

"Yes, and I wonder what she wanted to talk to him about."

"Humm. Yeah," Lynn said.

When she didn't say more, I added, "What do you think Ben was doing at the house? He seemed pretty familiar with where things went in the desk and was quick to put those papers away."

"Alex told me he works in finance, and I think he said Ben was helping Mrs. Drover with some investments. Maybe that has something to do with why he was at the house today," Lynn said.

"Okay. That would make sense." I didn't add that I didn't understand why he seemed nervous about us being there also.

I dropped Lynn off at her condo, telling her to call me if Alex was unable to take her to pick up her car the next day. By the time I got home I was famished, having missed my own dinner time, however I played with Bruno for a little while to make up for being so late coming home. After I fixed a quick omelet for myself, I called Justin. I was elated that I'd found an explanation for what happened to my scarf but felt awful that what was a nice gesture on Justin's part would now forever be associated with something so horrible.

I explained to him my very unsettling experience at the police department.

He sounded as if he could barely get his words out when I finished, "What! How could they think you had anything to do with the murder? You didn't even really know the woman!"

I cut in when he stopped to take a breath, "In all fairness, they had to follow up on the evidence they found at the scene. Detective Crane seemed sure the scarf belonged to Lynn before I admitted it was mine. He seems focused on pinning Mrs. Drover's murder on her." I suddenly flashed back to the sight of the blood-soaked scarf in the bag and felt queasy. I have certainly seen my share of blood, but it was the thought of whoever killed Mrs. Drover using something personal of mine to mop up her blood that upset me. "Anyway, Ms. Fredrick said she'll tell the police what happened. I'm sorry that the lovely scarf you gave me got ruined."

Justin said, "Don't worry about that! I'll buy you another one like it if you want."

I let my silence answer for me.

"Okay. Well, maybe something else, then," he said.

Chapter Thirteen

When I got to the office at Coretrack the next day to check the list of patients I had scheduled, my supervisor, Judy Pelzer, was on the phone.

"No. I'm sorry, but I can't give you that information. No. Absolutely not. Sir, if you continue to use that language, I'm going to have to end this call." She waited a few more seconds, then banged the phone receiver down. Her face had become flushed, and her hand appeared to be shaking. "How rude! I don't need to listen to that kind of abuse!"

"Who was that?" I asked. I had never seen Judy lose her temper before.

"They wouldn't say. It was a man, and he wanted to know if I had a Nora Smith working for me. When I insisted that I couldn't give him that information, he got verbally abusive." Judy was still obviously shaken by the call.

"Yeesh. Well, I hope he got the message, and he won't call back. Do you think he meant Nora Stevens?"

"Maybe," Judy said, "but in any case, I certainly wasn't going to tell him who works here unless he tells me who he is and what right he has to know."

I hadn't heard about any more complaints about Nora's care since Mr. Tabor claimed she had been a bit rough with his dressing change, but I hoped it wasn't another patient who was dissatisfied with the nursing care he'd received. I realized that I shouldn't just assume it had to do with Nora's nursing care, but that was the first explanation that came to mind. Of course, he may not have meant Nora Stevens, after all.

By the time I gathered my supplies for the day, Judy seemed to have regained her calm.

I was pleased that my morning visits went smoothly, and my day got even better at lunchtime when Sunny Cody called me.

"Just thought I'd let you know that we received a call from Muriel Fredricks. She confirmed that your scarf was in Mrs. Drover's possession when she was murdered. So, your story about having lost it checks out."

I let out a sigh of relief, "Thank you for letting me know. And thank you for standing up for me with Detective Crane when he was questioning me."

Sunny chuckled, "I have learned you are capable of many things, and I am witness to you being adept at plunging a sharp object into someone, but in this case, I'm sure you had nothing to do with Diana Drover's murder."

I laughed at her reference to me being involved in her medical care a few months previously after an attempt on her life. I do pride myself on my nearly painless injection technique. "What did Detective Crane say when Ms. Fredricks called?"

"I think the polite way to describe his reaction is 'deflated.' He was sure the bloody scarf would lead us to the murderer. Though he says that he still doesn't rule out Lynn Duncan. He says she could have mopped up the blood with it and hoped to incriminate you."

"Why is he focusing on Lynn? Aren't you investigating other suspects?" I said.

Her voice became more somber. "You know I can't tell you that. And don't think that gives you license to continue to do your own investigating. We'll find whoever did it."

I knew her insistence that I stay out of the investigation was reinforced by the fact she had undergone disciplinary action after she involved me in a case she was working on in the fall. While I knew it had only resulted in a small strike on what I was sure was her otherwise sterling record, I wondered if it had been the reason she wasn't assigned to be lead detective on the Drover murder.

I had just finished speaking to Sunny when I got another call.

"I heard what happened. The scarf and all. Like I told you before, you sure do get yourself into some touchy situations!"

I recognized Charlie Duggan's voice. "I take it you spoke to Justin. Well, this time I was just going about my business and I somehow got implicated in the murder."

"Well, glad you straightened it out," he said.

"Yes, for now. But it doesn't seem as if the police are any closer to finding who killed Mrs. Drover, and they are still considering Lynn a suspect."

"I got a hold of my friend Bill, the one whose wife is into charity work. He said his wife did work with the Drover woman on some fundraiser for the local art league last fall. He said his wife said she was a real piece of work. Half the people on the committee were scared of her, the other half tolerated her but couldn't wait until the event was over, and they didn't have to deal with her again. She did have a run-in with the committee chairman, a guy named Randall Moreland. They got into a real shouting match from what I was told, enough that one woman on the committee was all set to call the police before they calmed down on their own."

I grabbed my pen and a piece of paper. "You said his name was Randall Moreland?"

"Yeah, but don't bother trying to track him down. I checked him out already. He moved to Florida two months ago, so it doesn't look like he's the one who could have done her in."

The excitement I'd felt a minute ago drained quickly. "Well, thanks for talking to your friend, Charlie."

"Ahh, no problem. Besides your friend, do the police have anybody else in their sights? I'm guessing you have been doing some investigating on your own," he said.

"The police won't say who else they are looking at. But as a matter of fact, I did speak to a couple of people who I thought might have a reason to kill Mrs. Drover." I told him about my conversations with Wendy Reichs and Edgar Flint. "I'm pretty sure neither of them did it. Though, I got the feeling the maintenance man, Edgar, might be keeping some information back, but I couldn't be sure."

Charlie made a grunting noise, then said, "If it was me, I'd go talk to him again. I know when I was working security, if you wanted to know what was going on somewhere the place to start was by talking to the janitor. Maintenance people tend to blend into the background, and they notice when something ain't going as it should."

"Thanks, Charlie, I'll think about that." I remembered I'd told Edgar I might want some yard work done. He said I could get his number from Alex.

"Let me know if you learn anything interesting after you talk to him."

After we spoke about how his health was, and he tried to pry out of me how my relationship with his grandson was going, I hung up.

I called Lynn after work to ask her to get Edgar Flint's number from Alex. "You can let him know I spoke to Edgar about it at the funeral, and he said Alex would have it."

Lynn called me back within the hour. "Alex gave me the number right away when I told him you had already approached Edgar about doing the work, but I could tell something was bothering him. I had to prod him a little to tell me what it was, but he is upset now that he knows his mother planned to come to speak to him about something on the day she was killed. I think that he has some twisted idea that if he had known she was going to the cottage, he could have somehow been able to prevent her being murdered. He thinks that if it was an intruder who killed her, he could have been there to stop it, or at least gotten someone to go to the cottage with her so she wouldn't have been alone."

"But that is crazy. We don't know why or who killed her. And he's right, it could have been someone who planned to rob the place, even though the police don't seem to be going in that direction," I said.

"I know. I tried to tell him that. And that if he had been there, he could have been another victim. He seemed upset that he never found out what she wanted to tell him, also. He feels that it must have been important because she wanted to speak to him in person."

"So, you must have told him that the police brought you in to question you about the bloody scarf they discovered at the murder scene. What did he say when he learned it belonged to me?"

"I went in person to tell him right away the next morning. I didn't want him to hear it from the police or anyone else. He looked shaken at first, but I was quick to tell him the whole story." She paused for a moment, "After his initial shock, however, I could swear he also looked relieved."

I hesitated to say what I was thinking, "You don't think—"

"That he thought it might belong to me?" Lynn's voice caught on the end of her question. "No. I can't let myself think that. I can't."

"I agree. I don't think you should read anything into his reaction." I tried to reassure myself that he had called the accusations against Lynn ridiculous and was sticking to that opinion.

Lynn continued, "I explained how we went to the house in Westport to see if that was where you lost your scarf. When I got to the part about Ben being there, he looked surprised, though he tried to hide it. Then he said the same thing I told you, that Ben was helping his mother with some financial matters and must have been there to get some papers he needed to settle the estate."

I still thought it odd that Ben seemed uneasy when we showed up there. Though some people are uncomfortable being in someone else's house when they aren't there. Especially since, in this case, his aunt was gone for good. "That is the most likely explanation, then."

"My guess is that you want Edgar's number to see what he noticed the day he found Mrs. Drover's body that he hasn't shared with anyone else. Or have you had a sudden urge to relandscape your yard?" Lynn said.

I laughed, "No, you're right. I thought it was worth a shot to see if he might be more likely to talk to someone who was no threat to him. Even if he sticks to the same story, he told the police, sometimes just reading a person's body language when they are telling you something can be revealing."

"Well, good luck. Let me know right away what you think after you talk to him."

After I ended the call with Lynn, I looked at the time and decided to wait to call Edgar until the following day after work.

* * *

The following morning, when I got to the office at Coretrack Homecare, Judy was using her shoulder to clamp her phone to her ear and was frantically typing something into her computer. Debbie walked in shortly after me, and Judy mouthed, "Wait here a minute" to both of us.

After she hung up, Judy said, "Nora called in again today. She said she had a sudden emergency and wouldn't be able to come in. I'm trying to rearrange everyone else's schedule to accommodate the most urgent appointments."

Debbie and I were able to identify a couple of our own patients who we knew would be able to wait another day or so to be seen, or who could be checked on with a phone call. After a bit of juggling with the schedule, it looked like if everyone who was scheduled to work that day picked up one more appointment all the patients could be seen.

I wondered what Nora's emergency was and hoped she was able to straighten it out all right. In spite of my initial uneasy feeling about her, or maybe because of my so far unconfirmed suspicions, I had begun to feel guilty about the assumptions I'd made about her. I also felt a little sorry for her. I didn't know if she had made any friends since moving here and wondered if she had anyone she could rely on for help if she needed it.

I didn't have much more time to worry about Nora that day, as it was indeed very busy. I was glad to hear that Mrs. Chatham, the patient I was covering for Nora, had only good things to say about her and the care she gave. There were a few glitches with two of my own patients having to do with missed appointments and misunderstood medication instructions, but they were, thankfully, satisfactorily resolved.

I was glad that Justin and I had plans to go out for dinner that night, as by the time I got home, I didn't feel like cooking even my usual simple fare for myself. I couldn't cut short my playtime with Bruno, however, and after a game of fetch in the backyard and a quick walk, I felt recharged.

While I was waiting for Justin to arrive, I called the number Lynn had given me for Edgar Flint. I got his voicemail and left a message telling him that I wanted some type of hedge but would leave it to him to suggest the best kind. I asked him to let me know when he could come out to do the work.

I hadn't seen Justin in a few days, and in spite of the fact I prided myself on my self-sufficiency, I was surprised by how comforted I felt when I answered the door, and he drew me into his arms. We had had a falling out several months earlier, mainly due to my stubborn insistence I was perfectly capable of taking care of myself no matter the situation, and Justin's insistence on protecting me. Over time, we had come to a compromise where I agreed to consider the consequences of my sometimes bold actions, and he agreed to trust my judgment more. This solution seemed to be working. Most of the time. But I hadn't realized just how tense the past few weeks had made me until I was able to relax in his arms.

I kissed him and pulled him into the house. "I'm so glad to see you!"

"Whoa! I'm glad to see you, too." He kissed me again and began to guide me toward the sofa. "We don't have to go out. We can stay here if you like." He gave me a devilish grin.

Just then, my stomach growled, and I pulled away from him. "Don't take this the wrong way, but as good as that sounds, a plate of penne alla vodka with chicken sounds as good."

Bruno began to bark and run around us, no doubt annoyed Justin had not taken time to greet him when he arrived. Justin bent to pet him and scratch under his chin. "Do you hear what your mom said? She's ready to throw me over for a plate of pasta!"

"Well, we can see how you do in that competition—later." I gave him my own suggestive grin.

* * *

Once we were driving toward Café Fiore', Justin said, "How is Lynn doing? Have the police gone on to concentrate on another suspect in the murder?"

"Detective Crane still seems to be focusing on Lynn, though I know they have also questioned other people." I wanted Justin's opinion on something else that had been bothering me. "I'm a little worried about Lynn and Alex, though."

Justin glanced over at me. "In what way?"

I wanted to be sure my initial feeling that Alex might not be the right man for Lynn was not clouding my assessment now. "From what Lynn has told me, it seems that Alex isn't sure Lynn had nothing to do with his mother's murder. He hasn't come right out and said that, but for instance, he keeps pressuring her as to why the police keep interviewing her. When the bloody scarf was found at the murder scene, Lynn said she got the feeling that he thought it might be hers until she told him it was mine and explained how it got there."

We had reached the restaurant, and Justin pulled into a parking space. "That doesn't sound good for their relationship. What does Lynn say about it?"

"She always has an explanation or an excuse for the way he is acting, but I can see she is worried about it," I said.

Justin paused before getting out of the car. "What are your thoughts on the matter?"

"I think she is trying desperately to convince herself that their relationship will work, but the fact that he seems to have any doubts about her innocence is certainly a red flag as far as I'm concerned."

He grabbed my hand as we headed toward the entrance to the restaurant. "I agree with you. But all you can do is be there for her when she comes to that realization herself."

I sighed, "I only hope she does before it's too late and she's hurt again."

After a delicious meal, once we got back to my house and a very successful effort on Justin's part to make me forget all my worries, I fell into a dreamless sleep.

Chapter Fourteen

The next day, I got home from work to find a truck with the logo "Flint Landscaping and Property Maintenance" in my driveway, and Edgar already making a survey of my yard.

My backyard was fenced in, so I didn't need anything planted there; I didn't want to obscure the view of my front yard and house on the side of my neighbor Karen Walters. Karen kept a good eye on my property, even if I sometimes didn't appreciate just how well she watched the goings on at my place. Also, her daughter, Jenny, took care of Bruno after she got home from school, and I wanted to keep it as easy as possible for her to access my yard. The property on the west side of my house was rented by a couple who kept very much to themselves. I figured a couple of shrubs on that side wouldn't hurt.

"Hi Edgar. Thanks for coming out so quickly." I held out my hand.

"Well, since you are a friend of Doctor Drover, I hated to keep you waiting. I brought some shrubs that I think will suit what you're looking for."

I could see that he had several small burlap-wrapped boxwoods in the bed of his truck. I pointed to the property line on the west side of my driveway. "I thought maybe we could plant those there."

He nodded, "Okay, whatever you want. These are small now, but they will give you a nice privacy screen in no time." He headed toward his truck.

I could hear Bruno barking inside, and went in to get him. After a joyful welcome home from Bruno, I snapped his leash on, telling him, "I want you to be your most endearing. I need to get this man to talk to me." I hoped Edgar was a dog lover.

I needn't have worried. We walked over to where Edgar was beginning to dig the first hole, and he turned toward us, and I could see his expression melt at the sight of Bruno.

"Hey, buddy. You're a good boy, aren't you? Yes." Edgar bent to stroke Bruno's head, and Bruno wiggled with joy. "Nice dog. I have an old coon hound at home. Roscoe. He's my best friend."

I smiled. "Yes, I know what you mean." I bent to stroke Bruno also. "You know all my secrets and more, don't you, buddy?"

Edgar went back to digging, and I took Bruno to sniff around the front yard a bit, then we went over to stand by where Edgar was placing the first shrub. He was of average height and slim but looked wiry, and gray hair peeked out from under his cap. I judged him to be in his early to mid-fifties. "Alex said you have worked for the Drovers for a long time. You must have gotten to really know the family over the years."

"Yep. Mrs. Drover hired me to care for the property right after I started my business. I appreciated the work, and she talked me up to her friends in the area, too. Got me more business.

I wasn't long out of high school and not too much older than Dr. Drover and his cousins then." He chuckled, "Sometimes when they were at the cottage in the summer, if I wasn't rushing to another job, the kids and I would play wiffle ball in the side yard, or I'd help them get their old rowboat down to the shore. Their mothers never said anything about it. Maybe they were glad someone was keeping their kids busy for a little bit."

It sounded like he had a genuine affection for the family. It must have been a real blow when he got let go. And more so when he found Mrs. Drover's body. "It must be hard for you, the way things turned out."

"Yep." He was working pretty fast. He was on to his third shrub, and I hadn't found out what he was hiding about what happened that day. "You must know the property quite well. Did anything seem out of place, or did you notice anything odd before you went in the house to speak to Mrs. Drover?"

He stopped working for just a moment, but then went back to packing the dirt around the shrub he had just planted. "I understand the police found some blood on the front porch, but I went in the back way, so I don't know if it was there when I got there. When I went inside, I noticed some papers and things on the floor near the desk in the alcove. My first thought was Mrs. Drover must have been really upset about something to not straighten up that mess. Once I found…her…I didn't spend any more time in there. Ran outside and called the police right away. I was pretty shook up, can't be sure anything else I noticed was even real or I just imagined it."

"Yes. I know that can happen when someone has had a shock. What did you think you saw?"

He just kept working, ignoring my question. I wasn't sure if I'd pushed him too far, and he wasn't going to answer. Then he said, "I did think there was a lot of sand tracked up onto the back porch. I'd swept it the day before. I thought maybe Mrs. Drover had been down to the beach in front of the house, or it could have been the wind blew it up there. When I went to get my tools from the boat house shed…" He stopped to toss a rock he'd uncovered toward a small pile he had started next to where he set his tools. "There have been problems with local kids breaking into properties in that area when the owners aren't there. That's one of the jobs I had, to make sure the property was secure. The lock was off the boathouse door. I must have forgotten to lock it the last time I was there."

"Was anything disturbed in the boathouse? Your tools were all there?"

He grunted as he placed the last shrub in its hole. "Almost done." He gave me a tight smile, "Could I trouble you for a glass of water?"

"Sure." I realized we had probably reached the end of what he was going to tell me about that day. It was obvious that something he saw in the boathouse bothered him. I wondered if whatever it was could have been the murder weapon that, as far as I knew, was still missing. But then why not tell the police about it? Unless he was worried one of his tools had been used to kill Mrs. Drover. That gave me pause, it certainly would incriminate him, and I knew he was nervous about that. I was sure the police had searched the boathouse for a weapon, though.

I left Bruno in the house with his favorite toy, and I brought Edgar his water. He had filled in around the shrub before I got back outside. After he finished drinking, I said, "What made you think some local kids had been in the boathouse?"

"Like I said, I was not thinking exactly straight after what I just saw. I'm not sure what I thought, and the police didn't notice anything out of place there. Like you said, I must have been in shock." He handed me back the empty glass. "Thank you."

He wrote up the bill, and while I made out the check, he gave me instructions on how to care for the newly planted shrubs.

He hoisted himself into his truck and said, "Let me know if you want any other work done." He waved as he pulled away.

I wasn't sure I'd gained much more information about what Edgar was keeping to himself, but one thing I knew: I would love to take a look in that boathouse myself.

* * *

I called Lynn and invited her to stop over for tea after her last art class that evening.

I heard her car pull into the driveway and had the water on to boil before she walked in the door.

"Nice new hedge you have. I take it Edgar was here today." She eased herself into one of the kitchen chairs.

"Yes. But I didn't get too much more out of him. He is still keeping something back, though I don't know why. He seemed to really be fond of both Mrs. Drover and her whole family. I can't think why he wouldn't tell the police everything he remembered about that day. One thing he insinuated was that he noticed something in the boathouse that bothered him. He wouldn't say what, though. He tried to pass it off as vandalism, or a false memory, but I think he is sure about what he saw."

"Maybe he's afraid that whoever the murderer is will come after him if they think he can identify them," Lynn said.

"Hmm. Maybe. But I don't think that's it." I poured the tea and got the milk out of the refrigerator. "He mentioned seeing papers scattered across the floor by a desk. Did you hear anything about that?"

Lynn nodded. "Yes. The police asked Alex about them. He didn't know what they were, but the police said from what they could see, they looked like someone was writing a family history or something. Apparently, they looked old. Alex asked the police if they could return them after the case was solved. He said he was eager to see what they contained."

I had a sudden thought, "Maybe that was what his mother wanted to talk to him about. Maybe she wanted to tell him she had found them and to figure out what to do with them."

"It could be," Lynn said, "but she mentioned she planned to talk to Alex before she went to the cottage. That would mean she already had the papers. Where and when did she find them, then?"

"Okay, that's a good point." We both drank our tea in quiet for a few minutes. "Alex didn't mention if the police told him they had found the murder weapon yet, did he? I wonder if Edgar noticed one of his tools missing from the boathouse. Or something else that is usually stored there," I said.

"No, as far as I know, the murder weapon is still missing. The police admitted that 'it doesn't look' like my palette knife was used to kill Mrs. Drover, but they added, 'if I didn't mind, they needed to hang on to it for a bit longer.' When she was killed, the police said the murder weapon was something with a long blade. What would be in the boathouse that would fit that description?"

I thought for a moment. "It could definitely be one of Edgar's tools. The blades of a garden shears are long."

"Yes, but they made it sound like it was a single blade."

"He must have a utility knife he uses. I'm sure the police checked that, though, and ruled it out."

"Assuming it was a knife that was used to kill her, it could have been any kind of knife, and whoever did it must have taken it with them."

"True. I wonder what Edgar noticed that he didn't want to share, then?" I hesitated before asking her about what I had been thinking. "Do you think there's any possibility we could get into the boathouse to look around ourselves?"

Lynn drew in her breath sharply and shook her head. "I don't know if that's such a good idea. I know the police aren't allowing anyone back into the cottage itself. If he finds out we went into the boat house, Detective Crane is likely to turn it around somehow so it looks as if we are doing something to further incriminate ourselves. Despite Mrs. Cullen's daughter's explanation of how your scarf ended up at the murder scene, I think you are still on his radar, too."

I knew she was probably right, but the sooner the murder was solved, the sooner the dark cloud of suspicion would be lifted from over her head. Both our heads, as she had just pointed out. "Just think about it, okay?"

Just then, Lynn's phone rang. I could hear her agreeing to whatever the person on the other end was saying, but she sounded a bit dejected. After she ended the call, she said, "That was Alex. I was supposed to meet him at his place this evening. He says he needs to meet Ben to discuss a family matter, and he is pretty sure he won't be home until late, so it might be better if I don't come over until tomorrow. We were supposed to make a final decision tonight on the caterer for the wedding."

"One day longer most likely won't cause you to lose your first choice." I was trying to think of something encouraging to say to her. All the wedding planning had been put on hold after Mrs. Drover's death, but I was sure by now Lynn was ready to find something good to look forward to for her and Alex.

"You're probably right." She stood to place her tea mug in the dishwasher, preparing to leave. "It's more that…maybe I'm just being oversensitive, but I could swear I heard a woman's voice in the background as we were speaking."

"You're right. You are being oversensitive. There may be a logical explanation. If they are meeting at a bar or a restaurant, it wouldn't be unusual for there to be voices in the background," I said. I wondered if Lynn was starting to feel some doubts about her relationship with Alex now, also.

"Thanks for talking me off the ledge again. I guess I'm letting all the recent stress get to me," Lynn said.

"Do you know what Alex and Ben were meeting about?"

"It might be something to do with Mrs. Drover's estate. I know the family is supposed to meet at attorney Sander's office this week to go over her will. Maybe tonight Ben and Alex are meeting to talk about whatever Ben was working on for Alex's mother."

Bruno seemed to have had enough of the conversation at this point, as he jumped up into my lap and began to lick my face. "Okay. I know we were ignoring you!" I rubbed his ears and placed him back on the floor. "Let's walk Auntie Lynn out."

Lynn picked up her purse and jacket and said, "Since I'm not meeting Alex tonight, I might as well see if I can get a little bit of work done on the painting I'm working on."

"How are you liking the studio you rented? Is it convenient having a separate place to work?"

"I love it," Lynn said, "though I'm a little nervous working there after it gets dark. I think I'm just jumpy because of what is going on with the murder and all, but things looked like they had been moved around a little." She laughed, "At first, I wondered if the landlord was checking to make sure I was using the space for what I said I was using it for and not for some illegal master plan."

"Was anything missing?"

"No. And the more I thought about it, I wasn't sure I hadn't left things the way I found them," she said.

"Still…"

"I know, I'll be careful."

It was still light out, and I could hear the red-winged blackbirds calling back and forth to each other in the reeds and bushes across the road. Lynn stopped to look around before she got into her car. "Don't get me wrong, I love my new condo, but I kind of miss this place." She tipped her chin toward the little shrubs Edgar had just put in, "Despite your actual reason for having Edgar plant them, I think those are going to look very nice."

Chapter Fifteen

I saw Gina Baker again as part of my patient assignment the following day and was amazed at the difference in her. Her surgical site was healing well, and she said now she was able to get by with over-the-counter pain meds during the day, needing her prescription meds only at night.

"I'm sorry I was such a complainer the day you first came to check on me. I just couldn't deal with the pain as well as I expected. Thank you for straightening out my med situation." She looked embarrassed for a moment. "I did find one of my pain pills stuck between the cushions on my sofa. I must have dropped it when I was taking one from the vial those first couple of days. I was still a bit shaky."

Now, I felt maybe I had been too quick to suspect Nora. Though it seemed unlikely, Gina could have dropped several of the pills that had been missing without noticing. However, I had not heard of any other problems with any of Nora's other patient's meds, so had to admit my suspicions may be unfounded. "There is no question you were in a lot of pain, so no need to apologize for your reaction. I'm glad your doctor was able to prescribe something that worked to help you."

Gina was my last patient of the day, and I was glad to end on a positive note. When I got back to Coretrack after work, I noticed Nora Stevens leaving the building. She was walking toward her car with her head down and seemed deep in thought. I wondered if she had straightened out whatever the personal issue was that she had the other day.

"Hi, Nora." She seemed not to have heard me, so I increased my pace to come up beside her and tapped her gently on the arm. "Hi."

She leapt away from me and spun around quickly, letting out a startled "Hunh!" Then she looked around as if expecting an armed attack.

"I'm so sorry! I didn't mean to startle you. I called out, but you must not have heard me."

She had her hand to her chest. "No, I didn't. Give me a minute to get my heart rate under control."

I realized I must really have given her a scare. "Is everything all right? Can I do anything for you? You seemed preoccupied."

"No. I'm fine." She gave me a weak smile. "Did you need something?"

"No, I saw you, and I thought I would check on how things were going at work…and all."

"It's going fine. Is there some kind of problem? Did I forget to chart something?" She looked apprehensive.

"No, no. Nothing like that. Like I said, I just wanted to touch base with you, see if you needed help with anything."

"No. Everything is okay. Thank you for asking." She smiled and turned to walk toward her car in the parking lot again.

I walked beside her until we reached her car, "Would you like to go for a cup of tea, or coffee? It'll give us a chance to just relax, and I'd love it if we just had a chance to talk and get to know each other a little better. I'll just check in at the office first, and then I know a great place we can go." I surprised myself with the invitation, but I realized I probably should have asked her before this to go for a cup of coffee in order to welcome her to the agency. I thought if I reached out and made an effort to get to know her better, any feelings I had about there being something not right about her would be dispelled. Or, in the worst case scenario, confirmed.

She stopped before unlocking her car, looking as if she was struggling with her decision. "Thank you, but I think I'd better just get home." She gave me a polite smile, but then quickly opened her car door and loaded her laptop and work bag into the front passenger seat.

I wasn't sure if she was upset because of me approaching her the other day about what happened with Gina Baker or if it was something else that was bothering her. "Okay. Maybe another time?"

"Sure." She buckled up and shut the car door.

I watched her as she backed up and left the parking lot, feeling a mixture of guilt that I had not been friendlier to her earlier and offense that my efforts now were being rebuffed.

I had just started walking toward the building to sign out and happened to glance toward the road again when it looked like a dark blue SUV pulled out from the side of the road by the parking lot and seemed to speed up after Nora's car. I shook my head, convinced that I had come to see malicious intent everywhere lately. On the heels of this thought, though, came another: that while the events of the past year had made me much more suspicious of people, it had also taught me that often those suspicions were warranted.

It had been cloudy for most of the day, but on my way home, the sun broke through. I decided a longer-than-usual walk with Bruno might help clear some of my own mental clouds and help me put the things that had been worrying me in some kind of perspective.

Once I got home, I changed into my jeans and a sweatshirt and grabbed Bruno's leash to load him into the car for the drive to the bike path at Hammonasset Beach State Park. I planned to walk the almost two miles, starting at Meigs Point to West Beach. The path was more crowded than I thought it would be. It looked like I was far from the only one who decided to take advantage of the sunny afternoon. Most of the people we encountered were accompanied by their dogs, and Bruno was in his glory greeting them all. We had gotten about halfway to West Beach when I saw a familiar figure approaching, walking an energetic brown lab puppy. The dog was bouncing from one side of the path to the other, apparently not sure which side held the most interesting smells.

I heard a firm command of, "No, Beanie. Heel. Heel." The puppy stopped to look at Sunny Cody, skittered over to sit by her for a moment, then jumped up and began to pull her down the path toward us again.

Bruno spun around in a circle as Beanie, now twice his size, hopped around him. I bent to pet the very excited puppy. "Hi, Beanie! You are getting so big!"

"Sorry. She doesn't seem to remember all the commands she executes so perfectly with her trainer," Sunny said.

"But look at her, she's so sweet!" I said as she gave my hands a thorough licking.

"Yes. Good thing." She bent to pet her also.

I straightened up and looked behind Sunny. "Where is Katie? She isn't with you?" Sunny had gotten Beanie for her four-year-old daughter, and I knew the dog and little girl were usually inseparable.

She smiled, "No. not today. She's at a birthday party. Her social schedule is quite full these days. This one," she motioned toward the puppy, "needed to blow off some steam, so I thought we'd take a nice long walk before I have to pick up Katie at the party."

Both dogs had settled to sit at our feet now, though I could see a couple with a golden retriever puppy approaching and didn't think Beanie would be still much longer.

I was searching for a way to ask if there was anything she could tell me about the progress of the investigation into Mrs. Drover's murder, when Sunny said, "Before you ask, I can't tell you anything more about the investigation. Mostly because I don't have access to what is going on with it. Crane is keeping anything he finds out close to his vest at this point." She didn't look happy about it.

"Why isn't he sharing information with you? Aren't you on the team?"

She cleared her throat and looked off down the path, "Yes, well, he complained to the captain that I seemed to have too much of an involvement with some of the suspects and that I was trying to take over the investigation. He claimed that my judgment was being affected by personal matters." She stopped to take a large rock the puppy was chewing out of Beanie's mouth. She threw it into the brush with a great deal of force. "The captain asked me to step back a little; he said he understood my desire to be more deeply involved in the investigation, but in this case, it might be better to do as Crane asked."

"I'm sorry. I didn't mean to put you in a difficult situation, but I can't just stand by and watch Lynn get accused of a horrendous crime, one she certainly did not commit."

The dogs were getting restless, and Sunny motioned that we should start walking with them again.

After we had gone a few steps, I said, "I have to say, I would feel a lot better if you were leading the investigation." I hesitated a minute, not sure if I should mention what I'd learned from Edgar, then said, "I spoke to Edgar Flint, the maintenance man for the cottage."

Sunny gave me a sharp look.

"He did some landscaping at my house and we got to talking. There is something I'm not sure he mentioned when he was interviewed after the murder." I told her he hinted that it had something to do with what he saw in the boathouse when he went to speak to Mrs. Drover the day of the murder. "He didn't tell me the specifics, but whatever it is struck a chord with him."

She sighed, "I trust your instincts, but I know the boathouse was thoroughly searched the day of the murder, and nothing was found. We asked Mr. Flint, and he denied anything was missing. Are you saying he lied?"

"I don't know, but maybe it wouldn't hurt to take a second look."

"I'll pass that along, though I don't know how Crane is going to receive that suggestion."

"Can I ask if the neighbor who saw Lynn at the house that day saw anyone else there either before or after Lynn? Edgar thought Mrs. Drover might have spent some time down on the beach that day. He said there was sand tracked up to the back porch. Maybe someone saw if she was with someone else."

Sunny hesitated before replying, "The neighbor said she was out all day prior to seeing Lynn at the house, so she couldn't tell us if anyone else had been there. She mentioned that she usually kept to herself and didn't have much to do with Mrs. Drover. They had some kind of disagreement when the neighbor first moved in, and the relationship had been chilly ever since. However, since there have been several break ins in the area over the past few months, she said when she actually saw someone on the porch next door, she felt she had to investigate."

"How about the neighbors on the other side? Did they see anyone?"

"No. The house was empty at that time. The owners are seasonal and hadn't opened the house for the summer yet. That is all I can tell you. I may not be fully involved in the investigation at this time, but you know I can't divulge information I do have that could potentially help identify the killer."

"I understand." I did, but I also felt any bits of information I could squeeze out of her might help.

We had gotten back to the start of the path by Meigs point now, and I thought Bruno and I had gotten enough exercise so didn't need to retrace our steps.

Beanie looked like she had finally calmed down, and Detective Cody said, "It was nice meeting you here. I have to pick up Katie shortly, so I better go now." As she started to walk away, she turned and said, "I'd tell you again to stay out of the investigation, but I know you won't listen. Just try to stay out of Detective Crane's way. And be careful."

Chapter Sixteen

The next morning, I woke up to the sound of my phone ringing. I reached over to check who was calling and saw it was Coretrack Homecare. I felt a moment of panic that I had overslept. I was sure I was scheduled to be off today, though. When I answered the call, Judy sounded frazzled.

"Sorry to bother you on your day off, but I wonder if you could come in for a while this morning. Nora Stevens was a no-show, and she isn't answering her phone. It looks like a couple of her patients really must be seen today, and everyone else's schedule is full."

I sat up in bed, and Bruno got up from where he had been snuggled against my hip to watch me from the foot of the bed. "Sure. Let me shower and take care of Bruno, and I'll be right there."

"Thanks. You're a lifesaver," Judy said.

On the way to Coretrack, I thought about the fact that Nora seemed to be turning out to be pretty unreliable. She had called out twice in a short period of time, granted it may have been for good reason, but now she hadn't shown up at all. She seemed fine when I saw her the previous day. I hoped she was alright, but it was irresponsible of her to just not show up for work without calling to let Judy know what was going on.

I saw Judy's eyes light up when I walked into her office. "Thank you again for coming in. I think that if you can just see these four patients, we can reschedule the others. I'll try to contact Nora again to see what happened. Maybe she just got her days mixed up."

I could see why Judy didn't want to postpone the care visits to the four patients she wanted me to cover for Nora. They all needed IV meds to be administered, and two had just been discharged from the hospital and were having problems with wound care or understanding the post-kidney transplant regime their doctor recommended. However, I was able to get everyone seen, and any problems they were having straightened out by late morning.

When I got back to the office, I checked in with Judy. "Any luck getting in touch with Nora?" I asked.

Judy looked up from her computer screen. "No. I tried to call her again, but still no answer." She looked a bit worried now, "I'm concerned about what is going on with her. I know she has made a practice of keeping to herself since she started work here, but in the past few days, she has seemed distracted. Yesterday, after she left, Catherine found her driver's license on the floor outside the office. Now she hasn't shown up for work, and I can't get in contact with her."

I had to agree with Judy; it did seem like something was going on with Nora, and it was more than the standoffishness that she still exhibited. Maybe the best course of action would be to contact the police and ask them to do a wellness check on her, but since I was the one who oriented her to the job when she first came to work here, I still felt a sense of responsibility for her. Also, given what I knew of her desire for privacy, I wasn't sure how Nora would react to the police showing up at her door. "I could take her license to her, and that way I can make sure she is okay," I said.

Judy hesitated a moment, "Are you sure you wouldn't mind? I *would* feel better knowing it was just a misunderstanding on her part about her schedule." Judy handed me Nora's driver's license. I recognized the name of the road she lived on, Strawbow Road. I had seen a few patients in the area and had driven by it before.

"Sure. I'll tell her we want to make sure she is all right since you couldn't get in touch with her and that we knew she would need her driver's license. I'll call you after I see her and let you know what happened."

Nora lived in a secluded part of North Madison. When I got to Strawbow Road, I saw one car driving down the pothole-filled road some distance ahead of me; otherwise the road was deserted. The houses I passed were spaced far apart, and a good many had 'For Sale' signs posted in front of them. It was difficult at first for me to find Nora's address since the number on her mailbox was partially occluded by bushes. Her house was set back from the road and bordered on both sides by a brushy area. My first thought was that it must be a big difference from where she lived in Arizona—or Colorado—or Washington or wherever it was that she actually lived before coming to Connecticut. The house was small, perhaps once a cottage, and it was painted a light gray with faded blue shutters framing the windows. A small enclosed screened-in front porch with a slightly sagging roof was at the front. When I went up to the door to knock, I found the door to the porch was locked. The bamboo shades pulled down over the screened windows made it impossible to see inside. I didn't hear any noise coming from inside the house or see any lights on. It occurred to me that Nora might not even be home.

I rapped loudly on the porch door. "Nora! It's Melanie Bass. Are you here?" There was no answer. I stepped back off the two steps leading to the porch and tried calling out again, watching the windows of the house for someone to look out.

"Nora, It's Melanie. I have something I need to give you. Are you home?" I thought this time I saw one of the curtains in the window twitch. I went back up to stand outside the porch door. A few seconds later, Nora squeezed out of the barely opened front door and strode over to unlock and open the door to the porch. She gripped my arm and pulled, rather than guided, me onto the porch, shutting the door behind us.

"Hi. What are you doing here?" Her voice was strained.

She certainly looked physically well, if ready to jump out of her skin. "You dropped your driver's license at work yesterday. I thought I would bring it to you." I held out the license.

"Oh. Well, thank you." She took it and shoved it into the pocket of her jeans.

"Judy was a bit worried also; you were scheduled to work today and—"

"No, I'm...oh. Heavens! I'm so sorry. I thought I was working tomorrow."

"Judy was also concerned because when you didn't show up for work, she tried to call you, and couldn't get an answer," I said. Just then, I thought I heard someone say something from inside the house. I craned my neck to try to see inside the partially open front door. "Oh, I'm sorry. I thought you lived alone."

"Yes. That's right. It must be the TV." She stepped over to close the front door completely. "My old phone was giving me problems, so I had to get a new one. I must have forgotten to give Judy my new number. I'll call and let her know what it is."

"Okay. Good." I hadn't heard any noise like a TV on before, and it sounded like a female voice saying, "Nora…okay?"

Even though she seemed to be fine, just eager for me to leave, I asked her anyway, "So you are all right? I promised Judy I'd make sure."

She gave me a very unconvincing smile. "Yes. I'm fine. Thank her for her concern, and I'm sorry for not showing up at work today." She tapped her temple. "Just a glitch in memory." She walked toward the porch door. "And thank you so much for bringing me my license. I can't believe I dropped it."

She yanked the door open for me, but before I could step out, she leaned forward to peek out, as if she was checking to make sure no one else was waiting in her front yard. "See you at work."

My visit to Nora had done nothing to dispel my feelings that there was something strange going on with her. However, she looked well enough, and she insisted she didn't need help, so I guessed I'd just have to chalk it up to the fact that some people are just…different. I called Judy and let her know Nora was fine and had been confused about what day she was working. I knew I should feel satisfied that I had done all I could to reach out to Nora, that if she didn't want to accept help, there was nothing more I could do. As I drove toward home, I realized I was getting sick of people keeping secrets. First Edgar Flint, and now Nora. Because I was sure that Nora did have a secret, one that she was guarding closely.

Chapter Seventeen

I had the next day off and was eager to hear if Lynn and Alex had booked the caterer for the wedding. I knew she wanted to have Glen's Gourmet do it and wondered if Alex agreed and they were able to book them. It was a bit less than four months until their wedding in August, and I knew it could be tight as far as being able to book their preferred caterer. I called Lynn to see if she wanted to go out to breakfast so we could talk.

"Oh, I'd love to meet you for breakfast, but Alex wanted me to come with him to Attorney Sander's office so they can go over his mother's will. I'm meeting him at Highlife Derm shortly. As far as the caterer, we went with Theresa's Culinary Triumph. Alex said it was recommended to him by a friend. He said that his friend heard complaints about Glen's Gourmet, that there were issues with them not always delivering what they promised."

"That's too bad about Glen's. I always heard good things about their food. How do you feel about the one Alex's friend recommended?"

"It will be fine. Alex has let me make all the other decisions about the wedding, even though his mot…even when we had strong suggestions to the contrary." She chuckled, "Though I really was looking forward to the Filet Mignon with Merlot Demi-Glace on Glen's menu. I heard it was to die for. Oh, dear. I guess I shouldn't put it that way."

I laughed, "You probably aren't going to remember too much about what you eat anyway. You'll be so wrapped up in the excitement of the day."

"True. Though I distinctly remember the awful Chicken Parmesan I had at the luncheon Doug and I had to celebrate after our ceremony. Let's just say I was not at my best on our first night as man and wife."

I laughed, "I take it you checked to make sure Chicken Parm is not on Theresa's menu?"

"First thing I looked at! I'm sorry, but I have to leave now if I'm going to be on time to meet Alex when I said I would."

"I'm glad Alex asked you to come with him to the attorney's office. Let me know how things go."

I had my heart set on going out for breakfast, and I hadn't had much time lately to catch up with any of my friends from work. I knew Catherine was also off today, so I called her to see if she wanted to meet me at Christie's in Madison for brunch. We started off by talking about work, how things had finally calmed down a bit from a few weeks previously, and how happy we were that our co-worker, Elsa, was finally pregnant after trying for so long. It wasn't long, however, before the conversation turned to Nora Stevens.

"After I found her driver's license on the floor in the hallway outside the office, I tried to catch her to tell her she had dropped it, but she was already gone by the time I got to the parking lot," Catherine said. "She's a bit odd, but I feel sorry for her. She is all alone, and in a new place. I did try to start a conversation with her a couple of times. She was polite, but it was obvious she just wanted to keep things focused on work."

"I know. I get the feeling she doesn't seem too eager to make connections with people here." I thought of what happened at her house when I brought her license. "I don't think she is all alone, though. I was sure I heard another voice coming from her house when I was there yesterday. She said it was her TV, but it sounded to me like someone calling from inside the house."

"Really. Then maybe we're wrong, and she has made at least one friend since she moved here. I hope so." Catherine took a sip of her tea. "Speaking of friends, how is your friend, Lynn? I hope things are being straightened out with her …problem."

I knew she had been holding off asking about what was going on with the murder, probably hoping I'd bring it up first. I had avoided saying much about the whole investigation into Mrs. Drover's death to anyone at work. Lynn's name had never been released as a suspect, but word had somehow gotten around that she had been questioned in relation to the crime. "She's eager to see the murderer arrested, and she's been cooperating with the police any way she can. It's been a strain on both her and Dr. Drover, but they are hoping the police will solve the case soon."

I could tell by the look she gave me that Catherine was looking for a few more details, but she took my cue and let the subject drop. "Well, give her my best wishes."

To redirect the conversation, I asked about the trip to France Catherine had just taken with her sister. By the time she finished explaining the sites they had visited and all the food they had, I was hungry all over again. And I wanted a glass of wine. After we paid the bill, we decided that next time, we would meet for dinner and invite a few more of our co-workers.

Mid-afternoon, I heard a car pull into my driveway. There was a quick knock at the door, and Lynn popped her head in. "Are you free for a few minutes? I wanted to let you know what happened today at the attorney's office."

"Yes. Definitely. Let me put on the kettle."

"No tea for me, thanks. I just finished lunch," she put her hand over her midsection. "Though, on second thought, it might help settle my stomach."

I got out two cups and placed tea bags in them. "What happened to make your stomach upset? Is it something to do with Mrs. Drover's will?"

"No. Not the will itself. That was fairly straightforward. It started when I got to High Life Dermatology to meet Alex. He was finishing with a patient, so I was chatting with Bethany at the front desk while I waited. I could tell right away that there was something she was dying to tell me. At first, we just talked about the new lady Malcolm Devlin, one of Alex's partners, was seeing and how he seemed so happy now. But then she gave me a look and said, 'I hope Dr. Drover wasn't upset that I was a little curt with his friend the other day.'"

Lynn took the milk I handed her and put a splash in her tea. "I had no idea what she was talking about, so I said, 'What friend is that?' Bethany then went into an explanation of how a woman came in the day before and said she was here to see Alex, and when Bethany told her that he had a patient scheduled in a couple of minutes, the woman waved her hand in dismissal and said, 'Oh. He'll see me first, don't worry,' and strode right into his office. It turns out it was Celia Pound." She waited for me to respond.

"Celia? What was she doing there?" From what I had seen of her so far, I had no problem with believing she would push her way into Alex's office, but why?

"I asked Alex what she was doing at his office the previous day. He said she had a question about something, but that it wasn't important. Why was I asking?" Lynn paused to take a few sips of her tea, "I told him from what I'd heard, she seemed to have acted like she had a right to just barge in and see him any time she wanted. He just laughed and put his hand over mine and said, 'That's just Celia. She has always acted that way with people.'"

"What did you say then?"

"I didn't respond. Alex acted like I was making a big deal out of nothing, and I thought maybe I was. But then, guess who was already waiting in Attorney Sander's office with Alex's family? Celia. And Edgar Flint."

"Wait. Celia was there? And *Edgar Flint?*" I put my mug down hard. "Why?"

"It turns out Mrs. Drover left a specific painting from her Westport house to Celia. From the murmurs in the room afterward, I got the impression that it was quite valuable. Mrs. Drover specified that it not be put up for sale in the gallery Celia works for, however. Celia looked pleased when she learned it was left to her, but then not so much when the attorney told her the terms of the inheritance. Edgar looked like he had no idea why he was there, but according to her will, Mrs. Drover left him a generous sum. When he heard that, he seemed overwhelmed. Ben reached over to pat his shoulder and assure him his aunt was thankful for all his service over the years. Edgar looked at him wide-eyed, then just got up and left the room without saying a word."

"It does sound as if he was stunned by the inheritance. I'm glad she thought of him, though." I made a mental note that Edgar did benefit from Mrs. Drover's death after all. Though I still didn't feel he was the killer.

"Jill offered to go after him to make sure he was all right, but Alex's Aunt Eleanor said to just give him a minute."

"Okay, well, that explains why they were there. What about the rest of her will? You said it was pretty straightforward."

"She bequeathed certain pieces of her jewelry that had been in the family for years to her sister Eleanor and her nieces, Olivia and Jill. No surprise, Alex is to receive the rest of her estate and the Westport house."

"And, of course, the cottage," I said, "though I know it will be hard for him to go there now."

She shook her head, "No. The cottage passes to Ben. The attorney went over the initial document Alex's great-grandfather drafted. The cottage in Madison is inherited by the oldest living child in the next generation. Alex's grandfather and mother were the oldest of their generation, but Ben is six months older than Alex, so the cottage goes to him."

"Wow. Did Alex know that he wouldn't inherit it?"

"Yes, evidently. Everyone in the family seemed to expect that it would be Ben, but I was a bit surprised. It shouldn't change things too much, however. It is also in the original will that the cottage should continue to be available for use by the whole family, as it always has been. As you said, I don't think Alex is too eager to go there any time soon; however, after what happened."

"So other than Edgar and Celia also being there, it sounds as if things went as you expected. What happened to upset you?" I said.

"Celia. That's who. Ben suggested that Alex and I, along with his sisters and mother, go out to lunch once we were through at the attorney's office. Alex's Aunt Eleanor excused herself, saying she was tired and not very hungry, but Celia piped right up, 'I'll be glad to come.'"

I took a sip of my now cold tea. "And..."

Lynn rolled her eyes, "Of course, she grabbed a seat on one side of Alex while I was on the other. I could tell Olivia and Jill were a little uncomfortable at first sitting across from me, but thankfully, no one raised the topic of the investigation into the murder. Alex asked Ben if he had gone for his tux fitting yet, but before he could answer, Celia said, 'Yes, I heard the wedding is going on as planned now.' She turned to Alex then and said, 'Did you book Theresa's Culinary Triumph as I suggested?' She acted as if I wasn't even there or should have a say in choosing the caterer! *She* was the friend who convinced him to go with Theresa's. I don't believe the nerve of her! Barging into our wedding planning!" She had started to raise her voice a bit, and Bruno rushed over to see what was wrong.

"And..." I said.

She picked Bruno up into her lap and began petting him. "And I guess I'm a bit upset with Alex for talking to her about it and then taking her advice. Like I said, I just want her to stay out of our business."

I couldn't say I blamed her. It sounded like 'old friend' or not, she was going to have to tell Alex how she felt about Celia continuing to be involved in their lives. "I hope she didn't cause any more trouble at the luncheon."

"No, Jill must have picked up on how she was upsetting me and asked Celia about a project she is working on. Something to do with a new art gallery. I tuned out after a few minutes. Thankfully, Jill kept her attention away from Alex and me for the rest of the lunch. As everyone got up to leave, it looked like Celia was about to give Alex a goodbye hug, but I held on so tight to his arm that she had to settle for a wave as we walked away. I did look back to see that she had snagged Ben and was pulling him toward the bar. He looked like he had been taken hostage."

I laughed, "Poor Ben. Tell me again how Celia got involved with the family?"

"Childhood friends. I guess her family owned a cottage on the beach, not far from the one Alex's family owns. They were quite wealthy also and were friends with Alex's parents before they divorced. She hung out with Alex and his cousins during the summer, and I guess when they were teens, Alex and Celia became an item. Alex swears it wasn't that serious, but Celia acts as if she was the love of his life."

"She never married?" I asked.

"No. I asked Alex what the story was with her once, he said he thought she was too immersed in her work and busy flying off to exotic places to settle down."

"That is encouraging. With any luck, she will dive back into whatever project she has going on now and leave you and Alex alone." I had a sudden thought. "Alex didn't invite her to the wedding, did he?"

"His mother did. Before...you know. We were making out the guest list, and she insisted. She said it was a courtesy to an old family friend. I've been trying to think of a way to keep her away, though. Do you know of any diseases she might suddenly contract? Something she could come down with right before the wedding?"

I knew Lynn was kidding, but I thought of her wish to keep Mrs. Drover from interfering in the wedding and what ultimately happened.

She must have read my thoughts and said, "This time maybe not something so severe. Just something to keep her out of commission for a few days."

Chapter Eighteen

The next couple of days were so busy at work, I didn't have time to think about what Nora's problem was, or even what was going on with the investigation into Mrs. Drover's murder. I hadn't heard from Lynn since the day she came to tell me about the will, so I assumed there were no new developments in the case. At least ones that involved her having to speak to Detective Crane yet again.

To unwind after my third crazy day in a row, I took Bruno for a walk on Windy Reed Road, the dirt and gravel road through tidal marsh and wooded trails that was a short distance from our house. I could still hear the peepers near the stream that runs through the wooded area to the side of the road. They had started a couple of weeks before, announcing that spring was really here, and the loud chorus of the little frogs always made me feel happy.

As Bruno and I approached the house after our walk, I saw the Flint Landscaping and Property Management truck in my driveway. It looked like Edgar was still sitting in the truck, staring straight ahead. I had no idea what he was doing there. Bruno began to bark as we got closer, and Edgar slowly opened the door to the truck and got out.

"Hi. I'm surprised to see you today. My check didn't bounce or anything, did it?"

He chuckled and said, "No, nothing like that."

My thoughts started racing, trying to think of a way to bring up the subject again of what he might know and had not said about the day of Mrs. Drover's murder.

He assumed a serious expression again and nodded to me, saying, "I gotta thank you. One of your neighbors down the road saw my truck here and the work I did and called me for a job. So—thank you." He looked toward the west side of the driveway. "Thought since I was in the neighborhood anyway, I'd stop by and see how the boxwoods I planted were doing."

It had only been a matter of several days since he had planted them, so I had a feeling that wasn't the reason he had stopped in. "I've been following all your instructions, so they seem to be doing fine." In fact, the only care they needed at this point was watering, and I was pretty sure I was going to be able to handle that.

"Good." He rocked back on his heels a bit, looking around my front yard and avoiding looking at me.

Since he didn't say anything else, or look like he was about to leave, I took a chance and said, "I heard that Mrs. Drover left you a small inheritance. She must have thought highly of you."

His eyes began to fill with tears, and he blinked several times. "She wasn't always an easy one to deal with, but we got on okay. I never did find out why she let me go, but in the end, I guess I owe her."

He glanced quickly toward me, then away again. "I hear you are standing by your friend, trying to help clear her name. That's good. I think you need to watch out for your friends. Hard though, sometimes when..." He let his voice trail off.

"When what?"

"What if there is a conflict of interest, you know? Or maybe it means having to excuse something you shouldn't?"

"What do you mean? Is this about Lynn?" I felt a cramp in my stomach. He couldn't possibly be hiding something he knew that would implicate Lynn further.

He looked right at me then. "No. Nothing to do with her."

Then I realized what he meant. "Did you notice something that day that has to do with a friend of yours?"

He suddenly looked very uncomfortable. Bruno had been patient up until this point, but he started to bark again and was trying to pull me toward the house. "I could use a hot drink. I only have instant, but why don't you come in for a cup of coffee."

He didn't answer but followed behind me as I led him toward the kitchen. "Have a seat. I'll boil the water."

I set milk and sugar down in front of him, and he didn't say anything until after he fixed his coffee. It took him a couple of false starts, and he kept fidgeting in his seat as if trying to decide whether to stay or bolt for the door, but then he said, "The sand that was tracked onto the back porch was in the shape of footprints. Some medium-size, some large, like a man's size. When I got to the house that day to speak to Mrs. Drover about why she let me go, I went into the boathouse first. I saw right away the rowboat had been used recently. There was still a bit of water pooled in one end. Mrs. Drover never went out in that boat. Matter of fact, there is only one person who still uses it, and his wet, sandy shoes were tucked under the sawhorses supporting the boat. I didn't think twice about it, I threw the shoes in the bin we keep to hold the wet or dirty shoes people take off." He took two big slugs of his coffee. "He always told me going out in the boat helps him think, calm down when he is upset."

Alex was at work that day, and no way would he kill his own mother anyway. "Who was it, Edgar?" He'd said "he". If not Alex, then I could guess who else would be used to taking out the rowboat. "Was it Ben?"

He gave one quick nod. "Of all the kids, the two of us used to like to hang out together the most. He always begged me to finish up my work quick so we could play ball or ask if I could go out in the boat with him." He stopped talking and stared down into his coffee for a few minutes. "I don't think he killed Mrs. Drover; I can't believe he would do that. But why didn't he tell the police he was at the cottage earlier that day?" He looked at me as if he expected me to answer.

"Is that what you noticed? The boat and the shoes? Why didn't you tell the police when they questioned you?" I also wondered why he was telling me now, why he didn't finally go to the police with the information.

"When I saw that Ben must have been there earlier, I thought he would tell the police what he was doing there. Like I said, I believe he had nothing to do with what happened, and when he didn't mention it to the police, I thought maybe he had a good reason. I didn't want to make trouble for him." He stopped talking for a moment, then said, "I don't think they had been getting along lately. I overheard Ben yelling at Mrs. Drover the day before when I came to mow the grass."

I was beginning to feel excited. "That was the day before the murder? What were they arguing about?" I hated to think Ben was involved. Having met him, I never would think Ben would harm, let alone kill his aunt, but Edgar was right, then why not come forward and tell the police he was there that day.

"They weren't really arguing, exactly. Ben was raising his voice, but Mrs. D sounded calm, like she was trying to explain something to him. I couldn't hear what they were saying. I figured it was none of my business, so I moved out of earshot. I remember, though, Ben left in a hurry that day, racing out of the driveway." Some of the tension seemed to have left his body; he had stopped fidgeting now that he had said what he had to say.

"You're sure the footprints are from the day you found her? Could they be from the previous day?"

He shook his head, "No. I swept the back after he left the day before. Mrs. Drover said she was having someone over and wanted the place to look good. The bottom of the boat and the shoes were wet. Someone was out in the boat that day. Even though I told you I wasn't sure, I know I locked the boathouse when I left the day before. Ben has a spare key since he is usually the only other one to go in there."

"Why are you telling me this now?" I was glad to hear what he had been holding back, but curious as to what changed his mind.

"Like I said, I owe Mrs. Drover. Especially since she made sure I would be taken care of by leaving me that money in her will." He looked plaintively at me, "I don't want to hurt Ben. He's kind of like a little brother to me. The police need to know, though."

"But I'm not the police, so...'

He looked horrified, "I can't go to the police! Especially now that I was named in Mrs. D's will. With my record, they'll think I did it for sure! That I found out about the money she was going to leave me. At the least, they might charge me for withholding evidence. You been scrounging around for information. I need you to go to the police with what I told you."

I had no idea how that would work since I would have to tell them how I came by that information. I thought of something else. "Edgar, did you tell Ben what you noticed? Question him about why he didn't let the police know he was there the day she was killed?"

He looked ashamed. "No…I. No. I couldn't. Like I said, I hoped he would just tell them himself."

Considering that Ben had had ample time to come forward, that didn't look like it was going to happen. "Okay. Thank you for telling me what you saw. I'll try to find a way I can give the information to the police without involving you."

He got up and gave a slight bow toward me, "I appreciate it."

I held the door as he left and waved as he backed out. I was sure the police must have spoken to Ben after his aunt's murder. But what did he tell them?

I called Lynn right away, hoping to catch her at home.

She was a little out of breath when she answered. "I was on my way to bring the rest of my painting things to my new studio. What's going on?"

"Edgar Flint was just here. It seems he is feeling guilty since he found out Mrs. Drover left him a tidy sum in her will. He confessed that the day he found her body he went into the boathouse first and noticed the rowboat they keep there had been used recently. He also noticed sandy man-sized footprints on the back porch and wet shoes in the boathouse. They belong to Ben." I paused for her response.

"Ben? He never told Alex he had been there that day." She was obviously surprised.

"He never told the police either, according to Edgar."

"Why wouldn't he tell the police?" She hesitated, "I can't believe…did Edgar think he was the one who killed her?"

"No. He insists it wasn't Ben. But it obviously bothers him that Ben wasn't forthcoming with the police." I didn't have to add that his keeping quiet did nothing to take some of the suspicion off of her. "Do you know Ben's last name?"

"Woodrow. Why?"

"I'd love to know why he kept quiet about being at the cottage that day, and assuming he had nothing to do with her murder himself, if he saw something that could help the police find the killer."

"I guess that means you're planning to speak to him before you notify the police. I want to come."

"No. I think it's better if I go alone. It could be even more awkward than it already will be if you are there. He's going to be the best man at your wedding, and I don't want him to be angry at you if he has a reasonable explanation. It will obviously look as if you're accusing him of something." It was going to be awkward at the wedding no matter how it ended: the bride was a suspect in the murder of the groom's mother, and the maid of honor was accusing the best man.

"His office is in New Haven, right?" I said.

"Yes, it's on Whalley Avenue. Whitley Financial." She paused for a moment, "Even though his being involved would let me off the hook, I really hope he has a good explanation for what he was doing there and why he didn't mention it. I like Ben, and it will crush Alex if it turns out he had anything to do with Mrs. Drover's murder."

"I'll let you know if he tells me anything." I just hoped Ben would agree to go to the police himself, I wasn't too happy about what I felt I had to do otherwise.

Chapter Nineteen

The next day, I waited until mid-morning to head to Whitley Financial. I knew I was taking a chance that at that time of day Ben wouldn't be tied up with a string of meetings, but no one likes to be accosted with uncomfortable questions before they have had their morning coffee.

His office was in a busy section of New Haven; however, I was lucky enough to be able to squeeze into a parking space between two delivery trucks across the street. As I approached his building, I dodged workers out for a breath of fresh air on their coffee break, moms pushing strollers, and street people rushing up to me to bestow a blessing and then ask for any spare change I might have.

The office for his firm was on the fifth floor of the building, and I exited the elevator into a suite tastefully decorated in beige and chocolate brown. The receptionist at the main desk looked up from her computer screen as I approached.

"Good morning, I'm here to see Mr. Woodrow." I gave her my brightest smile.

"Sheila will help you." She returned my smile and motioned me to a receptionist at another desk.

I repeated my request to see Ben Woodrow, and his receptionist answered, "Do you have an appointment?"

"No. But if you could ask him if he could spare a couple of minutes, I'd appreciate it. I'm a friend of his; my name is Melanie Bass." "Friend" was stretching it a bit, and my mission today would most likely prevent us ever becoming friends.

Either I caught him at a good time, or he was so curious about what I was doing there, he saw me right away.

Ben stood and came around his desk as I entered. He held out his hand and said, "Melanie. Once again, I'm surprised to see you. What can I do for you?"

He appeared so open and welcoming I had to remind myself that he might be obstructing justice in a murder case. A murder case where Lynn was presently the prime suspect. "Thanks for seeing me." I had been wrestling with a way he wouldn't know I had gotten my information from Edgar, but it seemed impossible. Also, it might work as leverage to get the truth out of him. He motioned toward the chair opposite him.

"I recently had some work done by Edgar Flint. We got to talking about your aunt and what happened the day of her murder." Ben seemed to be trying to maintain a neutral "I'm listening" expression, but his hands, which had been casually clasped on his desk, were now gripping each other firmly. I continued, "He says that he is sure you were at the cottage that morning." I waited for his response.

He gave me a puzzled look, which I didn't find very convincing. "Why would he say…"

"He said he is sure you took out the boat that morning, that you are the only one besides him who has a key to the boathouse. Also, he found your wet shoes were by the boat." I had to agree with Edgar; Ben didn't seem like the violent type, but I tensed up, waiting for his response.

Ben sighed and looked down at the top of his desk before looking up at me again. "Something had upset me recently. I like to go out in the rowboat to think. Concentrating on rowing helps work off some of the stress and helps me focus. I did take the boat out that day, but I didn't go into the cottage."

"Edgar said he saw footprints on the back porch that looked like they could belong to you."

He looked annoyed now. "I was going to go in and speak to my aunt, but once I got up onto the porch, I decided against it. I returned the boat to where it belonged and left."

"What made you so upset that day? Why didn't you go inside to talk to your aunt?" I tried to channel Detective Cody.

Ben leaned back in his chair, "That is none of your business. It doesn't matter now, anyway. I really don't need to answer any more of your questions." He began to get up, I assume, to put me out of his office.

I quickly said, "Why didn't you tell the police you were at the cottage when they questioned you?"

He sat down again, "I didn't think it was important. I didn't see anyone else there, and as I told you, I never even saw my aunt. I would be no help in the investigation." He sounded a tad defensive.

"Meanwhile, Lynn is being questioned by the police and is one of their prime suspects for also just being there. She, too, 'never even saw your aunt.'"

"But she had blood on her hands…so to speak." He looked directly at me then.

I was over feeling any hesitation about going to the police with what I knew now. "Either you go to the police and tell them what you told me, or Edgar will do it. He kept quiet when he was questioned because he thought you would own up to it. He thinks the world of you, and it will hurt him, and maybe get him in serious trouble if he needs to do it, but he will." I was betting on the fact that Ben had some affection for Edgar.

We sat in silence for a few moments. Ben began playing with a paper clip. I was about to get up and leave, convinced there was nothing more I could do, when he said, "I'll go myself. But as I told you, I can't see how anything I tell them will make a difference."

"Good." I nodded and let myself out. I believed he would finally admit to the police he had been at the cottage that day, but doubted he would admit that there had been tension between them before she was killed.

* * *

I called Lynn as soon as I got home to let her know what had happened with Ben. That he had confirmed what Edgar told me, and that he would go to the police with the information.

"Do you believe him about not going into the cottage that day?" Lynn said.

"I don't know. According to Edgar, Ben and Mrs. Drover were having a disagreement over something. I wonder if they usually were at odds. The day of the brunch in Westport I saw them in a heated discussion as I left. I assumed it had to do with her behavior toward you, but maybe it was over something else. Did Alex ever mention his mother and Ben not getting along?"

"No. As a matter of fact, like I told you, Ben was helping her with some financial agreement or something. Maybe they disagreed about that," she said.

A disagreement over professional advice didn't seem like motive enough for murder. "Maybe." Besides, if she asked for his help, I wouldn't think she would argue with him when he gave it to her. "I think we better see if Ben does go to the police before you mention what we found out to Alex."

"I hope Ben has the decency to tell him himself. I don't want to get in the middle of that."

* * *

The day was cool but sunny, and after lunch, I intended to take Bruno for a walk at Hammonasset Beach, but I found myself bypassing the entrance to the park and heading toward Sea Shell Road. As I headed toward Alex's family's place, I passed a number of smaller beach houses that were more like what I pictured when I thought of a cottage, but also some huge residences that appeared to have been recently built. Even if it hadn't been the house I was looking for, I would have stopped to get a better look at 23 Sea Shore Drive. It wasn't the largest house, and it had obviously seen some wear, but I found it to be the most striking of all the houses I had passed. It was a weathered slate grey with white trim, three stories high, and had a porch that looked to be a wrap-around. However, it was the feeling I got when I looked at it, a sense of history and grace, that made it the most impressive to me. Lynn had used the word 'welcoming' to describe it when she came, and that was the same sense I had.

I pulled into the paved circular drive and parked. I knew from what Lynn told me that no one was allowed to enter the cottage until the police had finished their investigation. I'm sure that the police would not be thrilled that I was even exploring the property itself, but I convinced myself taking a quick look wouldn't hurt. Especially if no one saw me here.

I snapped on Bruno's leash and took him out of the car to look around with me. I wasn't sure what I was looking for, but I just felt the need to actually see the place. Even from where I stood in the driveway, there was a gorgeous view of Long Island Sound. A short distance off to the left, at the head of a sloped walkway leading to the beach, was what they must call the boat house. It wasn't an actual boathouse where you could pull your craft right in, but a large shed painted the same gray as the house. As I continued to scan the grounds, I had to give Edgar credit; he had done a meticulous job of maintaining the landscaping. I couldn't imagine why Mrs. Drover wouldn't want to keep him on. I approached the house then to get a better look and couldn't help but flinch a little as I saw the porch Lynn had described. I resisted the urge to climb the stairs and check the railing for a protruding nail or screw.

I led Bruno toward the back of the house, eager to get a look at the section of the house that faced the beach. I was right, the porch did wrap around the house to the back. This was the section where Edgar found the footprints. There wasn't much furniture out on the porch, Lynn said the house hadn't been fully opened for the season yet, but the porch swing situated to one side of the large oak door severely tempted me. I could imagine sitting there and watching the sea birds dive for fish, the tides change, and boats sailing out on Long Island Sound. I loved my little house near the tidal marsh, but I suddenly realized that this was very much like the house I'd imagined Artie and I would build one day. Well, maybe not quite as grand, and as it turned out, it was never to be with Artie, but still, I had daydreams of something like this.

Bruno suddenly started to wag his tail frantically and let out a short, friendly bark.

"Yoo-hoo! Hello?" A woman's voice called out, and a middle-aged woman in tailored beige slacks and a navy blue blazer came around the side of the house. "Hi. I was driving past, and I thought I saw a car here." She approached me, holding out her hand.

I shook her proffered hand, though I had no idea who she was or what she wanted, not to mention being a bit embarrassed by the fact I was trespassing.

"What a cute dog!" She bent to pet Bruno, then straightened up to say, "I'm Gloria Shames with Shames Realty. It was awful what happened to poor Mrs. Drover! I was shocked when I heard about it. And they say it was murder." She whispered the last word. "Well, that might put a bit of tarnish on the appeal of the house, but I guess it's all in how you spin it." She stopped and smiled at me, "I just wanted to check and make sure the family still wants to proceed with the sale of the property. Mrs. Drover never delivered the final papers to me before she died, but I will be glad to draw up a new set." She looked at me expectantly.

Mrs. Drover had planned on selling the cottage? Did Alex know? Did anyone know? My surprise must have shown on my face.

"You are one of the nieces, aren't you? She did discuss her plans with the family, didn't she?"

"No. I mean, I am not one of her nieces, and I don't know who she told about wanting to sell the cottage."

Ms. Shames looked slightly annoyed, "When I saw you here, I just assumed you were part of the family." She looked me over again and then said, "Are you by chance here because you are interested in this property? I can take your information and …"

I interrupted her, "No, I'm a friend of the family." I didn't go into my reason for being there, and luckily, she didn't ask.

"I don't suppose you know who I should contact now about getting it on the market."

"Mrs. Drover's nephew, Ben Woodrow, might be able to help you. I have his work address, but I'm afraid I don't know his number."

She pulled out her phone, and it looked like she was entering his name. "No problem, I'll get his number." Without saying another word, she walked up the steps onto the porch and began peering in one of the windows. "I'll have to get a look inside soon, of course, to make sure things were properly cleaned up. Well, one step at a time." She smiled and said," Have a good afternoon," and bustled off to her car.

I stood looking around the property for a few minutes, mulling over what I had just learned. Ben and his aunt had been at odds over something before she was killed; he was 'helping' her with some paperwork, and Ben was now in possession of the deed to the cottage. The property was obviously worth a great deal of money. Certainly, enough money to make someone go to extreme ends to get it. I wondered if Ben had been pressuring her to sell, or if she was the one to want to sell the property, and he was against it. Either way, it now seemed there was a lot more significance to Ben being at the cottage the morning Mrs. Drover was killed.

Chapter Twenty

On the way home from the cottage on Sea Shell Road, I wrestled with the decision of whether I should give Ben a day or two to go to Detective Crane and confess that he was at the cottage the morning of his aunt's murder. Given that I now knew he had a pretty good motive to kill her, I was trying to decide if I needed to go right to the police myself. Suddenly, a deer leapt out in front of me, and I had to slam on the brakes to avoid hitting it. I stopped in time to see it dart into the brush at the side of the road but heard the screech of brakes behind me and braced for the impact. Instead, a light gray Mercedes raced around me and took off down the road at a high rate of speed.

"Yeesh! Bruno, are you all right?" He gave a short bark in response, and though a bit shaken by what had just happened, I continued on my way, eager to get home. A short while later, I heard the blare of a car horn and looked in my rear-view mirror to see that a car had pulled out of a commercial building parking lot, cutting off the vehicle that had been behind me. It looked like the Mercedes that nearly hit me. The gray car seemed to be following me now, and I tensed up as I thought of all the incidences of road rage that had ended in violence lately.

My quick stop had certainly been unavoidable. I couldn't imagine what the Mercedes driver's problem was. I kept checking the rearview mirror to see that the car continued to be a short distance behind me. I tried to make out who was behind the wheel but couldn't even tell if it was a man or woman. The car turned off Route One when I did, but when I turned down Starbridge Lane, the Mercedes continued on. I sighed with relief as I finally pulled into my driveway, again amazed at how easily people were driven to act irrationally these days when they felt wronged by someone.

I forgot about the road rage incident as I fed Bruno and took him out. My mind was more on Ben and the possibility that he was guilty of Mrs. Drover's murder. I still hadn't decided if I should just go to the police myself. Justin and I were going to a movie that night, and I thought I'd tell him what I now knew and see what he said. I was meeting him at the movie theater since he was working late and wouldn't have time to shower and change and then pick me up in time to make the movie. When I went out to my car, I found a folded piece of paper under the windshield wiper.

"LET THE POLICE DO THEIR JOB. STAY OUT OF IT."

The note wasn't signed. The words were much what Detective Crane had told me, though I doubted he would just leave a note to drive home his point. I had spoken to several people about the investigation, none of them had been too happy to be questioned about any involvement in Mrs. Drover's murder. However, I couldn't think of anyone who would leave me a note. Edgar knew where I lived, but he had asked me to go to the police with what he had told me. I considered that it could have been left by Ben, but again he was more likely to talk to me in person. Whoever it was, it left me a bit unnerved. Just wanting to be rid of it, I started to crumple the paper up and intended to toss it in the garbage pail but changed my mind and instead threw it on the front seat before I left. Maybe it wouldn't hurt to tell Sunny Cody about it and see what she had to say.

After the movie, when we stopped for coffee and tea, I explained to Justin what I had learned about Ben, and he gave me the advice I expected.

"You need to go to the police with the information you have. Ben had an opportunity after the murder to explain himself and didn't do it. Even if Detective Crane doesn't feel he can act on the information you give him yet, it should at least cause him to question Ben more thoroughly."

I hesitated before I told Justin about the note left on my car because I knew it would get him worried once again, but I had agreed that I wouldn't keep anything from him regarding my involvement in solving Mrs. Drover's murder.

"I found a note on my car this evening telling me to let the police handle the investigation. It wasn't signed. You didn't leave it, did you?" I thought maybe making a joke about it would decrease how upset he would get. Even though I was getting more concerned the more I thought about it.

Justin stopped eating with a forkful of apple pie halfway to his mouth. "Someone left you a threatening note?"

"It wasn't really threatening, it just repeated what the police have…"

"Yes, but whoever left it knows where you live. You need to let the police know right away." Justin put his fork down and gave me a stern look. "Please."

"Okay. I will. I was going to contact Sunny Cody, but maybe when I speak to Detective Crane to tell him about Ben, I'll mention it."

We spent the rest of the evening talking about the movie we had just seen and making plans for the weekend, but I couldn't fully relax now. I began to wonder if the car following me earlier was really a case of road rage, or if the driver had begun to follow me earlier, after I left the cottage on Sea Shell Road.

* * *

The next day after work, I went to speak to Detective Crane. The officer at the desk said he was in a meeting and offered to take down any information I wanted to leave for him. Forty minutes later, I was beginning to regret my decision to wait to speak to him in person when he finally appeared and took me into a small interrogation room.

"What is it you want to tell me? I only have a few minutes, so please get right to the point." He motioned me to a chair, but continued to stand, arms crossed.

"I spoke to Ben Woodrow, and he admitted he was at the cottage where Mrs. Drover was murdered on the morning she was killed. I don't think he—"

The detective didn't give me time to finish. "He was here this morning and admitted that, so we are aware. While I'm not happy he kept that information from us initially, we are following up on his story now. So, thank you for stopping in, but we can take it from here." He turned toward the door and looked as if he was about to leave.

I blurted out, "Did he also tell you he inherited the cottage, and that he and Mrs. Drover were having a dispute before her death over whether or not it was to be sold?" I was confident now that was what Ben and Mrs. Drover were arguing about.

Detective Crane hesitated, then said, "Yes. I am aware of that."

Judging by the initial startled look he gave me when I told him, I was certain he was lying. "Then don't you think that would possibly give Ben a motive to want his aunt dead?"

I had his full attention now, "That's something we will decide once we view all the evidence. As I've told you multiple times, *we* will evaluate the evidence and decide who will be charged. Thank you for coming in, but I need to attend to another matter right now."

I was obviously being dismissed, but I felt more confident now that Lynn and I, might be lower on his list of suspects. I realized after I left that I hadn't mentioned the note I found on my car.

I needed to let Lynn know about Mrs. Drover planning to sell the cottage. I suspected Alex didn't know either and that that might be what his mother wanted to tell him in person before she was killed. If Ben was against the sale, I had to agree with him. I couldn't imagine why she would want to sell it; it was a lovely place, at least what I had seen of it. And why now? It had been in the family for years.

By the time I called Lynn to tell her what I found out, she knew already.

"I was with Alex when Ben stopped over to tell him about being at the cottage that morning. He said he wanted to let Alex know because he said he had gone to the police and admitted he had failed to notify them earlier. Ben looked at me when he said that, and even though I tried to look innocent, I mustn't have been doing a very good job. Alex somehow guessed I already knew about Ben and hadn't told him. Let me just say, he was not very happy with either Ben or me."

"Did Ben tell him about Mrs. Drover putting the cottage on the market? How did he react?" I asked.

"Alex was furious with Ben over him not telling the truth right away. He accused him of being deceitful and keeping secrets from him, not to mention important information from the police. They got into a huge argument. Ben shouted at Alex, saying that he wasn't the only one keeping secrets. He asked him if he knew his mother had been wasting the money she inherited on poor investments and said he had been trying desperately to get her spending under control. He said that he found out that in order to finance another harebrained project, she planned to sell part of their heritage right out from under them. That she planned to put the cottage on the market."

Lynn sounded like she was holding back tears now. "I have never seen Alex so angry. He called Ben a liar and shouted at him to leave. After Ben stormed out, I tried to calm Alex down. I told him I didn't know about her wanting to sell the cottage. He said he couldn't talk about it with me then. He said he needed time on his own to think, and he asked me to leave. He said he would call me later, but I haven't heard from him yet."

"I'm sure when he has had some time to work through what he just found out, he'll call you." I hoped so.

"I'm going to give him a couple more hours and then I am going to call him and tell him we need to talk about this. Maybe I should have told him what I knew about Ben, as soon as we found out, but they have always been close, and I didn't want to be the one to upset him. It kind of made me feel like I would be squealing on Ben."

"I think you are right to call Alex if he doesn't call you soon." I waited a moment, then said, "It sounds like Ben and Mrs. Drover's disagreement must have started over her handling of her finances. I wonder if the blow-up Edgar witnessed happened when Ben found out about her plans to sell the cottage."

"Yes. I suppose that could be why Ben was at the Westport house the evening we were there. Trying to find out what else she had been doing with her money." Lynn said.

"Or," I said, "maybe he was looking for the contract Mrs. Drover was to send to the realtor. Ms. Shames said she never got the signed document."

"But it wouldn't be valid now anyway since Mrs. Drover is dead, and Ben's name is on the deed," Lynn said.

"Exactly."

Chapter Twenty-One

I sent Lynn a text before I left for work the next day: *Did U speak to Alex?* Her response was quick *Yes. Call me after work. Worried.*

I didn't know how to take Lynn's response. Was she worried about Alex? Their relationship? Now, I was curious about what had happened when she spoke to him. I called her on my lunch break.

"I waited a little while after I spoke to you, then I couldn't stand it any longer and went to Alex's place to speak to him. To my surprise, he wasn't alone. Celia Pound was there," Lynn said.

"What was she doing there?"

"She left as soon as I arrived, but I asked Alex the same question. There were two empty coffee cups on the kitchen table. I didn't hide the fact that it upset me to find her there, and I asked Alex why she was there and that it looked like they had been having quite a cozy chat. Alex became defensive. He said that the police had asked Ben to come back in for further questioning, and she had heard about it and wanted to make sure Alex was all right now that his cousin was a suspect." Lynn sounded livid. "I reminded him that he wanted time to think alone, and yet he didn't have any problem with Celia coming over. I told him if he needed to talk about it with someone, he should have called me. I would have come right away to be with him. We got into an argument, and I stormed out this time. He called me afterward to apologize, but now, the more I think about it, the more upset I get again. We're going to be married; he should be able to talk about anything with me." She paused for a moment as if something had just occurred to her. "I guess that was probably his point, too, as far as me telling him about Ben."

She wasn't wrong. However, Celia was beginning to look more and more like she was trying to throw up a roadblock in their relationship. I didn't comment on that because I think Lynn was getting the same feeling. "I told Detective Crane about Ben finding out about Mrs. Drover's plans to sell the cottage. I pointed out that it certainly looks like he has a motive for killing his aunt now. What did Alex say? Does he believe Ben may be guilty?"

"I think he is hurt that Ben kept all that information about his mother from him and also that she kept it from him herself. However, I think he can't believe Ben would kill her. He said *Celia* tried to reassure him Ben would never do that; that was why she stopped over."

"Hmm." I wasn't convinced.

"The look she gave me as she left let me know who *her* prime suspect was, though. I said something about Celia needing to get her hooks out of Alex, and that's what started the argument. He said that I was being unreasonably jealous, that, in fact, he was pretty sure Celia had her eye on Ben, not him, and how could I not trust him? It pretty much escalated from there." Lynn said. "Anyway, like I said, later on, we apologized to each other, and he is taking me out to dinner tonight so we can talk about what still needs to be settled for the wedding."

She didn't sound as enthused as she usually did when she mentioned the wedding. "That's a good thing, isn't it?" I wondered if she had been more upset by the confrontation with Alex than she let on.

"Yes, of course!" I thought her cheerfulness sounded a bit forced.

My lunch break was nearly over, so I said, "Okay. Well, call me if you hear anything more about Ben, or if you need to talk about anything else."

I had an appointment that afternoon with one of my favorite patients, Mrs. Paine. The eighty-four-year-old always had interesting, if occasionally long-winded, stories to tell while I was examining her. I was due to check on her vital signs today as well as how she was doing since she fell and sprained her left wrist. I had always felt Mrs. Paine was spry for her age, but I worried now that her balance and strength might be starting to be a problem.

As she led me into her living room, she told me what happened. "I was filling the bird feeder in my front yard and stepped back, tripping over that big rock that borders my garden. That rock has been there as long as I can remember. I feel like a fool for not being careful of it." She shook her head as she took a seat on the sofa.

As I sat beside her, I noticed she had a stack of children's books on her coffee table. She saw me looking and said, "Did I ever tell you I was a teacher? First and second grade."

"No, I don't think I knew that," I said. "I can picture you teaching young children, though. I bet you were good at it."

She smiled and said, "Yes, I believe I was. I really loved teaching that age group." She motioned to the books, "I was just going through these, getting them ready to donate to the library. I used a lot of these in my classroom, and some of them are classics now." She picked up one and stroked the cover. "My children and grandchildren, and even my great-grandchildren are getting too old for them. So, I thought, why not pass them on."

I noticed a couple in the stack that looked familiar from my own childhood. "That's a lovely idea, Mrs. Paine."

She was silent while I listened to her heart, then suddenly said, "How is your protégé, Nora, doing?"

I was taken slightly off guard, "She's fine, I think. She's not exactly my protégé, though."

She shook her head and sighed, "There's a young woman with something weighing on her." When I gave her a startled look, she continued, "Like I said, I taught for many years and got pretty good at telling when a student was going through a tough time or had something they were worried about. We get a little better at hiding it when we get older, but I can still tell."

I didn't know how to respond at first since I was pretty sure she was right about Nora. "I agree with you. But I think she's a very private person and finds it hard to respond to offers of help."

Mrs. Paine put her hand on my arm, "I know if anyone can break through her resistance, you can."

"Thank you, Mrs. Paine. I'll try." I wasn't sure if her confidence in me made me feel better or worse for my inability to figure out what was going on with Nora.

After I finished my examination of Mrs. Paine, and she assured me her wrist was feeling better, as well as the hip she'd bruised in her fall, I gathered my things and prepared to leave. I told her she needed to continue to sit and rest, but she insisted on walking me to the door.

"I think it's good for me to keep moving." She held up her right wrist with the smartwatch on it, "Time for me to stand, anyway."

I focused on the rest of my patients for the remainder of the day, even though I was eager to know if Detective Crane had shifted the focus of his investigation to Ben as a suspect in his aunt's murder. I wondered if Sunny Cody might have some information, even though she told me she had been pushed to the side of the investigation.

I was on my way to my car after work, thinking about whether Sunny would tell me anything, even if she did know what was going on when I was stopped by a man in a navy blue windbreaker and jeans.

"Hi. Sorry to bother you, but you work here, right?"

"Yes. What can I do for you?"

"I was wondering if you know Nora Smith, or maybe she is going by Stevens now."

"May I ask why you want to know?" I remembered Judy's phone call from a guy looking for Nora Smith a week or so ago.

He hunched his shoulders and gave me a mournful look, "I'm her brother. I've been overseas for a while, and we lost touch. I was able to trace her to this agency, but I'm afraid I don't have her current address."

I gave him a skeptical look. "Why don't you call her, then?"

He patted his pockets, "I'm not having the greatest day, I lost my phone somewhere on the way here. I would love to just surprise her and show up."

He looked like he was just a bit older than Nora and had the same light brown hair and blue eyes as her, but he was tall and solid-looking compared to Nora's slight build. I wasn't buying a bit of what he said. However, since no one seemed to know much of anything about her personal life, Nora might very well have a brother who she was estranged from.

"I'm sorry, but I can't help you. If I see Nora, I'll be glad to give her a message for you, though. Why don't you give me a way she can contact you?"

I was reaching in my bag for my phone to type in his contact info when he started to walk away.

"Forget about it. I'll manage to get a hold of her on my own." The friendly, non-threatening tone was gone now.

As soon as I got into my car, I tried calling Nora. There was no answer. Did the woman never pick up her phone? I texted then: *"your brother (?) was at the coretrack office looking for you. Not sure of situation. gave him no info."*

I was almost home when I had second thoughts about what happened with the guy in the parking lot. I had a bad feeling about him now, and Nora had not answered my text. I turned around and headed toward her house in North Madison, intending to speak to her in person. I felt a bit annoyed. There was quite enough drama going on around me already with Lynn being accused of a murder. I didn't need to get involved in Nora's family dispute.

I was just turning down Strawbow Road when I heard my phone signal a new text: *"I don't have a brother!!!!"*

It felt like someone had put their cold hand on the back of my neck. I had just recently dealt with a stalker who was watching Lynn this past fall. At least, we thought he was a stalker. I had another thought. Since Nora seemed cagey about her past, maybe the guy in the parking lot was investigating her for some reason. I continued toward her house, determined to get at least a bit more information about her past out of her this time.

When I knocked, Nora came out immediately and pulled me into the house. She looked much paler than usual, and as soon as she let go of my arm, she clasped her hands in front of her chest as if trying to hold herself together. She didn't offer me a seat, but instead, I stood watching as she paced back and forth across the room. Her voice was strained as she asked, "What did this guy look like? Did he come into the office, or did you see him outside? Did you tell him where we live?"

I could hear someone closing a drawer or a cupboard in the kitchen. "He came up to me as I was going to my car. He was tall, late twenties or early thirties, brownish hair, and blue eyes. Like I said, I didn't give him any information about you. He gave me some story about being your estranged brother."

Just then, another woman came into the living room. It was hard to guess her age, because the first thing I noticed was that it looked like she had been run over by a truck. Her right arm was in a sling, she had yellow and green bruises all over her face and neck, and she limped as she came to stand by Nora. "He found us, didn't he?"

Nora nodded and said, "I'm afraid so." She put her arms around the woman. They went to sit together on the sofa, and Nora helped the other woman lower herself into her seat. Then she motioned for me to take the chair opposite them. Nora said to the woman, "This is Melanie. I work with her." Then, looking at me, she tipped her chin up defiantly and said, "This is Maryjane. My partner."

Maryjane glanced at Nora as if asking for permission, then said, "The man who was asking for Nora is Zane Kirkwood. We were married. Are still married, I guess. I wanted a divorce." She motioned to her face with her good hand. "When I told him that, he did this. He *really* didn't like that I was leaving him for another woman."

Nora placed her hand on the woman's back and began to rub it." We met at the homecare agency where we both used to work."

Maryjane said then, "Nora found out what Zane was doing to me, and she kept urging me to leave him. I appreciated having someone care about me and having someone I could talk to about what was going on." She turned and smiled at Nora, "I felt I could tell her anything, and she let me know she felt the same way. We were going to just leave town together, but somehow Zane found out about us, and as I said, he went into a rage."

I was appalled at the beating she must have taken, "Did you report him to the police? I'm sure he could be arrested for what he did."

Maryjane made a "humph" sound, then said, "That's true. Unless you live in a small town and your husband is one of their few police officers. This was the result of only the latest, and worst, of the beatings. Reporting him didn't turn out to do me any good in the past."

There were a thousand questions going through my mind, and just as quickly, several of the answers came to me. I looked at Nora, "I assume Zane has been trying to find you, that is why you have been lying low. But why not report him to the police here? I'm sure they will help you."

Nora said, "I did. Or at least I tried, but since he hadn't shown up yet, he was only a potential threat. They said to let them know if he appeared and if he continued any threatening behavior."

"And you are sure this Zane is still trying to get you to come back with him?" I said.

They both answered, "Yes."

"But why?"

Maryjane answered, "Because he's possessive and likes power over people. I think he has serious mental health issues. He said our marriage was over when *he* said it was over. This isn't the first time I tried to leave him. He tracked me down and, once he found me, made me sorry for leaving. He told me if I tried it again, he would kill me." She took Nora's hand, "It wasn't until I met Nora that I had the courage to leave him again. She gave me courage." She shifted on the sofa, then, as if she was getting uncomfortable sitting.

"Did you go to the emergency room to get those injuries looked at when they happened?" I said.

Maryjane shook her head, "No. They keep records, and would ask a lot of questions about how I got my injuries. Like I said, Zane is a cop, and if it was reported, he would hear about it." She looked at Nora again. "We are both RNs and can handle my injuries ourselves."

Even though Maryjane seemed to be slowly healing, I was sure she really needed to have seen a doctor for what her husband had done to her. I had another thought. Nora had been in town for a while, but from the way Maryjane still looked, her injuries must have been very painful even up until recently. Mrs. Baker's missing narcotics looked even less like a case of misplaced or dropped pills now. Before I could question Nora to see if she had slipped a few pills out of Mrs. Baker's supply to give to Maryjane, I heard the crunch of gravel as a car pulled into the driveway.

Nora jumped up out of her seat, and the look of panic on her face made me leap up, also.

"I take it you were not expecting anyone," I said.

Nora said, "No," and went to peek out from behind the curtain covering one of the windows facing the driveway. "Go into the bedroom," she whispered to Maryjane.

Maryjane was having a bit of difficulty getting up from the sofa, so I helped her up and watched her as she limped away toward another part of the house.

I went to the other window facing the driveway and peeked out just as the man in the blue windbreaker got out of the car. He looked a lot bigger to me now than he had when I first met him. "That's the guy who stopped me in the parking lot," I whispered.

The sound Nora made told me that it was Zane. She moved away from the window and motioned for me to do the same, then she went over to the front door and threw the deadbolt.

"I don't know how he found you. I don't think he could have followed me," I said. Not that it mattered now how he found out where she lived.

There was a hammering at the door to the screened-in porch. Nora put her finger to her lips.

He was going to know someone was here. Nora's car must have been pulled around back or something, but my car was right in front. "Nora! Open the door!"

Nora looked at me and shook her head.

The hammering became louder, followed by a splintering sound as if he must have forced the door open.

I ran to where I left my purse in the chair I had been sitting in and pulled out my phone. Before I could call 911, however, Nora grabbed it from my hand. "Wait a minute."

There was a banging at the front door of the house now, and the man was yelling, "Come on, Nora, I know you're in there." He waited a minute, then said, "Maryjane? I just want to talk. I promise."

Nora yelled back, "Maryjane's not here. I don't know where she went. She left me."

I could hear him laughing on the other side of the door. "Sure she did." Then, there was a loud bang at the door again. "Let me in!" I could hear a thudding as he tried to break down the front door. Luckily, it held.

Maryjane came limping back into the room carrying a baseball bat. "Here, one of you take this. I don't think I can swing it hard enough." She handed it to Nora.

I took a deep breath and yelled, "Sir, you need to leave now, or I'm going to call the police." I motioned to Nora to hand me my phone, but she shook her head and tossed it across the room back onto the sofa.

"Wait. I think he may leave now." Nora looked panicked.

Maryjane spoke up. "Nora, I think we better call…"

"No!" Nora waved the bat at me. "Don't call the police!"

I took a few steps away from her. "Okay, I won't."

The hammering at the door had stopped, and I thought maybe he had left after all, when there was the sound of breaking glass coming from another part of the house.

I didn't care what Nora said. I scrambled to get my phone. Nora raised the bat and took up a stance in front of Maryjane and me. She turned once to glare at me, and I said, "I'm not calling 911, see." I held up my phone with just one name highlighted: "Sunny Cody." As soon as she looked away, I pressed Sunny's number and held the phone by my side. I heard a soft squawk of, "Melanie? Hello?" but didn't answer, fervently hoping she wouldn't just hang up.

I said, "Let's go before he gets in here. My car is right out front. I think he means to harm us." I spoke loudly, hoping Sunny was listening.

We had just started backing toward the door when Zane appeared from the rear of the house. I saw he recognized me immediately, and he smirked and said, "It seems not all of your colleagues are as suspicious as you are. Look, I'm not going to hurt you. I just need to speak to my wife."

I pulled Maryjane a few steps closer to the door, "How did you find her? I never told you she was at 59 Strawbow Road."

He looked at me and saw right away that I had my phone by my side and must have figured out what I was doing. He said, "Hand me the phone miss." When I held onto it, he said loudly, "Officer on the scene, no further help needed."

Nora swung the bat at him, but she missed. He grabbed the bat and shoved her to the floor, then lunged for me, grabbing the phone from my hand.

Maryjane dove for the door, but her hip must have given out, and she fell. Holding the bat, he motioned to me and said, "Help her up. Then, all of you take a seat on the sofa."

It didn't seem that we had a choice at the moment, so we did as we were told. "The police are going to be here any time now," I said. I prayed Sunny had heard what was going on and called it in.

He stood over us and said, "If they do show up, I'll be sure to tell them I'm just here to rescue my wife from her abductor." He looked at Maryjane, "Right?"

Maryjane flinched but said, "No. I'm going to—'

"Quiet!" He looked at Nora then, "I have quite the story to tell them about you, also, Nora, don't I?"

Nora looked at him defiantly, but I could tell she was scared.

"Nora doesn't want the authorities involved any more than I do. It turns out there is a little scandal she's involved in regarding fraud in getting a nursing license. She'll have some charges of her own to face."

Both Maryjane and I turned to look at Nora.

She ducked her head and said nothing.

Zane continued, "Just come with me, Maryjane. There doesn't have to be a problem here." He reached to grab Maryjane's arm, but Nora launched herself up off the sofa and tackled him, saying, "Run!"

I grabbed Maryjane to help her up off the sofa, but Nora had only caused Zane to stagger back a bit, and I heard the thump as he whacked her with the bat.

"Police! Open the door!"

I let go of Maryjane, so I could unlock the door. Zane turned to run back toward the rear of the house, but Nora grabbed his leg and tripped him.

I jumped back, arms raised, as Officer Bridges and a young policeman I'd never met burst through the door.

Zane dropped the bat and put his hands up as soon as the police were in the room. "I don't want any trouble. I'm an officer of the law myself. I'm just here to pick up my wife. As you can see, she is injured and may need medical attention. I want to make sure she is all right and then take her home."

Maryjane scoffed and said to Zane, "Well, you would know all about how I got these injuries!" She turned to Officer Bridges, "I have no intention of going anywhere with this man. He broke into our house, threatened us, and held us captive. I want him arrested." Any thoughts I had about Maryjane being timid were dispelled by her words and the look she gave Zane.

Zane's voice became cajoling, "Come on, Maryjane, we can—"

Officer Bridges didn't give him a chance to finish. "Let's go, Zane."

As the three of us watched, Zane was led out in handcuffs, but before he left, he yelled, "This is not over, Maryjane."

We gave the short version of what had happened to Officer Bridges and promised to come into the station to make a full statement. No one said anything at first as the police car pulled away. Nora winced as she helped Maryjane to the sofa again to sit. Zane must have connected to her shoulder pretty hard when he hit her with the bat.

I went to stand in front of her and said, "Let me palpate your clavicle and your shoulder. He could have fractured something."

She pulled away, "No. It's fine." She moved her arm slowly to show me. "I'm not going to get it checked out, and don't even bother arguing with me."

I realized she wasn't going to change her mind about going to the emergency room, so I said, "Then I guess we all better go down to the police station like Officer Bridges said so that we can give our statement as to what happened."

They both nodded. Nora did not look happy at the prospect, though.

"Nora, what he said about you—?" I started to ask her.

"I'll resign from Coretrack. We have to leave here now anyway; you heard what he said."

Maryjane took Nora's hand. "Is it true? I mean, did you…are you really licensed as an RN?"

Nora looked defiant again. "I passed the licensing exam. I just never actually graduated from an accredited program." She looked at me. "You know that I'm a good nurse!"

I remembered reading about several nursing school programs that were selling false transcripts. The schools were fined and closed down, but I wasn't sure what action was being taken with the people who bought the transcripts. Like she said, wherever she got her knowledge, she was able to pass the licensing exam. My next thought was that Judy would probably need to be sedated when she found out about this.

"Nora, you can't keep practicing as an RN. You have to contact the Nursing Board and find out what your options are." I felt terrible for her, but also appalled at what she did.

Maryjane said, "I'll help you. We can fix this somehow."

Nora just nodded and said, "Let's go and make our statement against Zane."

I offered to drive, but Nora said she was fine, and she and Maryjane would take her car.

I felt a bit shaken as I drove to the police station to give my statement. I knew Nora was hiding something, but I had not suspected it had anything to do with obtaining her RN license fraudulently. Or that she was in actual danger from someone tracking her and her partner. It made me question what I might have missed in trying to help Lynn prove her innocence in Mrs. Drover's murder.

* * *

Judy took the news about Nora better than I expected. She was obviously upset, but immediately set about calling the Nursing Board herself to let them know about Nora and then checked with the agency's lawyers to find out what liability, if any, Coretrack might have connected to her working for the agency. She stressed to them that the agency had checked and found Nora did indeed have a nursing license and had hired her in good faith.

Over the next few days, the news got out about Nora, and it had all my co-workers talking, though out of Judy's earshot.

"I can't believe she was able to fake it like that."

"Does anyone know if she worked in some other capacity in healthcare? Is that how she passed her licensing exam?"

"How did she do it? I failed twice before I passed!" One of my colleagues wailed.

Between the amazement at her fraud and the fact that she was on the run with her partner's husband in hot pursuit, Nora became the biggest topic of discussion for several days. I was somehow seen as an expert on her history, but answered any questions put to me about her with as little elaboration as possible.

I waited anxiously for Nora to come back to work, even if it was just to pick up what personal belongings she'd left there. She never returned. I heard through Detective Cody the police couldn't find her or Maryjane to follow up on the complaint against Zane Kirkwood.

The whole experience left me with a whole bucket of mixed feelings about Nora. I hadn't even found out if her last name was Stevens or Smith, or if the small town she and Maryjane were talking about was in Arizona, like she said, or somewhere else. I was sure if I asked Sunny Cody she would find the answers, but it somehow didn't matter now. By pouring my heart out to Bruno and Justin, I was able to unload at least some of my guilt at not being able to help her sooner, as well as my anger at her for her lies and deception. Mostly, once I got over what had happened, I hoped she was going to be all right wherever she was now.

Chapter Twenty-Two

The day after the episode with Nora and Maryjane, I called Lynn to find out how things were going with Alex and to let her know what had happened to me.

"Wow! Are you sure you're all right? He didn't hurt you, did he?" Lynn said.

"No. He was certainly threatening, but the only one he hit was Nora. At least this time, poor Maryjane had obviously been worked over pretty badly before she left him." I cringed once again, thinking about what Zane must have done to her and how trapped she must have felt to stay with him.

"So, I guess it turns out this Nora was keeping a lot of secrets. That seems to be a theme lately, huh? Secrets?"

I knew what she was referring to. "How did Alex seem when you went out to dinner? Was he still upset with Ben, and his mother?"

"I told him that I thought his mother was going to tell him about planning to sell the cottage the day she was killed. I said I was sure her intention wasn't to keep that from him. Hearing that seemed to make him feel a little better." Lynn said.

"Good. When I went to the police station to give my statement about Zane Kirkwood breaking into Nora's house and holding us captive, I tried to fish around a little. I wanted to see if I could find out what was going on with their investigation of Ben. I didn't have any luck. Officer Bridges made it very clear that I was there only to relate the events that occurred at 59 Strawbow Road. The police haven't contacted you again about anything to do with the murder, have they?"

"No. I have to admit I'm feeling a little relieved now that it looks like Ben may become their chief suspect. Though, I still find it hard to believe he did it."

"What did Alex say about Ben? Does he think that he was involved in his mother's murder?"

"I don't think he wants to. He's still very hurt that Ben kept it from him that his mother planned to sell the cottage and that he was there the morning of Mrs. Drover's murder. He claims to believe him about not going into the house that day."

I was curious how Ben's being a suspect in the murder was going to affect their wedding plans. Though Lynn being a suspect certainly would derail it even more. "Is Alex still set on Ben serving as best man?"

"Yes. The other evening we discussed it and decided that we should proceed with our wedding as planned. We are both sure the police will find the real murderer soon, and even with all the setbacks we've had, we are counting on being married on August fifteenth."

I was keeping my fingers crossed that nothing else happened to ruin Lynn and Alex's plans.

* * *

I had the weekend off, and Lynn made an appointment for any alterations that were needed on her bridal gown and my maid of honor dress. We planned it as a girls' day out. Lynn and I both had fittings scheduled for late morning on Saturday, then we had plans to go out for lunch. She also said that before she dropped me off again at my house, she wanted to show me the studio she was renting in downtown Guilford.

When Lynn came out of the dressing room in the wedding gown she had chosen, I gasped. She looked gorgeous. She turned slowly in front of me, "Too much? Be honest."

I shook my head. "No. I think it is perfect."

Mrs. Cady, the proprietor of the shop, echoed my opinion, "That dress was made for you."

140

Lynn looked hesitant, "Maybe I should have gone with a champagne or ivory color. After all, I've been married before."

"No. You deserve to wear white for at least one ceremony," I said.

Mrs. Cady piped in, "Honey, if every bride thought that way, the white gown would go the way of the dodo. Now let's see what we need to adjust here." She began to tweak the gown here and there, pinning each tuck as she made it.

"Okay, if you're sure." Lynn beamed as she stared at herself in the mirror.

After Lynn's dress was done, it was my turn. I had to admit I couldn't wait for Justin to see me in the teal tea-length dress I had chosen. I grinned at Lynn over Mrs. Cady's head as the seamstress bent to pin up my hem "just a teenie bit."

"I think we did good!" I said.

We were both lucky, and neither her gown nor my dress needed much adjustment, so we were done with our fittings in a short time. We went to Lenny and Joe's Fish Tale for lunch, and after we each devoured a delicious helping of fried shrimp and French fries, Lynn drove us to the space she had rented as an artist's studio not far from the Guilford green. Lynn was more relaxed than I'd seen her in a while, and I realized we had not discussed anything to do with Mrs. Drover's murder or the investigation all morning.

"The space is small, and I am still arranging things as I want them, but I'm selling more paintings and even have a couple of commissions now, so I thought it was time I had an official workspace."

"I agree. I think renting the studio was a good idea. I'm so excited for you that your painting career is taking off."

"Thank you." Lynn took a deep breath and let it out, "I can't help but feel that finally things are working out. Not only is my art selling, but I love teaching my art classes, and now the wedding is back on track. "

I knew that neither one of us wanted to mention the one big issue that still wasn't resolved.

We were almost at the studio when Lynn said, "I'm sorry I haven't had time to bring you here earlier."

I grunted, "Well, it isn't as if we both haven't had a lot going on."

"No kidding. Anyway, I love having a little space to go where its only purpose is for my art."

The studio was in a small building among several other shops and a couple of restaurants. When we pulled into the shared parking lot, there were two police cars there. It looked like the officers were just getting out of their cars.

"I wonder what's going on." Lynn's knuckles were white as she gripped the wheel. "Someone got their purse snatched in this parking lot last week."

"It could just be an accident in the parking lot or something." I didn't want to tell her that even though I didn't get a good look at him, I thought one of the officers looked like Detective Crane.

Lynn pulled into the first available slot, stopping rather abruptly. "Oh no. It looks like they are going toward my studio." She jumped out of the car, and I was right behind her.

"Excuse me! Officers! What happened?" Lynn took a step back, nearly knocking me over as one of the officers turned. "Detective Crane."

"I'm glad you're here, Ms. Duncan. Would you mind opening the door for us? We have a warrant to search the premises of this establishment." He took a document from his coat pocket and shoved it toward Lynn.

We both answered together, "What? Why?" I looked over her shoulder at the paper in her hand. Neither of us took the time to read it, but it looked legitimate.

"We have reason to believe there may be evidence in your studio related to our ongoing murder investigation. Please open the door. Otherwise, we will need to force entry."

Two other policemen stood by waiting patiently, gloved for the search. I recognized one as Officer Bridges, who only days before had come to the rescue at Nora Steven's house. He met my eyes briefly, then looked away, a blush starting to creep up his neck.

Lynn's hands shook as she tried to fit the key into the lock. "I don't understand. Why are you looking here?"

I asked Detective Crane, "What are you looking for? Lynn rented this place after Mrs. Drover was killed. There is nothing here that could possibly link to her murder."

CHAPTER TWENTY-TWO

He gave me a tight smile, "Then there is nothing to worry about, is there?"

Lynn stepped into the studio and flicked on an overhead light. The two officers went in behind Lynn, followed by Detective Crane. He turned to me as he entered, "If you are going to stay here, Ms. Bass, don't touch anything, stay out of the way, and please keep your comments to yourself."

The studio was small, as Lynn had said, but it was perfect for what she wanted. There were several finished paintings lined up along one wall, and the one she was working on was on the easel in the center of the room. Her rolling chair sat in front of the easel, and her paint supplies were on a rolling table pushed against another wall. There was one easy chair I recognized as being from her condo and a couple of boxes she hadn't unpacked yet in one corner.

Lynn came to stand beside me, and I reached for her hand and squeezed it. "Don't worry."

Officer Bridges went around the room checking behind each of the paintings along the wall; the other officer, whose name tag read 'London', went over to peek under the table containing her paints. Detective Crane stood watch over Lynn and me as we stood stiffly, side by side.

My surprise and initial apprehension had now turned to anger. What reason did the police have to harass Lynn yet again, looking for evidence that did not exist? Finally, I couldn't hold my tongue any longer, "This is ridiculous! I have no idea what you expect to find, but you can see there is nothing…"

Officer Bridges had moved to examine the things Lynn hadn't unpacked yet. He pulled something out of one of the boxes and turned, holding up a Prada beach bag. "What's this?"

He shook it, and it appeared there was something heavy weighing it down. Detective Crane grabbed it from his hand.

Lynn dropped my hand and, taking a step toward him, said, "Where did that come from? It's not mine."

Detective Crane opened the bag, and his eyes widened. He reached a gloved hand in and pulled out some kind of implement with a long, sharp blade. It was strange looking: the blade was triangle-shaped, and the handle where the grip was looked like a pair of brass knuckles. I could almost make out a date and some initials that were stamped on the side of the grip.

I let out a gasp, and I felt Lynn slump against me.

Officer Bridges whistled softly, "That's a trench knife. They used them in the First World War." Detective Crane gave him a questioning look. "My dad collects military paraphernalia. He's been searching for one of those online for years; they stopped making them after World War I, and it's hard to find an authentic one."

Lynn croaked out, "I have no idea how that got here. I have never seen that before."

Detective Crane said nothing, turning the knife in his hands. I could see something crusted around the guard between the blade and the handle. He turned to Officer Bridges, "Put this in an evidence bag." His voice was soft as he said to Lynn, "Ms. Duncan, I'm going to have to ask you to come with me."

I watched, stunned, as they put handcuffs on Lynn and started to lead her away. "I'll call a lawyer...and Alex," I said.

Tears were dripping down Lynn's face, and she looked totally baffled by what was happening. She nodded in reply.

Chapter Twenty-Three

Two more police cars had arrived as Lynn was led to one of the original vehicles. Officer Bridges guided her gently into the back of his cruiser and he turned to give me a sympathetic look before he closed the door. I yelled to Lynn, "Don't give any kind of statement until your lawyer gets there."

I thought I saw her nod again.

I stopped Detective Crane before he climbed into his own vehicle. "Can I at least get the car keys from Lynn? I don't have my car here."

He retrieved Lynn's purse and handed me the keys. "You'll have to wait until her car has been searched before you can leave. Until then, stay out of my officers' way."

The look he gave me made me think he was accusing me of somehow being complicit in hiding what was likely the murder weapon. "I understand." I figured there was nothing to gain by responding to his hostility with any of my own.

I turned to see Officer London and another policeman checking under floor mats, the spare tire compartment, and the glove box of Lynn's car. Luckily, their search didn't take long. Though she could create quite a mess in the throes of working on one of her paintings, Lynn kept a meticulously clean car.

"Nothing here," Officer London announced.

Detective Crane had already sped away after Officer Bridges' car, so I climbed behind the wheel of Lynn's car and headed toward home, fervently running through my mental list of any defense attorneys I had heard of. One very good candidate came to mind.

I barely greeted Bruno after I dashed into the house. I plunked myself down at the kitchen counter and scrolled through my phone until I found the number I was looking for. I had gone to high school with Amamda Reilly, now Booth, and was sure she had gone on to law school. I was pretty sure she had an office in Clinton, which is the next town over. I quickly googled her to check what type of law she practiced and was happy to see it was criminal defense.

Her office was closed for the weekend, but I left a message with her answering service and was relieved when I got a speedy callback. I picked up Bruno to hold him in my lap as I spoke to her. Mostly to calm myself, but also to make up for ignoring him when I got home.

After a quick greeting, Amanda cut to the chase, "I'm assuming you didn't call me just to catch up on our lives. How can I help you?"

I summarized what had happened: Mrs. Drover being murdered, Lynn becoming a suspect due to her rocky relationship with her future mother-in-law, and the fact that the police had no real evidence to link her to the crime—until today. I was amazed I had been able to maintain my calm through it all until I got to the bit about the knife they found. My voice shook as I said, "They found a very frightening-looking knife in a beach bag in her studio. Lynn is clueless about how it got there. They have her at the station now. I told her not to say anything until you got there."

"Good." It sounded as if Amanda was scratching down a few notes as we spoke.

I took a deep breath, "I found out that Mrs. Drover's nephew, Ben, had good reason to want her dead. I think maybe...'

Amanda's voice was firm, "Let's just worry about what is going on with your friend right now and not worry about who may have or may not have been the murderer. Why did the police believe they would find evidence at her studio?"

"I don't know. I asked, but they never answered the question."

"Okay, why don't I go to speak with your friend? Lynn Duncan, right? Also, maybe I can find out what caused the police to do the search. I am assuming she wants to retain my services?"

I was sure of what Lynn's answer would be. "Yes. Definitely." I suddenly felt the first spark of hope since I saw Officer Bridges pull that beach bag out of the box of Lynn's things.

After I hung up with Amanda, I moved on to the next thing I needed to do. I dreaded having to make the call to Alex to let him know what had happened to Lynn. She still maintained he had no doubts about her lack of involvement in his mother's murder. I wasn't as sure about him.

"Melanie! Hi! How was your girls' day out with Lynn? I'm waiting for her to get here now; where is she?"

There was no way to sugarcoat it. "She's at the police station. She's been arrested. They found a weapon in her studio, and they think she hid it there."

"What! How? She's been arrested?"

"Yes. They found a knife in a beach bag among her things. She told them she had never seen it before."

He was silent for a beat or two, then said, "A knife? Does she have any idea how it got there?"

I repeated what I had just told him. "No. She has no idea where it came from or who put it there."

"The police think it is the knife that was used to kill my mother?"

I thought that would be obvious to him, but kept my voice calm as I answered, "Yes. That's what they are saying."

"This is a lot to take in. What will happen now? Should I go to the police station?"

I couldn't help thinking that it is probably a good thing there weren't many emergencies in dermatology, because Alex would be useless. I tried to keep the anger out of my voice, "Yes. She needs you there to support her. I'm not sure when they'll let you see her, but she needs you there to offer her encouragement. I've already called a lawyer. I'm going to go down there also to see what is going on."

"All right. The lawyer is a good idea. I'll meet you at the station."

My plan was to take Bruno out, get him settled with his chewy bone, and call my young neighbor, Jenny, to come and spend some time with him while

I was gone. Before I could call her, however, she was at my door.

She looked panicked. "Help! My mom just fainted or something! She said she wasn't feeling well, and then she kind of stumbled and fell down. Hurry!"

I grabbed my work bag and ran next door with her. By the time we got into the house Karen was sitting up on the floor and was trying to pull herself up onto one of the kitchen chairs.

"It's okay, Karen. Just sit there a minute. I'm going to take your blood pressure, okay?" As I wrapped the cuff around her arm, I noticed that she looked pale. Her blood pressure was a bit low, but not dangerously so.

Jenny stood by my side, "She threw up last night and again a couple of times this morning. I told her maybe she should call the doctor, but she didn't want to. I was going to call 911, but I saw you were home, so I went to get you first."

Karen looked embarrassed, "No, don't call 911. I'm fine, just the stomach flu." She tried to get up again and this time I helped her into the chair. Her color had started to improve a little by now.

I felt torn about what to do. Karen probably was dehydrated and could benefit from some IV fluid, but I kept thinking of Lynn being arrested and at the police station now. However, there was no question that Karen needed my attention first. "I think you should be seen; I can drive you to the ER if you like."

Karen shook her head, "No. Thank you, but I can call my sister Nancy to take me to the walk-in clinic to get checked out."

Jenny said, "If you want, I can drive you, Mom."

Karen lost some of the color she had started to regain, "Absolutely not! You only have a learner's permit. Your aunt will do it."

While we waited for her sister to arrive, I was able to get Karen to take a few sips of a drink containing electrolytes and keep it down. When Nancy arrived, she took charge and bustled both Karen and Jenny out to her car.

* * *

When I got to the station, I was relieved to see that Alex was already there.

However, he was not in the sympathetic and supportive state that I had hoped to find. He was pacing back and forth in the waiting area outside the front desk. When he saw me, he stopped and glared at me.

"It wasn't just any knife they found! The police asked me if I had ever seen it before, and I told them it was my great-grandfather's! How the hell did Lynn get hold of it? The police said it was right in with her work supplies, the ones she brought directly from her condo!"

"Wait a minute! How can you even think that Lynn had anything to do with getting the knife from anywhere? Someone else put the knife in her things." I kept my voice down. I didn't want to be asked to leave the station, but I put as much venom into it as possible.

He took a deep breath and said, "I don't want to believe she had anything to do with what happened to my mother, but she was there that day, and the knife was kept at the cottage. It used to hang on the wall, but my mother took it down and put it away somewhere when she found us kids playing with it one day. Lynn and my mother did not get along, and—"

"Quiet!" I tipped my head toward the officer sitting behind the Plexiglas shield at the front desk. "I know this is very upsetting, but just think about what you are saying."

He stopped pacing suddenly, and, looking toward where the desk officer sat, said, "Okay. You're right."

My doubts about Alex were obviously well-founded. It would break her heart if Lynn heard what he was saying now. I spoke softly, "You know, your cousin Ben also was at the house, and he would know about the knife. I find him much more likely to be guilty."

Alex looked like all the steam had gone out of him. He went over to a bench against the wall and slumped down on it, rubbing his face with both hands. "Great. One of the two people in my life who are most important to me may have killed my mother."

It was unbelievable how he had turned Lynn's problem around to be about him. Although I could sympathize with him to a point, his feelings were not the most important thing to consider right now. Once she finally got out of this mess, I was going to have a very painful talk with Lynn about Alex.

The door to one of the interview rooms opened, and Amanda Booth strode out. I hadn't seen her in several years, but the first word that sprang to mind was "confident." In school, she had always been on the honor roll, and she was quiet but not shy. We had a great time at our ten-year high school reunion, and I learned she was also a lot of fun. Today, she was in her professional mode, and I knew I'd made the right choice when I'd called her.

I rushed over to her, "How is Lynn?"

"Nervous, but she has calmed down a bit. She filled me in on what has happened so far, at least her version of it. I told her I would start looking into the case immediately and be back on Monday."

Alex had come to stand next to me. "Monday? You mean they are keeping her here?"

"Amanda, this is Alex Drover, Lynn's fiancé."

Amanda turned to him and said, "Yes, I'm afraid she has to wait for official charges to be made and for bail to be set. The courts won't open until Monday. She was distressed to learn that but has since come to accept that she'll need to stay in custody at least until then."

Alex went to approach the officer at the desk to ask if he could speak to Lynn now that her lawyer had seen her. I walked with Amanda as she headed toward the exit from the police station.

"Thank you, Amanda. I feel better knowing you are going to represent Lynn. This is…"

"I know, a nightmare. I will do my best for her. Meanwhile, I know she appreciates your support. As bad as this looks, try not to worry too much." She gave me a quick hug and began to leave, but as she reached the door, she turned around again. "Oh. I spoke to a Detective Crane, who said they had a call from someone who works for the cleaning service. They said as they were cleaning the place, they saw something strange in Lynn's studio."

As I turned from seeing Amanda out, Alex stormed over to me. "They said I can't see Lynn while she is in custody! They said only her lawyer is allowed to visit her. I told them who I was, but they said it didn't make any difference!" Without another word, he marched out of the station.

My heart sank. I desperately wanted to talk to Lynn to make sure she was really doing all right. Just then, I saw Sunny Cody approach the front desk carrying a stack of forms, and I rushed over to speak to her.

"Sunny! I mean, Detective Cody, would it be possible for me to see Lynn Duncan now? I just want to see how she is doing."

She glanced over to the officer manning the front desk and said, "No. Absolutely not. As Officer Poldonski has already told Dr. Drover, only her legal council is allowed to speak with her right now."

"Not even for a few minutes?" I knew as soon as I said it that I had no right to ask her to bend the rules.

Sunny put her forms down and came out to speak to me. "I can't. I'm sorry, but it would be a big breach of protocol, and not only would I get reprimanded for it, but it could adversely affect her case, too."

"Okay, but what happens now? Lynn did not hide that knife in her studio, someone else put it there. Has Detective Crane spoken again to Ben Woodrow? He had a motive to want his aunt dead; he knew about the knife at the cottage, and he admits he was there the day Mrs. Drover was killed. He could have…"

"We did look at him, but he has an alibi. His secretary swore he was at the office at 9 AM and was in various meetings all day. Mrs. Drover's time of death was early afternoon." Sunny looked at me sympathetically, "All I can tell you is that the knife has been sent to check for fingerprints and analysis to confirm the blood on the hilt belongs to Mrs. Drover. Let's hope there are some fingerprints, and they don't belong to your friend."

"Will you at least tell Lynn that I was here and that I said we will figure this out."

"I will." Sunny cleared her throat and then said, "There's something that doesn't…" Detective Crane walked through the front door, and Sunny didn't finish what she was saying.

He walked by us without saying anything. After he was out of hearing range, Sunny said, "I promise, I'll keep an eye on Lynn to make sure she is as comfortable as possible while she's here."

Amanda Booth said that someone from the cleaning service called the police, and that led them to search her studio. I figured that I could start with whoever those cleaners were.

Chapter Twenty-Four

I tried calling the rental company the next day to find out what cleaning service they used, but since it was Sunday, the office was closed. I was trying to decide if there was anything else I could do to find out how the knife got into Lynn's studio when Justin called me. He suggested Bruno and I take a walk with Jasper and him.

"We can do the Greenway Trail or walk the bike trail at Hammonasset. You choose."

I hadn't slept well the previous night. I kept worrying about what was happening with Lynn, and there had been a knot of tension building between my shoulder blades since I got up that morning. "I think a long walk will do me good, and Bruno could use a little more of my attention these days." The thought of spending the afternoon with Justin made me immediately feel a little better. "Also, I would love to spend a little time with you today. Bruno isn't the only one I have been neglecting lately. Why don't we meet you at Meigs Point at Hammonasset?"

I was right about the walk doing me good. As we walked, Justin listened to my explanation of what had happened to Lynn after our lovely morning out. "I just don't know who would have placed that knife in Lynn's studio, or why." I explained my failed effort to contact the leasing company to find the cleaning company they used and that I planned to try again on Monday.

"Calling the cleaning company is a good idea. I wonder if the person who found the beach bag looked inside. Otherwise, how would they know it was suspicious?" he said.

"That's a good point. If it was in a box, they wouldn't have reason to look inside the beach bag, or even to touch the bag itself."

"Also," he said, "who could have put it there? Who would have the most to gain by Lynn being arrested for the murder?"

"The first person who comes to mind is Ben. He supposedly has an alibi, but up until the knife was found in Lynn's things, he looked like the most likely suspect. He also had access to the cottage and knew about his great-grandfather's knife. I don't know how he could have gotten it into Lynn's things, though."

Although the day was mild and sunny when we started out, the wind had picked up now and it looked like we were about to get a rainstorm. Justin said, "Why don't you meet me back at my place. We can order in pizza for lunch, and we can brainstorm some more about how the knife got into Lynn's studio."

The rain started to fall just as I was buckling Bruno into his seat restraint. When I got to Justin's, he and Jasper were already there. Jasper, worn out by the walk, had plopped down into his bed in the living room. Bruno was still full of energy and delighted to see Miss Scarlett, Justin's Maine Coon cat. Miss Scarlett was not as happy to see Bruno, so we spent the first few minutes making peace between the two and finding a safe spot for Miss Scarlett to hide away.

As we ate our pizza, we took up our discussion of how the knife got where it was found. "It isn't as if Ben has access to the building where Lynn's rental is," I said.

"That may be true, but Ben is fairly wealthy, isn't he? Money can buy a lot of services, and if it is enough, often there are no questions asked about why something is being done," Justin said.

"You've been around your grandfather too much! You are beginning to think like him. What you say is true, though. How is your grandfather, by the way? I haven't seen him since we had dinner on his birthday."

Justin grinned. "Oh, didn't I tell you? He has a new lady friend."

"What! No! Where did he meet her?"

"They met at a community center luncheon. She is a widow, a retired 911 operator from New Haven who lives in Guilford now. Her name is Loretta. I haven't seen too much of him lately, either. She has him going with her to the theater, mystery night dinners, and author readings at the local bookstores. He says she is running him ragged, but he looks better than I've seen him since my grandmother died five years ago."

I was delighted. "I need to call him and tease him about his love life, considering the way he butted into our relationship."

The rest of the afternoon, we watched a movie on TV, snuggling on the sofa and making up for not having seen much of each other lately. By the time I left Justin's, I had begun to feel more relaxed and more sure of where I should start to find out who set up Lynn. Justin made a good point about someone being hired to plant the beach bag containing the murder weapon in Lynn's studio. So, as I had originally planned, the place to start was with the person who made the call to the police.

* * *

At work on Monday, focusing on each patient and their needs helped a little to keep my mind off what was going on with Lynn. At lunch time, I tried calling her to see if she had been released on bail, but my call went right to voicemail.

When I couldn't reach Lynn, I tried calling The Hudson Company, who owned the building where Lynn was renting her studio. I was connected to Mr. Ross, who when I inquired about what cleaning service he used to clean the company's properties, was very forthcoming. I lied and told him I was opening a new hair salon in town and needed a cleaning service. I'm sure that helped.

"We use a company called Tidy Titans. So far, we've been very pleased with them, but then we only started using them a few months ago. We generally only use them to do a thorough cleaning and sanitizing once a client moves out, and we are preparing to relist the property, though."

"Oh, I see, so you don't schedule regular cleanings of your properties? Would there ever be a reason that you would request the company to send someone to do a touch-up or anything in a property that was already occupied?"

"No. We expect the tenants to do the day-to-day upkeep of the property. Were you looking for a company to do more frequent cleaning of your shop?"

"Thank you. You have been very helpful." I quickly hung up.

When I called Tidy Titans, the person who answered the phone sounded harried. I didn't use any type of ruse this time, but just admitted I was calling with a few questions about them having cleaned a property on Water Street in Guilford.

"Miss, if you are calling with a complaint, I'll direct you to our website, where we welcome your input. I don't take—"

"No. It's nothing like that. I spoke to Mr. Ross at Hudson Company and he said your company does the cleaning on units after the previous tenants have moved out."

"Yeah."

"Are you ever employed by tenants to do cleanings in between, for upkeep or anything?"

I could hear another line ringing in the background, but the woman appeared to be ignoring it. "It's against company policy for our workers to do work not booked through this office, but I know some of our people might do a little moonlighting. I figure it's none of my business what they do on their own time." I could hear a phone ringing in the background again.

"Did any of your workers report finding something suspicious at unit—?"

She didn't let me finish. "If our people reported all the suspicious and disgusting things we find left at the places we clean, we would need a whole other department to deal with it. I really am a little swamped right now. Like I said—go to our website if you have any more questions." She abruptly ended the call.

After speaking to Miss Just call Our Website at Tidy Titans, I called Sunny Cody. I wanted to let her know what I had found out from Mr. Ross and to ask her what she started to say to me while I was at the police station on Saturday. I got right to the point when she answered. "I know you said that Detective Crane is supposed to be leading the investigation, but I wonder if you have any more information you want to share with me. I thought you were about to say something the other day at the police station before Detective Crane walked in."

She took a minute before she answered, and I thought I heard a door closing. "I was just going to say that there was something fishy about the murder weapon suddenly showing up in Lynn's studio like it did."

I felt a flush of excitement, "I thought the same thing. Also, I called the company that cleans the properties owned by the Hudson Company, and the cleaning company had no record of a worker reporting anything unusual in Lynn's studio. The leasing company said that that particular property hadn't—"

"I know the property hadn't been scheduled to be cleaned since Lynn Duncan signed the lease. I checked with the cleaning company also, and they had no record of a complaint having been called in to us." Sunny sounded annoyed now. "If Crane finds out you are still snooping around trying to absolve Lynn of the murder, he's going to think I put you up to it. Then he will make sure I am totally locked out of the case."

"Can I at least ask if the results on the fingerprints on the knife are back yet?" I hoped she hadn't noticed that I'd made no promises about not trying to find out who really killed Mrs. Drover.

She sighed, "The blood on the knife matched that of Mrs. Drover, and no other blood belonging to anyone else was found. There were no usable fingerprints on the handle or blade. Both had apparently been wiped clean. I am only telling you this because we had to make the report available to Lynn's attorney, whom I am certain will share that information with her."

I cheered inwardly at this bit of news. "That's good news for Lynn, isn't it? I mean, there is no proof she handled the knife."

"There is also no proof she didn't, but at least there is nothing at this point to further incriminate her."

"What about in the cottage itself? Lynn said she never went inside. If her prints aren't there, how could she have killed Mrs. Drover?"

"There was a jumble of fingerprints inside the cottage itself. It will take some time to figure out those that can be explained and those that can't." I heard the sound of knocking in the background, and Sunny said, "I need to go. I'll let you know if I find out anything else that I am able to share with you."

* * *

I was relieved to finally hear from Lynn early that evening. "I'm sprung." She was trying to sound cheerful, but I could tell she was on the verge of tears. "Apparently, there were no usable fingerprints on the knife. Attorney Booth used the fact that it couldn't be proved I ever handled the knife and my lack of any kind of criminal record to get the judge to set a reasonable bail. At least she said it was reasonable considering that I was being charged with murder, but I was stunned at the amount the judge named. Alex showed up at the courthouse for the bail hearing. Once the bail was set, he agreed to contact a bail bondsman and take care of it."

Her voice got a little shaky now. "We…went back to his house. We had a big fight once we got there. He was acting like he thought I might actually be guilty! Afterward, I told him I needed to rest and a little time to think about everything that has happened over the past couple of days, so he drove me home."

I checked the clock; it was only 7 PM. "I want to hear the whole story. Would you mind if Bruno and I came over for a bit?"

"Please come! I could use a little Bruno therapy!" she said. "Besides, what I really need is to talk over with you what is going on—in the investigation and with Alex."

I stopped at a small market to get some of their homemade soup to bring to Lynn. I was pretty sure that with the kind of day she'd had, she most likely hadn't eaten anything. When I got to her condo, she opened the door before I even knocked. I handed her the bag with the soup in it. "It's still hot. Let's go into the kitchen, and while I get a bowl out, you sit down and start to tell me what happened."

Lynn did as I asked, stopping only to pick up Bruno and put him in her lap while I scooped out her soup. "I really like Amanda Booth; thank you for finding her. She is no-nonsense and gets right to the heart of the matter. If anyone can help me out of this mess, I think she can."

I placed the bowl in front of Lynn and put Bruno down on the floor next to her, where he very nicely rested his head on her feet.

"Anyway, I was so happy to see Alex was there this morning. Amanda talked me through what to expect before the judge came in, so that helped. I was relieved when the judge set bail, but I had no idea how I was going to pay it. As I said, Alex told me not to worry; he would take care of it. I felt grateful to be engaged to such a generous and capable man."

Hearing that raised him a notch in my opinion. However, judging from what Lynn had told me so far about what happened afterward, he still had a long way to go before I felt he deserved Lynn.

"That was how I felt then. If I'd known what was going to happen a bit later, I might have chosen to stay in jail." She took a deep breath and let it out slowly. "After I was released, we had a huge fight. He said he could understand if I lost my temper; his mother could certainly provoke people. Was it possible I just lashed out, not meaning to really hurt her?"

I could feel all the goodwill I'd started to have toward Alex evaporate in an instant. "Oh, Lynn!"

"I couldn't believe what he was saying! I lost my temper. I told him I thought he loved me, that he knew me. How could he think I would kill anyone, let alone the mother of someone who I planned to spend the rest of my life with?"

"What did he say to that?" I didn't even want to mention that he had been spewing those thoughts at the police station, where he could be overheard.

"He backed down then. He said he was confused and upset by what was going on in the investigation into his mother's death. He swore he didn't mean what he said. He didn't really believe I killed her; he hadn't been thinking clearly lately. He begged me to forgive him."

She stopped to eat a little bit more, then said. "I said I did. But I don't think I do. He claims he was confused, but some part of him must have believed it was possible." She put her spoon down. "I am not sure what I want to do now as far as our relationship. How can I marry someone who would think me capable of such a terrible act? Even if he only thought so for a short time."

Even though I had the same feeling, I reached across the table, put my hand on her arm, and said, "That's something you have to decide for yourself. You were right to ask him for some time to really search your feelings."

She looked teary-eyed again, "None of what I decide will matter if I am convicted of Diana Drover's murder and I have to spend the rest of my life in prison."

I didn't want to admit to her that I was scared, too. "You didn't do it, and we will find a way to prove it." I continued, "I called the rental company for your building to get the name of the cleaning service that takes care of it. It turns out they only use the cleaners when someone moves out to do a terminal cleaning." I winced at the irony of the word they used. "So, it wasn't someone from that service who called the police since they wouldn't have had a reason to go back into your studio."

She looked like something was suddenly occurring to her. "A few days ago, I stopped in to drop off a few new canvases I bought. I thought things looked…different. Not where I left them. But then I figured I was just imagining things, I've been pretty distracted lately between the things going on with the investigation and the wedding."

"But maybe you were right. That could be when someone planted the murder weapon. We have to call the police."

"I'm not sure if Detective Crane will believe me."

Just then, Bruno let out a sharp bark and ran to the door. Both Lynn and I got up to see what he was barking at. As we approached the door, I heard a car pulling away from in front of her condo. There was a small piece of paper lying on the floor at the base of the door. Lynn picked it up, looked at it, and then showed it to me.

MURDERER-YOU WILL NOT GET AWAY WITH IT.

It was printed, so there was no real handwriting to compare, but I thought it looked a lot like the printing on the note I found on my windshield warning me to stop looking into Mrs. Drover's murder.

I opened Lynn's front door to look out, but the car was long gone. I told her about the note I'd gotten also.

"You never mentioned getting a note. What did you do with it?"

It was still crumpled up in the cup holder of my car, and I went out to get it and showed it to her.

"It does kind of look like the same person wrote these," Lynn said.

"Whoever it is seems intent on making sure you are convicted of Mrs. Drover's murder." Once again, my suspicions went to Alex's cousin, Ben. He had avoided telling the police he was even at the cottage that day until pressured to do so. His secretary said he was at the office all day, but did he leave for lunch? Did she? He could have gone to confront his aunt about the sale of the cottage then, and things got out of hand.

I decided to take a trip back to Whitley Financial the next day, this time to talk to Shiela, Ben's secretary. But first, I wanted to make the police aware of the two notes we had gotten, along with Lynn's suspicion about someone having broken into her studio. No matter what they said, I wanted both things on the record. "I'm calling the police," I said.

Lynn lifted an eyebrow as she said, "I'm not sure how seriously the police are going to take what you tell them right now concerning anything that involves me. Besides, I'd just as soon stay as far from law enforcement as I can until I'm cleared."

I made the call, but Lynn was right on both counts. Officer Garcia came to take our complaint. He actually rolled his eyes when Lynn told him she thought someone had broken into her studio. He did look at both notes, but afterward he said, "I'll make a report, but it could just be a crank." I thought I saw him smirk then, "I'm afraid we can't control public opinion in these cases." He put his pad away and headed to his car, muttering something under his breath.

Lynn seemed upset after Officer Garcia left. "Don't worry. He may not believe us right now, but at least it will be on record about the notes and the suspected break-in," I said.

"It's not that. Or at least that's not all that is worrying me. I just hope that what we just told him doesn't backfire and makes it look like I'm trying to make up an explanation for the knife being there. My attorney said I have to avoid contact with all of Mrs. Drover's family, except Alex, of course. She said I need to stay away from the crime scene and anything at all to do with the murder while I'm out on bail. I hope this doesn't jeopardize my defense."

"I don't think it will. I'll tell them the truth; it was me who wanted to report them," I said. "As to you staying away from anything to do with the murder, that's a good idea." I smiled and patted her hand, "I don't have to stay away, however, no matter what notes or advice I get."

Chapter Twenty-Five

The next day, I waited until just a few minutes past noon to arrive at Whitley Financial. I was betting that was the usual time they took their lunch break. As I approached Ben's secretary's desk, I could see she was gathering her purse and jacket. With any luck, Ben would have left for lunch already, since it was Sheila I really wanted to question.

"Hi. Sheila, right? I'm not sure you remember me. My name is Melanie Bass. I'm a friend of Mr. Woodrow. I was hoping to get in to see him for a minute or two." I gave her an expectant smile.

"Oh, I'm sorry. He just left for lunch. I would tell you where he is going, and you could catch him there, but he is meeting a client." She grinned, "He usually doesn't do business at lunchtime. He says this is his time to relax and think, but this client insisted it was the only time he could talk to him."

"Oh, that's too bad. Maybe I can catch him later, then." I acted as if I was about to leave, then said, "Do you know when he will be back in the office?"

She shifted her jacket to her other arm to check her watch. "He usually takes an hour and a half. Unless he had to run a quick errand, then he might be a bit later getting back."

An hour and a half was plenty of time to get back to Madison, confront his aunt, and get back to the office. "I might as well get lunch too, then, since Ben isn't available right now. Is there a specific restaurant he likes around here?"

I saw her check her watch again, I was obviously cutting into her lunch hour. "He loves Chez Marie, but he isn't there today. Anyway, as I said, he has a working lunch and will be busy, so…"

Perfect. I could ask a few questions about Ben without worrying about bumping into him. "Thank you. I'll give Chez Marie a try." I gave her an apologetic smile, "You wouldn't remember if he took an extra-long lunch on April 12th, would you? That would be a couple of weeks ago."

"No. And I really must get to lunch." Her friendly manner was suddenly gone. "When Mr. Woodrow returns, I'll tell him you were here." She left without even being sure she had my name correct.

The restaurant was much busier than I expected when I got there. My surprise at how busy it was increased when I checked the prices on the menu, but then, most of the patrons looked like they were used to taking an hour-and-a-half lunches and probably writing off the expense. I was lucky. It looked like I would have a few minutes to speak to the hostess before someone came in behind me to be seated.

I rushed up to her, checking my watch as I reached her. "Hello. I'm looking for Mr. Benjamin Woodrow. I was supposed to meet him for lunch, and I'm afraid I'm already late."

Her brow furrowed as she looked down at her reservation list. "I don't see his name here today." She looked at me apologetically, "That's strange because Mr. Woodrow always has his secretary call to make a reservation when he dines with us."

"Oh. I'm sure he said this was where we were to meet for lunch." I looked as distressed as I could muster without becoming melodramatic. "He is going to be sooo angry with me, I'm afraid. I must be confused about where we were to have lunch. I was supposed to meet him here a few weeks ago, but I got the date wrong. He said April twelfth, and I had it as the fourteenth. I can't stand him up again!"

She looked as if she was just thinking of something. "Oh, I do remember him coming in not long ago and saying he was waiting for someone, but then he left right after his appetizer and didn't stay for the full-course meal. I remember it because he left so abruptly, I thought something was wrong. But he explained his guest had canceled and he needed to leave as he had something important to take care of."

I had to keep the look of satisfaction from showing on my face. Instead,

I said, "Oh, dear! I will definitely have to make this faux pas up to him!" I took out my phone as if I was about to call him. I nodded to her and said, "Thank you."

I had to get what I had just found out to the police. Ben's alibi was not as airtight as he claimed.

I planned to stop at the police station on my way home, but first, I wanted to check that Sunny Cody would be there. I didn't care that she was only peripherally involved in the case now. After the way Detective Crane had treated both Lynn and me, I didn't trust him to listen to what I had to say.

"Hi. Could you connect me to Detective Cody, please?"

The desk officer said, "Is this an emergency?" When I said it wasn't, he said, "I can connect you to her voicemail, but she is out of the station right now."

"Do you know when she will be back?"

"Sorry, no."

I was disappointed, but I decided I would try her again later. I wanted to talk to her in person when I tried to persuade her to get Detective Crane to look more closely at Ben Woodrow.

I needed to pick up some groceries on my way home, but I was starving. I never had gotten any lunch. I stopped at Dunkin Donuts for tea and a bagel with cream cheese before I hit the Stop and Shop to get what I needed.

I was distracted as I cruised the aisles at the grocery store. I was thinking about what I had learned about Ben's alibi and praying that I could get Sunny Cody to convince Detective Crane to look at other suspects in Mrs. Drover's murder. As I exited the canned goods aisle, I noticed a woman dressed in blue scrubs standing in front of the meat case. She turned to put something in her cart, and I was shocked to realize I recognized her.

"Maryjane?" The facial bruising from the beating her husband had given her was nearly gone, but I was sure it was her.

She turned to smile at me, "Melanie! I'm so glad I ran into you." She came over and gave me a quick hug. I was still too stunned at seeing her there to hug her back.

"But…I thought you left town."

"We did leave for a few days, but I convinced Nora that running away wasn't going to work for us long-term. It certainly didn't solve my problems with Zane. After we discussed it, we agreed that we liked it here, and at least for the foreseeable future, we are going to stay." She motioned to the way she was dressed, "As you can see, I'm back to work. I just started on a med surg floor at University Hospital."

I was happy for them, but also surprised at their decision. "Where's Nora? Is she all right?"

"Nora is doing much better. She was able to find a job as a home health aide for a lovely elderly lady. She was hired to stay with her and care for her during the day while the woman's daughter is at work in the city. She's also working on straightening out her issues with the Nursing Board. She's determined to do whatever is required to regain her RN. Even if it means actually attending nursing school this time so she can legitimately sit for her nursing boards." She laughed, "I'm sure she'll ace them. She really is a good nurse; she had me fooled, too."

"I'm glad to hear she has a plan to return to nursing."

Maryjane was quiet for a few seconds, then said, "Nora feels horrible about how things ended at Coretrack, and especially how she left things with you."

"Please tell her I said hello and that I would love to see her again."

"I know she wants to apologize to both you and Judy. I just think she needs a little more time to get her thoughts together and to get up the courage to face you."

I had another thought. "You said you are staying here, but what about Zane? He knows where you live. Has he given up on trying to convince you to return to him?"

"I took out a restraining order against him. Besides, it turns out Zane has more troubles than what happened to him here."

Having had the pleasure of meeting Zane, that didn't surprise me.

She looked around as if making sure no one else was listening in, then said, "I was not the only one he liked to get rough with. When they didn't get any satisfaction from the local police department, a few of the people he beat up during stops for trumped-up traffic violations went to the Arizona State

Police. It looks like his buddies in the local department didn't want to cover for him anymore, especially if it deflected attention from any unprofessional acts they might have been involved in themselves. Zane is on suspension and facing lawsuits from several of his victims."

"I'm glad that he is finally will have to answer for his deplorable actions. How did you find this out?"

"We finally returned to the police department here to pursue the charges we wanted brought against him. They told me I didn't have to worry about him bothering me anymore. That he was still back in Arizona trying to straighten out his problems there."

I was pleased that things were starting to work out for Maryjane and Nora. "Well, I'm so glad I ran into you today. Don't forget to tell Nora I was asking about her."

Maryjane smiled again and waved as she walked away, "I'll tell her."

Chapter Twenty-Six

My thoughts were buzzing by the time I got home. Between discovering Ben did have the opportunity to kill his aunt and the news that Nora Stevens was back in town, I was totally wound up. Bruno must have sensed this, because after greeting me with his usual enthusiasm, he began to race around the house, stopping only to snatch up one of his toys and then fling it up in the air, and then catch it again. I let him get out a bit more energy before I called him to me so I could take him outside.

I decided to wait an hour or two, before I called the police station again to see if Sunny was back from wherever she had been. I wondered if Ben really had been supposed to meet someone for lunch that day and got stood up. If so, was it another client, or about a personal matter? As far as spreading the news that Nora was back, I'd keep quiet unless someone mentioned having heard it first. I thought she deserved a chance to handle letting people know her situation in her own time.

After doing a couple of chores around the house, I called to see if Sunny was back yet. This time I was told that she had left again to attend to a personal emergency and the desk officer said he wasn't sure when she would be back. I was worried for Sunny now. I wondered what her emergency was and hoped her daughter, Katie, was all right.

I briefly considered trying to convince Detective Crane myself to look further into Ben's alibi, but Sunny's warnings about how he would react if he knew I was still poking around in his investigation made me quash that idea. He seemed to fully believe Lynn was the murderer. Or, at least, that was how it seemed to me.

I had gotten Ben to admit once before that he had not been completely open with the police. I knew I might be pushing my luck, but maybe I could come up with a way to get him to tell me where he really was during his lunch hour on the day of Mrs. Drover's murder. Though, if he was the killer, it might be chancy to push him too much.

I called Ben, asking him to meet me for coffee after work the next day. He didn't answer me at first, so I said, "I feel bad about how things ended with us the last time we spoke. I'm sorry I pressured you into admitting to the police you were at the cottage the morning of the murder."

What I was really sorry for was that he didn't admit it in the first place.

He still didn't respond. "This has to do with Alex and Lynn. We both care about them, and I wanted to get together to talk about what is going on between them."

He sighed and then said, "Okay. Though, I'm not exactly my cousin's favorite person right now. I can meet you at Starbucks in Madison at 5:30 tomorrow."

"That's perfect."

I arrived early and nursed a cup of tea as I waited. I was trying to come up with a way to ask about his whereabouts on the early afternoon of April twelfth without having him just get up and leave. I still hadn't thought of a good approach when I saw him enter the coffee shop.

After ordering his coffee, he slid into the seat opposite me. There was an elderly couple seated at a table right next to us, but as they got up to leave, I said, "Thank you for coming. I'm really worried about what is going to happen with Alex and Lynn. They are supposed to be getting married in a few months, and..."

Ben snorted. "Do you really think that is going to happen now? I've barely spoken to Alex lately, but from what I've heard, the only way Lynn will be able to marry him is in a jailhouse ceremony."

I fought to contain my anger. "I know things don't look good for her, but she is innocent. Though, I will say it would be helpful if your cousin was better about showing he believes in her innocence."

"Like I said, Alex and I aren't on the best of terms lately. So, I'm not sure how much weight he will put on what I tell him." He took a sip of coffee before continuing. "For what it's worth, I agree with you. I'm having a hard time believing Lynn is the killer."

I wasn't sure how to take that comment. If he was guilty, wouldn't he want to be sure she was accused to take any suspicion off of him? I decided to just take my chances and dive right into the real reason I invited him to coffee. "You said you were there early the morning your aunt was murdered; you admitted you wanted to go into the house to talk about something with her but changed your mind at the last minute. Did you, by any chance, go back later in the day, say at lunchtime, to have that discussion?"

"Wait a minute! I was at the office all day. I told the police this already. What are you insinuating?"

"I know you went to lunch at Chez Marie but left shortly after arriving. Where did you go?"

He began to stand up as if to leave, but then sat down again. "I don't know how you got that information, but it is none of your business where I went. It certainly wasn't back to the cottage, though."

I was glad we were in a public space; he had started to raise his voice, and a few of the other customers turned to look at us. I kept my voice at a normal level, "Were you really supposed to meet someone for lunch that day? Who?"

"That is also none of your business."

"But the police might be interested enough to make it their business."

He spoke in a harsh whisper now, "That's the second time you threatened me. I understand you want to clear your friend's name, but you are wrong about me. I didn't kill my aunt." He took a deep breath, "I did leave the restaurant early. I was supposed to meet a friend concerning a business deal they were proposing, but they canceled at the last minute. I went back to the office and checked out places in Key West where we could have Alex's bachelor weekend. And before you ask, no one else was back in the office yet after their lunch." He sat back in his chair and glared at me.

His story sounded convenient, but also plausible. "I suppose someone at the directory desk in your office building will be able to back up your story of you returning when you claim you did?" I had no intention of checking with whoever manned the front desk at this point, but I wanted to make him think I would.

"They might, but it gets pretty busy there during the day, and there is no reason I need to check in with them." He leaned forward across the table toward me. "Look, instead of you chasing me around trying to pin the murder on me, why don't we work together to find out who the real murderer is."

"What do you mean?"

"Like I said, I don't think Lynn is guilty either. Before she was killed, I started noticing some irregularities in some of my aunt's financial records. Amounts paid to unnamed sources. In some cases, large amounts. I questioned her about it, but she refused to tell me where the money was going. She said that it was her inheritance to do with as she saw fit."

I had visions of someone blackmailing her or some slick gigolo involving her in a romance scam. "Did you follow up on where the money was going?"

'What she said was true. I couldn't tell her how to spend her money. But then she told me she planned to sell the cottage. She said she had to do it to get the funds needed to take advantage of a great opportunity. I reminded her that the cottage was only in her care, that it was meant to be a family legacy passed down through the generations. We got into an argument. She wouldn't budge on her decision. I stormed out."

I remembered the fight Edgar overheard. "This was the day before she was killed?"

He nodded, "I keep thinking about that final argument and regret that my last words to her were angry ones."

"Why didn't you go in to talk to her that day?"

"I told you; it was early. I wasn't sure she would be awake yet, and, also I was still upset about what she told me the previous day. I just didn't want to get into it with her again. I thought I had a better chance of getting somewhere with her if I approached her calmly with my objections. I planned to talk to her again once I'd cooled down."

"What was the great opportunity she wanted to invest in?"

"She wouldn't tell me that, either. She said she wanted to wait until everything was settled and in place. She said it was something that she'd had an interest in for a long time. She said that once it was established, it would be a greater legacy than the cottage, that it would be something that bore the family name."

That did sound intriguing. Though, whatever it was it certainly sounded like an expensive one if she had to sell the cottage to pay for it.

He could be telling me a pack of lies, but why else would Diana suddenly decide to sell the property? "Do you think she was going to tell Alex about her plan to sell the cottage before she was killed? Her housekeeper said that Mrs. Drover planned to speak to her son about something."

"That may be. She took me totally by surprise, but I'm sure she would have wanted to tell Alex about it herself." He took a large gulp of his coffee, which I'm sure was cold by this time. "Lynn probably told you about the falling out Alex and I had. Alex seemed as shocked by the news that his mother wanted to sell the cottage as I was. I think that is one of the reasons he got so angry with me. I was the bearer of bad news."

"And you think that whatever it was she planned to do could be in some way connected to why she was killed?"

"I think if we find out why she wanted to sell the cottage, it might lead to someone who has information that could point us in the right direction."

I realized that, somehow, I'd entered into a partnership with someone that, up until that point, was my prime suspect for Diana Drover's murder. However, I was beginning to question whether he was the one to kill his aunt, and he had some ideas worth following up on. I just wanted to make sure that I didn't lose sight of the fact I could be wrong. What if he was guilty and leading me down a blind alley?

Ben said, "I think I need more coffee. Do you want more tea?"

When he returned to the table, he said, "I checked my aunt's Westport house for any paperwork to give me a clue as to what she wanted to invest in, but there was nothing there. I haven't been able to search the cottage in Madison because the police said they weren't through there yet. The last update they gave me, though, they said I would be able to go into the house in another day or two."

I wondered if they had decided there was nothing else to find since Lynn was being charged with the murder. "I heard that they found some papers scattered around the room where Mrs. Drover was murdered. Do you think there might be something in them?"

"They returned the papers to Alex. He let me see them, and they all look like they are part of a family history. I don't know who wrote it. It is handwritten, the pages are yellowed, and much of the ink faded, so it looks old. It could have been written by either our great-grandfather or our grandfather. From what I read, the building of the cottage had a great deal of meaning to my great-grandfather Keeley. He had just come home from World War One. While there, he had seen many of his friends killed. He looked at the cottage as a place where family and friends could always be welcome and celebrate good times. It was only a partial history, whether it was ever finished or not I don't know." He cleared his throat, "Anyway, there was nothing in them to tell me what my aunt was up to."

I had perked up at the mention that he, or someone, would soon be able to get into the cottage to look for more clues. I thought of something else. "What about the knife used to kill her? Alex said his mother had hidden it away somewhere; how would the killer know about it?" I didn't want to add that Ben certainly knew about it.

He grimaced, "When I went to speak to her the day before she was killed, I noticed she had it, along with the two medals her grandfather was awarded, sitting on the top of the desk at the cottage. I asked her about it, and she said she had been going through some old mementos. So, the knife would have been in plain sight."

Then, whoever killed her would not have had to look very far for a weapon. "How do you suppose it got into Lynn's studio?"

He shook his head, "I honestly have no idea."

It had not been publicly revealed yet that Lynn was being investigated for the murder, but it had been no secret either that she was a suspect. Could the real killer have heard about it and decided to set her up? How would they know about the studio she was renting? I thought about the notes left on my car and at Lynn's condo. I thought I was being followed the day my note was left. Could someone have been following Lynn also and knew where she went and what she did?

Ben interrupted my thoughts. "I'll see if I can look deeper into what my aunt's planned investment was. Maybe if we get an idea if that had anything to do with her murder, we can trace it back to who is trying to frame Lynn."

"All right. When you get word that you can go back into the cottage, I'd like to come." I could see the look of uncertainty on his face. "Please. Two sets of eyes are better than one, right?"

"All right." Just then, his cell phone dinged. He looked at the message, and I thought he blushed. "I need to go. I have someone…anxiously…awaiting me back at my place." He grabbed his jacket and said, "I'll call you when I hear about the cottage."

Chapter Twenty-Seven

Even though Lynn was forbidden to physically be around anything to do with Mrs. Drover's murder, I knew she would want an update on what I'd discovered. Bruno and I went to her condo early the next day.

The first thing I noticed after she let me in was that she had fresh flowers on nearly all the surfaces in her kitchen and living room. "Are you doing a side hustle as a florist now?" I asked.

She looked exhausted, like she hadn't been sleeping well, but she laughed. "No. Alex has been very remorseful about the comments he made after my release on bail."

"This is a lot of flowers!" I kept thinking about the phrase "he doth protest too much" but didn't say anything.

"Yes. It is." She put the kettle on and said, "Please tell me that you have been able to discover something that will help my case."

"As a matter of fact, I think I have." I told her about Ben having a gap in the timeline of his alibi, and his explanation about where he was during that time. Her lips tightened when I told her he claimed he was trying to arrange Alex's bachelor party.

"That's something that the police can check," she said.

"Yes, if I can convince them to look deeper into Ben's alibi. I'm sure they can get his search and phone history." I thought for a moment, then said, "I have to admit that I'm beginning to believe what Ben said, though. He said that he thought that in spite of what the police found, you are innocent. Then he totally threw me for a loop by offering to work with me to help find the real killer."

Lynn seemed to be considering what I just told her. "I'm glad to hear at least one other person thinks I'm innocent. But do you think he is trying to throw you off the scent by offering to work with you?"

"I thought of that. But something was really bothering him about the way his aunt was acting before she was killed. He said she was keeping some plan secret. It may have had nothing to do with her murder, but it is another avenue to explore."

Lynn smirked a little, "Looking back now, I realize that right before Alex's mother was killed, she hadn't been butting into our wedding plans as much as she had been before. Maybe she did have something else to distract her. At the time I was just glad she had stopped trying to push her suggestions for caterers and the only florists she felt worth using on us."

"In any case, if Ben will let me look around the cottage with him, maybe I can find something that will make the police want to reopen the investigation." However, I suddenly felt less sure that meeting Ben alone was such a good idea. In explaining my plan to Lynn, I realized what kind of a chance I was taking by believing his story. I didn't even want to think about what Justin's reaction would be when he found out I was going to a murder scene with someone who could potentially be the killer.

As if reading my thoughts, Lynn said, "I really want you to be able to get in there to find out if there is anything to point to the real murderer, but I can't let you put yourself in such a risky situation. Maybe there is another way to get you into the cottage. I can ask Alex if he will lend you the key and you could go on your own."

"That is a great idea!" I was sure I could come up with an excuse for why I changed my mind about going with him when Ben called me. "I can't get into the cottage anyway until the police give the all-clear. In the meantime, I can try to find out who was trying to frame you by planting the murder weapon in your studio. Think back to right before the police found the knife among your things. Was there anyone who seemed to be hanging around near the building, or watching you?"

"No, I never saw anything suspicious. After what happened last fall, I think

I would notice if someone was following me. As far as who might have been hanging around the building, I'm still not familiar with all the other people who have a business there, so I don't know who belongs and who doesn't." I could hear her sigh, "Besides, there are a lot of shops and little restaurants in the area, there are always all kinds of people who are coming and going."

She was right, but maybe someone who worked at one of the other businesses did notice something unusual before the knife was found. Also, I wanted to know who had called the police claiming to be from the cleaning company. "Do you remember the names of the businesses on either side of your studio? Maybe one of the people who work there noticed someone out of place."

She looked as if she was thinking for a moment. "There is a small coffee shop across from my studio. I never stopped in there, but it looks like it is usually pretty busy. There is a florist shop right next door to me on one side and a yoga studio on the other. I did talk to the woman who teaches yoga one day when I was there. She said her name is Amy, I think. She is very nice, if a little talkative. She seemed very interested in my painting and admired a few I had on display. She then went into a rather long-winded explanation about how she got involved in yoga and what it meant to her. I think she wanted me to enroll in one of her classes. Anyway, she mentioned that she was getting ready to move her business to a larger studio, so I don't know if she is still there."

The yoga teacher would be my first stop. In my experience, people who loved to talk also noticed a lot of what was going on around them. Though, I kept my fingers crossed that whoever had gained entry to Lynn's studio had done so when the woman wasn't in the midst of a yoga class and not paying attention.

My plans changed as soon as I got to Lynn's studio. There was a van pulled up in front of where the yoga studio must have been. It featured the outline of a very muscular man holding a bucket and mop aloft and was marked Tidy Titans. I remembered what Mr. Ross said about them primarily having the units cleaned after someone vacated the premises. I had evidently missed my opportunity to speak to Amy, the yoga instructor, but maybe someone on this crew knew if anyone had reported something they found to the police. I approached a young man putting a floor polisher back into the van. He lifted the polisher easily but looked half the size of the titan portrayed on the company logo.

"Hi. I was wondering if this is the team that usually cleans the buildings in this complex."

"Yeah. Usually. Why?" He reached down to grab some floor cleaner he had placed by his foot and put it into the back of the van.

"Have you ever been in the unit next door? Maybe someone requested an extra cleaning be done?"

He shook his head, "Nope. Not me."

Just then another, slightly older guy exited the building. He was huge. It looked like he could easily have modeled for the titan on the van. The first young man turned to him. "You did an extra job in unit 4C last week, didn't you?"

The other man nodded, "Yeah. It was all above board, though. The office got a call and said the tenant wanted the floors touched up. The tenant also asked if we could look for a box by the side of the building. They thought maybe they forgot to grab it when they were unloading some of their stuff from their car. The office said they asked if we found it, could we move it inside when we did the floors again."

I think my heart actually skipped a beat. "You said it was someone from the office at Tidy Titans who called you?"

"Yeah. That's where they said they were calling from. Who else would it be?"

I didn't answer. "Did you look in the box they asked you to put inside?"

His look became more guarded, "No. I just did what they asked. I figured it was just more paint and stuff. Looks like the tenant is an artist or something."

I tried to keep my voice calm, "Did you call the police to report finding something odd in the studio?"

"Why would I call the police? The only thing odd about the place was that the floor did not need doing again. Whoever is leasing it did a good job of putting tarps down, and all so as not to get paint all over."

"The person who called you about moving that box inside the studio, was it a man or a woman?"

"I don't know. Could have been either. It was just someone from the office. Why?"

The younger guy looked like he just remembered something and leaned over to whisper something to the other guy. I caught the words "police" and "weapon." The older man looked startled.

"That was here?" He looked at me then, "I don't know who you are, but I just do what the office says. I don't know anything about what happened here. I just started this job a month ago and I don't want any trouble. We got to go."

"I need you to tell the police what you just told me."

The young guy slammed the back of the van closed, and without saying another word, both men hopped in and drove away. I hadn't gotten any names, but I was sure the police could find out who they were. I dialed Sunny as soon as I got back in my car, but my call went to voicemail. I tried calling the desk at the police station then.

"It's very important that I speak with Detective Cody. Could you please ask her to call Melanie Bass when she comes in?"

The dispatcher hesitated a moment, but then said, "Detective Cody is out on family leave for the time being. Perhaps I should connect you to someone else."

I paused, not sure what to do, but finally, I said, "Would it be possible for me to speak to Detective Crane, then?'

I waited several minutes on hold before he picked up my call. "Yes, Ms. Bass, what can I do for you?"

"I know how the knife that was used to kill Mrs. Drover got into Lynn's studio. I spoke to the cleaners who take care of the complex where her studio is. One of them admitted he got a call from their front office saying that the tenant wanted some extra work done and that she left a box outside and asking if they could put it in her studio. Lynn never made that call, and the cleaning company only cleans after the tenant moves out. Someone else made that call, whoever it was is setting Lynn up." I tried to keep my voice even, but I realized I was out of breath and practically squeaking by the time I finished.

"That's a pretty wild theory. Who was this cleaning guy who told you this?" His voice was dripping with sarcasm.

"I didn't get his name, but you could call the company and find out." Even as I said it, I got the sinking feeling he wouldn't follow up.

"I understand that you really don't want to believe your friend is guilty, but she is being charged with the homicide, and it will be up to a jury to decide if Ms. Duncan is innocent or not."

I played one last card, "I'm sure Attorney Booth will be glad to speak to the gentleman who works for Tidy Titans. I think his account of how the murder weapon got into Lynn's possession will put significant doubt about Lynn's guilt in a jury's mind."

There were several seconds of silence, then Detective Crane sighed and said, "What is the name of this company?"

He had already ended the call before I realized I had failed to mention that there was a gap in the timeline of Ben Woodrow's alibi. I was still unsure whether I believed Ben's explanation of where he was and whether or not he was the one who killed Diana Drover. Amanda Booth was very happy when I called her to let her know what I found out from Mr. Tidy Titan. I had given it a bit of thought and realized that since there was a coffee shop directly across from Lynn's studio, whoever called the cleaners pretending to be from their office could have watched from there to make sure the box ended up in Lynn's studio. I shared this thought with Amanda, but as we agreed, since the shop was usually busy, it would be impossible to pinpoint who that might have been.

I tried to contain my elation at having solved the problem of how the knife got into Lynn's studio. It didn't explain who had actually killed Mrs. Drover, but it debunked the strongest evidence they had against Lynn.

Before heading home, I decided to swing by Sunny Cody's house. I stopped to pick up a small plant to bring her. I felt bad bothering her when she had problems of her own, but I wanted to make sure she was all right. Her car was in the driveway, so I went to ring her doorbell.

When she answered, it was obvious she hadn't been getting much sleep. "Hi. How are you doing? I heard you were having some family issues, and I wanted to make sure you are all right."

She motioned for me to come in, "My dad had a heart attack. He's had bypass surgery, and he is stable now, but I was just on my way to the hospital to relieve my mother."

"Oh. I'm sorry. Is there anything I can do?"

"No." She gave me a weak smile, "But once he comes home, I know a great nurse, who I'd like to request to do his follow-up visits."

"I'll be glad to. I don't want to bother you anymore right now, so just let me know how he is doing."

"No, no. I have a few minutes."

She went into the kitchen to get us both a glass of lemonade. When she came back into the living room, Katie's dog Beanie was following her. "Thankfully, Katie's best friend's family has been great about having her over to play while we deal with my dad." She sipped her drink. "Anything new with Lynn Duncan's case?"

I told her about Ben, explaining where he was during his lunch hour on the day Mrs. Drover was killed and about what I found out from the cleaning service. "I called Detective Crane with the information, but I'm not sure he plans to follow up on it."

She cursed under her breath, "Do you believe the guy who told you this?"

"Yes. I don't think he realized at first why I was asking about him going into the studio, and he volunteered the information about bringing the box in there."

"I'll make sure Crane follows up on the information you gave him. It puts credible doubt on major evidence. I'll make a call to the captain. I can frame it as something that, if once confirmed, could make our department look like buffoons if it comes to light that we didn't investigate the lead."

"Thank You."

"I'll see what we can do about confirming Ben Woodrow's story, also."

"I'm sorry. I didn't intend to bother you with this. You have enough on your plate right now." I had to admit I did suddenly feel a weight lift off my shoulders, though.

"No. It's important. Like I said, this throws doubt on the case against Lynn. Besides, it gives me something else to focus on besides sitting and worrying while I watch my father's heart monitor."

"Speaking of which, I'd better let you go relieve your mother. Let me know if there is anything I can do for you."

As I drove home, however, my joy at having an explanation for how the murder weapon got into Lynn's possession dampened. What if they couldn't find the guy who brought the box into Lynn's studio? He was pretty spooked when he realized that whatever was in the box was linked to a crime. What if he took off, afraid he'd be implicated somehow? I decided to put those worries aside for now. I had to let Lynn know what I had found out.

Chapter Twenty-Eight

It was almost dinner time when I got home. Bruno's dinner time, anyway. I took him out into the backyard to play for a few minutes before I fed him, and my neighbor Jenny saw us and came over.

"Hi, Melanie! Hello, Bruno!" Bruno began to wag his entire body and leap up, licking her hands. "I was just going to check and see if you were home yet, or if you needed me to feed Bruno for you." She squatted down to pet him and let him give her kisses.

I felt a stab of guilt, I really hadn't been spending as much time as I usually did with the poor dog. I was so glad I had such a caring dog walker. "Thanks, Jenny. I appreciate that you take such good care of Bruno for me when I'm not here."

"It's no problem. I love doing it." She stood up and smiled at me, "I think that after I finish high school, maybe I'll go to school to become a vet, just like Dr. McKenzie!"

"That's wonderful! You'll be an excellent veterinarian." The mention of Justin gave me a twinge. After I called Lynn, I still needed to talk to Justin about my plan to go to the cottage to look for something to point to Mrs. Drover's real murderer.

I fed Bruno and then gave Lynn a call. "Don't get too excited. We need to make sure the police verify his story, but one of the cleaners from Tidy Titans was the one who put the box with the beach bag containing the knife into your studio." I told her about talking to the men and how one of them was tricked by someone claiming to be calling from his employer.

It sounded as if she burst into tears. "Oh. Melanie, thank you! That's wonderful!"

"Well, I went to Detective Crane with it, and he was less than enthusiastic about the information. Until I told him I was also going to let your lawyer know what I found out. Also, I told Sunny Cody, and I know she'll make sure they follow up on it."

"I certainly hope so." She took a deep breath, "I called Alex right away after you left. I explained you have heard from Ben that they may be able to get into the cottage again soon. He was surprised; he said no one had notified him. Anyway, he thinks it's a good plan for you to go to the cottage to see if there is anything you find that will clear me and shift the blame to the real killer."

"Really? He didn't have any objections to me going there?"

She chuckled, "I think he would agree with anything I suggested at this point to prove his faith in my innocence."

"He didn't want to go to look around himself, did he?"

"No. I could hear the panic in his voice when I asked him that same thing. It is going to take more time until he can face going there. Anyway, I asked about the key. He called me back a little while later, saying he searched his house and can't find it."

"He has no idea where he left it?"

"No. He said he usually keeps it with several other keys on a keyboard in his kitchen, but it isn't there. He said he doesn't remember the last time he saw it. He hasn't been to the cottage in several months. He wonders if he left it on the side table by the door the last time he was there."

This put me back where I started as far as searching the cottage.

Lynn continued, "He was adamant, though, that you had nothing to worry about concerning going to the cottage with Ben. He said Ben told him he planned on booking something in Key West for the bachelor party, so that part of his story checks out. Also, Alex said in spite of their recent tiff, he could no more picture Ben hurting his mother than he would himself."

All very well, and I was hoping that was true, but I had been in enough situations by now where I had misjudged the amount of danger involved. "All right. I'll think of something. Somehow, I'll get into that cottage."

My next call was to Justin to invite him to stop over for dinner the following night. I knew it would be best if I talked to him in person to explain my plans.

As I traveled between patients the next day, I ran over in my mind ways I could explain my decision to meet Ben at the cottage in Madison. Each time I came up with what I thought was a rational explanation of why it was not a foolhardy decision, I could hear the squawk of his objection. Objections that were certainly based on common sense.

By the end of the day, I still hadn't come up with a convincing argument.

I made shrimp scampi for dinner, one of Justin's favorites. I knew that culinary manipulation was not going to be enough to fend off any protests he had about what I planned to do, but it wouldn't hurt to at least get him in a good mood.

I almost wavered on my whole plan to investigate the cottage myself as soon as Justin walked in the door. The feeling of both comfort and excitement I felt when he kissed me hello made me realize that part of the security I felt in my life now was due to him. Not that I felt I couldn't handle myself when I went out on a limb, but that he was always there holding a safety net.

"Ohhh! Something smells good!" he said as he straightened up after greeting Bruno.

"I hope the amount of garlic I used won't disrupt the rest of our evening," I said, wiggling an eyebrow.

"Never!"

Over dinner we talked about what each of our days was like, and I held off mentioning anything about Lynn's case until we were having tea and coffee. I was eager to let him know about finding out about the knife, but still trying to find a way to broach the subject of going to the cottage alone with Ben.

"I went to talk with some of the business owners around Lynn's studio to see if they noticed anything suspicious going on before the knife was found. I hit the jackpot! I spoke to the cleaning crew and found out one of the workers was tricked into bringing the suspicious box into her studio."

"Really? That's wonderful!" He beamed at me, but then gave me a stern look, "I assume you called the police."

"Right away. They need to take it from here. I think it will put a big dent in the evidence against Lynn."

"Good work! I hope it didn't involve any sleuthing in dark alleys."

He was getting a little too close to the next thing I needed to discuss with him. "No, the men were very cooperative, I just was lucky enough to ask the right questions." I waited until we went to sit in the living room until I said, "We still don't know who killed Mrs. Drover, though." I explained my theory that Ben Woodrow did have time to kill his aunt and my meeting with him where he denied it. That he claimed he was working on the bachelor party for Alex during his lunch hour that day. And finally, I was beginning to believe he might be telling the truth.

"You believe him? He could be making that up. Can his search or call history be checked?"

"I'm sure the police could do that. They could get a court order or something if they believe him to be a suspect. Up until now, Detective Crane has concentrated on Lynn." Justin had his arm around me as we talked, but now I inched away so I could look at him. "Ben thinks his aunt was involved in something that may have put her in jeopardy. He hasn't been able to find what that was by searching her house in Westport, but he can get access to the cottage in Madison pretty soon. I talked him into letting me go with him."

I waited for Justin's reaction. He remained calm and didn't speak for a minute. I briefly thought that he didn't see a problem with my going.

"So, let me get this straight: you plan to go to a fairly secluded spot, alone, with someone who may or may not be responsible for killing a family member? And he knows you are determined to find the killer?" He looked at me as if he was waiting for me to answer.

"I know it sounds reckless, but if he is the murderer and he is alone, he could clean up any lingering evidence before someone else finds it."

"And if you are there, he could also get rid of someone who could pin blame on him. Namely, you."

I began to argue with him, but he cut me off.

"I'm glad you told me before you just went ahead with your plan, and I assume you want to know what I think of it. No. It is not safe for you to go alone to meet this guy."

I had thought in advance of one argument for when he objected. "I will set up an arrangement where I keep in touch with Lynn to let her know everything is all right. It worked before." Sort of, I thought. "I am actually having doubts now about Ben being guilty, anyway."

He shook his head, "It's not safe. If he is guilty, he could hurt you before you can call for help. You can't go alone. I'll go with you."

I looked at him with amazement. "You will?"

"I told you I wanted to help you since you insist on being involved in this investigation. When Ben notifies you he is going to search the cottage, call me, and I'll arrange to meet you there."

I felt a sense of relief. I didn't care what Ben said when I showed up with Justin. If he objected, it would make me even more sure it was the best choice not to show up alone. "Okay. Deal." I leaned in to kiss him.

* * *

I was pleased to get a call from Justin's grandfather, Charlie Duggan, when I got home from work the following day. I hadn't had a chance to call him to tease him after I found out he was seeing a lady friend.

"What's this I hear about you cracking the case for the police? I'd say you were in the wrong profession, but you aren't bad at taking care of ornery patients, either," he said.

"Thanks, Charlie. I haven't exactly solved the murder, but I hope what I found out will be enough to get Lynn off for Mrs. Drover's murder," I said. "And what's this I hear about you charming a lovely lady into going out with you?"

"Oh, nah. It happened the other way around. Next thing I know, I'm being dragged to one thing, then another. The woman's a whirlwind. I was the one corralled when I wasn't paying attention."

"You don't sound too upset about it!"

"Well, you know…it's kinda nice having something to do besides sitting

187

around by myself listening to the police scanner, waiting for something big to happen. Loretta was a 911 operator; she still has a thing for following police business, too. Besides, she ain't too bad looking!"

"I'm really happy for you."

"Thanks, but never mind that. Justin says he's going with you to check out the murder scene, see if there is anything the cops missed. Says you were thinking of going alone with the victim's nephew, who just could turn out to be the killer."

"I'm not sure about Ben, but I have to say I'm glad Justin volunteered to come along."

"I'm glad you finally saw sense. I'd have insisted on going with you myself if he didn't," he said.

I believed him, too. "The only problem is I'm not sure what we're looking for."

"Well, you never do. Until you find it."

Charlie had spent over thirty years working in security and still liked to get involved in anything having to do with solving a crime. "Ben did mention looking for some paperwork that might tell us if his aunt was involved in something that put her in danger. Though, I would think that if there was anything to find, the police would have found it when they investigated."

"Maybe. Maybe not. Depends on how obvious it was."

I knew Charlie was right. But I was counting on the fact I'd recognize any clues I found in her paperwork, or if Ben did, that he would share the info with me.

I heard Charlie's doorbell ring in the background. "Gotta go. That's Loretta. We're going to some play at the Ivoryton Playhouse tonight. Be careful. Watch out for Justin, too."

I ended the call, glad to hear Charlie sounding so happy.

The call from Ben Woodrow came two days later. "I received notification from the police that I can get into the cottage now. I plan on going tomorrow. I can meet you there at noon. If you're still interested in taking a look around, that is."

"Yes. I want to see if there is anything there that can clear Lynn." I didn't add that I would be bringing along my own personal bodyguard to make sure I wasn't already in the presence of the murderer.

"I'm not sure what is left after the police went through everything, but I'm hoping there is something they missed that will give us some clues. There could be something still there that on the surface didn't look suspicious but could lead to why she was killed."

What he said sounded a lot like what Charlie had told me. "Okay. I'll meet you at the cottage at noon." I began to feel a sense of excitement at the thought of finally getting a chance to rummage around at the crime scene.

I called Justin as soon as I ended my call to let him know I would be meeting Ben the next day at the cottage.

"I'll reschedule my afternoon appointments, so I can meet you there. Do *not* go into the cottage with that guy until I get there."

"All right. Be sure to be there by noon though, otherwise it's going to look strange that I don't go inside with him." I also was worried that if there was anything that he didn't want me to see, Ben would have time to get rid of it before I got a chance to find it.

* * *

The next day, as I got ready to go to meet Ben, Bruno followed me to the door, letting out small plaintive yelps.

"You stay here. I have to go find something to help Auntie Lynn," I bent to stroke his head. When I straightened up and put my hand on the knob, he increased his whining and barking. This was not like him. He seemed to really be upset, most likely because I had been leaving him alone a lot lately. On the spur of the moment, I snapped on his leash, saying, "Okay. You can come. Uncle Justin can keep an eye on you while I do what I need to."

I had timed it so I got to the cottage fifteen minutes early, but there was a gray Mercedes that looked vaguely familiar, already parked in the circular driveway when I got there. It looked like Ben arrived early, also. I was more eager than ever to get inside, but I knew I had to keep my promise to wait for Justin.

I decided to take Bruno for a walk around the grounds while I waited. If Ben saw me, I would tell him I needed to walk my dog before we got started. I wanted to get a good look around the outside of the house first, anyway. Obviously, the police had done a thorough search, but again, I was hoping to notice something they might have missed.

We walked toward the back of the cottage, where it faced the water. I was once again struck by the view. It was a beautiful, warm day at the end of April, and this part of Long Island Sound seemed unusually calm. In the distance, I could see two sailboats gliding along. As I walked around to the side of the house, I noticed the house next door, the one which had been vacant when Mrs. Drover was killed, now looked like someone had moved in. There were lounge chairs set up on the back patio and a wheelchair parked next to the house. The wheelchair looked like one of the large wheeled all-terrain ones. The car in the driveway had out-of-state plates, but I couldn't make out where they were from. I wondered since these people were not from the area, if they had heard about the murder that had occurred on this property.

I checked my watch and realized it was a few minutes past noon, but Justin still hadn't arrived. I was just about to call him when my phone dinged and I saw he had sent me a text: *Emergency this AM. dog ate sock. needed surgery. be there ASAP. WAIT!!"*

I could feel a tightness in my chest. I needed to get inside the cottage before I lost my chance. I was surprised Ben hadn't already checked to see what I was doing out here. Unless, he didn't realize I had arrived already. I went back to the rear of the cottage and led Bruno up the stairs to the wrap-around porch. The drapes on the windows were open, and I peeked in one of them. Bruno seemed to think this was the best adventure ever and sat quietly at my side. From what I could see, it looked like the door opened to what once was called a great room. I didn't see anyone at first, but then I could make out a form moving back and forth at the far side of the room. It looked like a woman, though. I had assumed the car parked out front belonged to Ben, but was it one of his sisters instead?

I rapped twice on the door and then pushed it open and stepped inside. "Hello?" As I thought, the room I was now standing in looked like it was a combination family and living room. It had an open floor plan and seemed to take up the entire back part of the house.

At my greeting, the woman spun around, grabbing her chest as if I had startled her. It was Celia Pound.

"Hi. I was supposed to meet Ben here. Have you seen him?" I said.

She gave me a shaky smile, "No. He's not here." She seemed to have suddenly noticed Bruno. She looked at him as if he was something I'd dragged in on my shoe.

"You brought your dog?"

"Yes. He's well-behaved." As if on cue, Bruno once again sat patiently by my side.

Why was Celia here, and how had she gotten in? "Was the door unlocked when you got here?"

She raised her chin as if evaluating both me and Bruno. "Alex heard that the police were through with their investigation here, and he said I could look around."

That didn't explain how she got in. I thought Alex couldn't find his key.

She continued, "There are a good many valuable paintings and early twentieth century pieces here. I offered to get them appraised for the family."

I remembered she worked at an art gallery in the city. Looking around, I could see that she was right. However, I had not gotten the impression from Ben that they planned to sell any of the antiques here. I wondered if Alex had discussed the possibility with the rest of the family.

She had obviously regained her poise, as when she continued her voice sounded very commanding, "You said you were supposed to meet Ben? Why? If I may ask." She looked at me expectantly.

I didn't like her proprietary manner, and I realized that something about her had always rubbed me the wrong way. "I was hoping to find something to help clear Lynn Duncan's name; she is being wrongly accused." I had no intention of telling her that initially, but her attitude made me want to be blunt.

She grunted. "From what I heard, the evidence says differently." She walked away to examine one of the paintings beside the stonework fireplace.

I stopped myself from snapping back at her that the evidence had changed. I had learned that arguing with such people rarely altered their opinion. Besides, I realized I had just done what Justin asked me not to do; I had gone into the cottage without him. But Ben wasn't here, I reasoned, so I hadn't totally broken my promise. I turned away from watching what Celia was doing, and I shot Justin off a quick text: *In cottage. Ben not here yet. woman named Celia Pound here so not alone. Plus, I brought Bruno for extra protection! XX*

I didn't want to waste any more time since Ben hadn't gotten here yet. This way, I didn't have to look over my shoulder and worry he was about to do away with me.

Celia looked at Bruno again, who had started sniffing tentatively around the room, "He's very cute, but I am allergic to pet dander, so kindly keep your dog with you and away from me."

With that, she began to examine a side table in the room, pulling out drawers, feeling under the edge of the top surface, and peeking underneath. I assumed she was looking for defects or refurbishing that might decrease the value.

"Don't worry, he won't bother you." I signaled Bruno to follow me, and I went straight to an area I noticed in one part of the large room. The rear of the house was in shadow at this time of day, but the area that drew my attention had two large windows that looked out across the back lawn to the water. This was apparently used as a writing or office area. There was a small sitting chair, and a large kneehole desk with swivel chair positioned so that whoever sat there had a stunning view. The desk clearly dated from the early twentieth century. I knew this because Mrs. Paine had one like it in her house, and she told me once that it belonged to her grandfather. She had had it appraised, and although it was worth "a pretty penny," she told me there was no way she would ever sell it. I wondered if Celia had already had a look at this one.

Before I started rifling through the drawers, I checked to see what Celia was doing. She was still checking behind paintings and under the furniture in the other part of the room. She was acting a bit odd, but as long as she left me alone to look for…something …I didn't care what she did.

The desk had multiple drawers, six large and two banks of smaller ones set back above the writing surface of the desk. I looked in each of them and was disappointed to discover that they all had been nearly emptied out. There remained a few blank sheets of paper, some paper clips, and envelopes and stamps, but no calendars with suspicious appointments or canceled checks made out to our unknown business partner. It looked like the police had been thorough after all and left nothing behind which could implicate someone. I tapped on the bottoms of all the drawers and checked the back panel of the desk, looking for a secret compartment. If there was one, I couldn't find it.

I looked up to see that Celia must have retreated to another part of the first floor. I spied what looked like a formal dining room through one of the doorways out of the great room and assumed she might have gone to search in there for items of interest.

I had been in the house for nearly half an hour. I wondered why neither Justin nor Ben had arrived yet but was actually glad for a chance to look around on my own. I took advantage of the fact Celia seemed to be checking out the furnishings in another part of the house and climbed the stairs to the second level, Bruno pattering up the stairs behind me. Whatever updates that had been made to the house, the stairs seemed to be the original ones. They were not all evenly spaced, and I needed to use the banister and watch my step as I climbed them.

The open staircase was divided into two flights, with a small landing between them. I stopped at the first landing to look out over the room below, searching for a likely place where something could be hidden. Celia had been over the room pretty thoroughly, but she was looking for valuable items, not hidden clues. I would check the room again after I went through the upstairs.

I was immediately drawn to an area to the left at the top of the stairs. It was a cozy alcove that was obviously meant as a small library. There were two reading chairs facing each other and a large bookcase on one wall. The early afternoon light streamed in from two windows behind one of the chairs.

Whoever designed the cottage had taken into consideration the natural light that would be available at each time of day. Bruno sniffed around the base of the bookcase for a few moments, then perked his ears like he heard something and ran downstairs again. A few minutes later, I thought I heard a door close and wondered if Ben had finally arrived or if Justin was here now.

I called down, "Justin? Ben?" but got no response. Maybe Celia had gone outside, or in the best-case scenario, left. "Celia?" I heard a response from somewhere in the house.

"Yes?"

I decided to just keep looking for something incriminating or helpful. It would be easier before either Justin or Ben arrived and the search party got larger.

I could see that some of the books in the bookcase had been pulled out. It looked like they had once been arranged alphabetically, but now a few were haphazardly placed back in the bookcase, and a few seemed not pushed in all the way. This part of the house must have already been searched by the police. I pulled several books from different parts of the bookcase to look behind them, checking for anything that might be hidden there. My search didn't reveal anything, and again, no hidden panels.

After I put the books back in order, I noticed an old-looking edition of Pride and Prejudice sitting on a small side table by one of the chairs. Could it actually be a first edition? I picked it up and examined it, but it turned out to be an edition printed in 1923. It was in very good condition, and I figured it might be worth a good deal, anyway. On the inside flyleaf was an inscription:

> *To my darling but strongly opinionated Granddaughter, Diana, on her fourteenth birthday- This was your grandmother's, and I hope you will come to love it as much as she did.*
>
> *My advice to you as you get older is that you will find honey works better than vinegar.*
>
> *Your loving grandfather,*
>
> *J. Keeley.*

Apparently, Diana had always had a difficult personality. I flipped through the pages; this had always been one of my favorite novels, also. As I turned the pages, a piece of lavender-colored paper fell out. It looked as if it had been crumpled up, then straightened out again and folded in half. I opened it and noticed the date at the top: April 11, the day before Diana Drover's murder. The writing on it was spidery, but the penmanship excellent.

Diana:

You know how I am—a nervous Nellie. I felt in order to protect my investment I must have the Elaine de Kooning I bought from your protégé C. appraised. It turns out it is merely a lovely reproduction. I would not wish to insinuate that it was a deliberate deception, but in any case, I must warn you that I would hesitate to refer this woman to any of your other associates. I will contact you about recovering the funds (not all—it is a good reproduction!) I have remitted for the artwork. Or perhaps you can put me in contact with her, and I will make arrangements directly. Of course, we will keep this unfortunate occurrence between us.

Fondly,

Louise

Charlie's words about knowing what you were looking for when you found it echoed in my mind. I refolded the note again as I heard the creak of the stairs.

"I'd like that, please." Celia stepped toward me and reached to grab the note from my hand. I instinctively turned and jerked it away, shoving it into my jeans pocket.

I turned to face her. "Diana Drover was referring patrons to you." Was this something to do with the big project that she told Ben she was going to invest in? I took a chance and said, "She was also giving you funds. Why?"

I backed away a few feet from Celia and looked for something to defend myself, should I need it.

Her tone was defensive when she answered me. "I mentioned to her I planned to open my own gallery. She wanted to be involved. It was a legitimate deal. At first. All I had to do was to promise we'd name the gallery after her grandfather."

"Did she know all along that you were dealing in fraudulent art pieces?" I was willing to bet that she didn't, and now thought I knew who had a very good reason to want Diana Drover silenced.

"It was only the one time! I am not a crook! I explained that to her. We needed more money, and she wasn't sure she wanted to sell the cottage." Celia's mouth drew into a hard line. "After that old cow told her the Elaine de Kooning I sold her was a reproduction, Diana backed out of our deal. She also changed her mind about selling this place. She said she wouldn't have her family name associated with a criminal. She threatened to ruin me!" She took a couple of deep breaths as if trying to calm herself. "Give me that note."

She stepped toward me and reached out as if to grab the note from my pocket. I shoved her away. "No."

Celia pulled a small gun from beneath the bulky sweater she was wearing. "Give it to me. Now."

I realized that we had been at the cottage for quite some time now, and Ben still had not shown up. I had a bad feeling about that, but I said with as much confidence as I could muster, "Ben is supposed to be meeting me. He'll be here any time now."

She looked as if she was suppressing a smile, "I don't think so. I told him to meet me at the house in Westport. I told him that I had discovered something important his aunt had tucked away there. We have become quite close lately, and it didn't take much to get him to change his plans for today."

Justin. Had I talked him out of coming here by assuring him I was fine? That I was safe because I was here with Celia? "My boyfriend knows I'm here with you."

"This is an old house. An accidental injury would not be uncommon." She waved me toward the staircase.

I suddenly realized I could hear frantic barking coming from outside and that Bruno hadn't come back upstairs. "Bruno!"

Celia shrugged, "He went to the door. I think he needed to go out."

That explained the sound of the door closing I heard. I tried to take a couple of steps to dodge around her, but Celia stepped in front of me.

"Do you really think Mrs. Drover would scrap the whole project? She told Ben she was very excited about something she wanted to invest in." From what I knew of her, I had no doubt that Mrs. Drover wouldn't hesitate to expose Celia, but I was trying to stall for time while I thought of some way to distract her so I could get away.

Celia was visibly upset now, "Oh, she meant it. I admit I lost it first. I started toward her when she told me she was going to expose me, that she refused to throw good money after bad. As I came around the desk, she grabbed that old knife. I never would have hurt her. I only wanted her to listen; to make her understand the fake was only a one-time thing. We could make the establishment of the gallery work. But she wouldn't listen; she just kept talking, belittling me, angry about all the money she had invested already, waving that knife at me. I just had to shut her up."

Celia had me by the arm now; she wasn't much bigger than me, but she obviously had a better workout routine. She dragged me toward the stairs. On the climb up I had failed to truly appreciate how steep and twisty they were. I had been taken unawares and shoved down a staircase once before. I wasn't going without a fight this time, especially since I had no doubt Celia planned on this being a fatal fall.

I could hear Bruno barking and scratching at the front door. I tried using my free arm to brace myself against the wall at the top of the stairs, but she shoved the gun into my back. "I can shoot you instead and claim I thought you were an intruder. Either way, it can look like an accident."

I whipped around and hit the arm holding the gun, ducking down immediately after I did so. She fired a shot which went wild, then regained her balance and body slammed me into the railing at the top of the landing. I could hear it creak and feel it bend outward a little. I grabbed onto her sweater and fought to regain my balance.

The door suddenly burst open, and I heard a female voice say, "Melanie? What the…"

Bruno came barreling up the stairs, growling and barking as he tried to get in between Celia and me.

I heard an angry yelp as Celia tried to kick Bruno away. She pushed me toward the railing again and then turned and shot at the intruder. I heard a muffled scream but took the opportunity to grab for Celia's gun. As we grappled for it, I slammed her against the railing twice. I heard a screech as the nails holding it came out of the wood and then a thud as it totally gave way and Celia fell. I looked down to see she wasn't moving.

I raced down the stairs, Bruno right behind me as I rushed to check on the figure in the doorway.

Nora Stevens was pale, but sitting up now, her right hand putting pressure on her left arm. "What is going on? I saw that woman attacking you."

I went over to where Celia was crumpled on the floor. She was lying at an odd angle and unconscious, but I was glad to see she was still breathing. "I need to call 911." I found my phone on the landing at the top of the stairs, where it must have fallen out of my pocket when I struggled with Celia.

"Help! My name is Melanie Bass. I'm at 23 Sea Shell Road! A woman has been shot, and another woman is seriously injured after a fall." In spite of the circumstances, I felt a pang of guilt since I was the one responsible for Celia's injuries.

"Are you in any danger yourself, Ms. Bass?"

"No. Please send help right away. I'm going to hang up. I need to check on the injured women."

I didn't want to move Celia since I wasn't sure what injuries she sustained in the fall. She moaned as I checked her breathing and pulse again. I grabbed a throw blanket from one of the sofas and covered her before I went back to check on Nora.

Celia's shot had grazed her left arm, but the wound looked superficial. There was a lot to process about what had happened in the past several minutes, but the question that came to mind first was to ask Nora, "Where did *you* come from?"

"Next door. I take care of Mrs. Kinard during the day. I heard a dog barking and came over to let the people who live here know that their dog was loose outside." She nodded toward Celia. "Who is she, and why was she trying to kill both of us?"

I only had time to say, "I'll explain everything later," before there was someone else in the doorway.

"Melanie! What happened?" Justin had a look of total horror and bewilderment on his face.

Chapter Twenty-Nine

I could hear Celia moaning loudly. She had started to regain consciousness as the paramedics loaded her into the ambulance. Even though she had planned for it to be my broken body on the floor, I felt a moment of sympathy for her pain.

A second ambulance arrived to transport Nora to the emergency room, but it took some convincing to get her to agree to go to be treated. She insisted she couldn't leave Mrs. Kinard on her own. She explained that, just as Maryjane had told me, she was now working as a home healthcare aide. Finally, one of the police officers called Mrs. Kinard's daughter at work and promised to get someone to stay with the elderly woman until her daughter arrived.

I was relieved to see that one of the first police officers responding to the call was Officer Bridges.

He seemed to be surveying the scene, then approached me and said, "Ms. Bass, I can't tell you how eager I am to hear what happened here."

That was the first time I had ever heard him say anything remotely humorous. I thought he was trying to be humorous, anyway. I began with, "Ms. Pound was threatening me with a gun, and during the struggle, the banister broke, and she fell." I then proceeded to take him through why I was at the cottage and what had happened from the time I got there until he arrived. By the time I finished, Ben Woodrow had finally appeared.

He looked shell-shocked. "I don't understand. I texted you to say I couldn't make it and that we would have to come here another day."

I checked my phone to see I hadn't seen his text. "I'm sorry. A lot was going on, and I never saw it."

I noticed both Justin and Bruno made sure to stand closely by my side as I spoke to Ben.

He looked toward the departing ambulance, "But…Celia asked me to meet her at the house in Westport. Why was she here?"

"She said she was evaluating some of the antiques for sale, but I'm certain now that she was looking for something else."

"What did she want here?" he said.

I glanced toward the police officers who were examining the broken banister and the floor beneath it. "Your aunt was planning on investing in the gallery Celia planned to open. That was where her money was going and why she planned to sell the cottage. She canceled the deal at the last moment because she found out something about Celia. They had an argument and—"

I didn't get a chance to finish what I was saying as Officer Bridges approached us. "Mr. Woodrow, I'll need to get your statement now, if you don't mind."

From the look on Ben's face, I think he knew what I was going to say anyway.

I picked up Bruno and hugged him to me as the full weight of what had happened settled on me. Justin turned to me, and I expected him to lecture me about once again failing to realize how much jeopardy I had put myself into. I started to say, "I know, but I really didn't think…"

Justin put his arms around both me and Bruno. "Shhh. I'm sorry. I wasn't here. I promised to help you, to keep you safe."

I rested my head against his chest. "You had no choice; you were dealing with an emergency. I knew something was off with Celia. I should have listened to my gut feeling." I didn't add that I did end up doing what I came to the cottage for, however. So, I didn't fully regret my decision.

"Do me a favor, though. When you talk to that guy Ben again, I want to be with you," Justin said.

I looked up at him, "Why? He had nothing to do with his aunt's murder."

"I don't like the way he was looking at you and how close he was standing."

I laughed, "You have nothing to worry about, but okay."

* * *

I called Lynn as soon as I got home. I wished I could see her face when I relayed the whole story.

"I knew that Celia was up to no good. That…ugh!" she sounded enraged. "I provided a very convenient scapegoat, too. With me out of the picture, she could dig her claws into Alex again."

It did seem like that might have been her plan, but then, according to what she had admitted to me, she was involved with Ben now. I thought finding the best one to finance her gallery might have been her true motive. I had another thought, "You don't think Alex gave the key to the cottage to Celia, do you? And he didn't want to admit that to you when you asked?"

"No. No, I'm sure he wouldn't lie to me about that." Lynn paused for a moment as if to reassure herself of what she said. "Celia was at Alex's house several times. Maybe she took the key."

"That does sound like a more likely suggestion." I certainly hoped her theory was right.

Lynn said, "I'm sure the police will notify Alex of what happened at the cottage, but I'd like to be there when they do. If you don't mind, I think I need to call you back later. I'm going to go to his house now."

"Yes, please go. Let me know how he reacts to the news."

She hesitated a moment before she ended the call. "What do you think will happen to me now? Will the charges against me be dropped?"

"I think so, but you should talk to your lawyer about that." I just hoped Celia would confirm what she told me when the police were able to interview her. I had given Officer Bridges the note I found, which certainly showed motive.

* * *

Sunny Cody came to see me a few days later. "I wanted to let you know that they will be officially dropping the charges against Lynn Duncan. Celia Pound admitted to killing Diana Drover. She claims it was in self-defense, and I think she plans to try to get the charges reduced." She gave me a stern look, "I know Lynn's lawyer is informing her of this also, but you didn't hear this from me, okay?"

"Understood." I knew that even if she was convicted of manslaughter for killing Mrs. Drover, Celia still faced charges of attempted murder and assault for what she did to Nora and me. "Did Detective Crane ever contact the cleaning service to find out the name of the man who put the knife in Lynn's studio?"

"Yes, Crane did speak to the guy. He told him the same thing he told you. During questioning, Ms. Pound admitted calling the man."

"How is Celia?" I really hoped she hadn't sustained any permanent disability due to her fall from the second-floor landing. A fall I caused.

"My understanding is she will recover. It is unclear what, if any, long-term problems she may incur."

Sunny must have seen the look of guilt that crossed my face. She said, "As a police officer you learn early on that your primary job is to protect the lives of the innocent, and you can only be able to do that if you also protect your own life. I certainly think that applies in your case, too."

I knew what she said was true, and I knew I did what I had to in the moment, but it would take a little time to stop feeling responsible if Celia had trouble walking again or suffered from another infirmity. "Thank you."

I realized that Sunny must be back at work now. "I'm sorry, I never asked how your father is doing."

"They plan on releasing him from the hospital tomorrow or the next day, so I will hold you to your promise of doing his follow-up homecare," she said.

I smiled, "With pleasure."

As she prepared to leave, she said, "Oh. You can expect a call from Detective Crane."

I cringed at the thought, unsure of what he would want.

She said, "He wants to thank you for your dogged effort to find Mrs. Drover's murderer." She opened my front door, then turned and said, "I have found that he isn't always gracious in his apologies, but he does make an effort."

* * *

Lynn and I went out to lunch and to have a glass of wine at Rose's Vinyard to celebrate the charges against her being dropped. As we ate, I said, "I realized we never planned anything to do while Alex is going on his bachelor weekend. Shall we go away also, or do you want to invite some of the women from High Life Derm and from your art classes for a night out?"

Lynn took a large sip of her wine. "About that. There isn't going to be a wedding in August."

I couldn't keep the shock from showing on my face. "There isn't?" I hoped my relief wasn't as obvious. "I'm so sorry. I know you love him. What happened?"

"No, don't be sorry," she said, "I wonder if I convinced myself that I was in love with Alex. I do care about him, but..." she took a deep breath, twirling the stem of her wine glass. "I have been doing a lot of thinking. How even before Mrs. Drover's murder, Alex was always ready to excuse his mother's behavior, and after she was killed, I could see he had doubts about my innocence. I kept trying to ignore them, to bury my own hurt at his behavior."

I waited for her to continue.

"When the charges against me were dropped I felt such an overwhelming sense of relief, not only was I proven innocent, but I was free marry Alex now. That was when I gave into the realization it was the beautiful wedding I was looking forward to, not being married to Alex."

"So, you decided to call off the engagement."

"Yes. We had a long conversation last night. I told him how his doubts about me made me feel, what it did to me when his mother belittled me, and he tried to excuse her behavior."

"What did he say when you told him that?" I said.

"He denied it at first, defended his actions. I pointed out that showed how little he valued my feelings." She took another sip of wine. "I think he was genuinely upset and sad when I said I didn't want to marry him. But after we both shed a few tears, I think we both felt as if a final weight had been lifted. I know I did."

"I'm glad you finally realized that Alex should have been more supportive, but I'm sorry you had to go through so much to recognize that," I said.

"I guess I was just too focused on having my happy ever after. I should know better by now."

"I love that you always look for a happy ever after! But you deserve to find it with someone other than Alex," I said.

"Thanks. I wonder if we can get our money back for the dresses. Probably not." She looked at me, and we both laughed.

It wasn't until she reached for a piece of cheese with her left hand that I noticed her bare ring finger. She smirked, "He said I could keep the ring. I put it in a safe place, someday I may be ready to sell it."

I suddenly felt a wave of appreciation for Justin and our ever-growing relationship.

Lynn raised her glass in a toast, "Here's to true friends! Who knew what kind of adventures awaited us when we first met?"

I raised my glass to join her in the toast. "To friends!"

"So, what's next?" Lynn gave me a mischievous grin.

I took a deep breath. "Let's see if we can find something to do where the police don't need to get involved." I felt a little blip of apprehension in my stomach as I wondered if I had just tempted fate.

Acknowledgements

As always, thank you to my writers' group, Roberta Isleib and Ang Pompano, for excellent advice and unending support.

I want to thank Ret. Lieutenant William Burns of the Port Authority Police Department for answering my question about police procedural. Any mistakes in police work are my own. Eileen Doyle was an immense help with choosing the artist mentioned in this work. Thank you to Joseph Estrella RN for the information regarding what the day of a home healthcare nurse might look like. My editor at Level Best Books had some excellent suggestions—Thank You, Shawn Reilly Simmons. A big thank you to the Sinc-CT write-in group for giving me companionship, a sense of accountability, and helping to start the writing day off right.

I was very lucky that my own mother-in-law was not like Mrs. Drover, and I hope I bear no resemblance to Mrs. Drover myself in dealing with my own daughters-in-law!

Finally, a huge thank you to my family for their love and support.

About the Author

Christine Falcone's short stories have appeared in publications such as *Imagine, Lancrom Review,* and *Deadfall: Crime Stories by New England* writers. *Cutting Remarks* is the third in her Melanie Bass Mystery series. Prior to her retirement she worked for nearly forty years as an RN in a Neonatal Intensive Care Unit. She lives on the Connecticut Shoreline with her family and her dog Toby who is not nearly as well behaved as Bruno, the beloved canine in her mystery series.

AUTHOR WEBSITE:

  christinefalcone.com

SOCIAL MEDIA HANDLE:

  Facebook: Christine Falcone Author

Also by Christine Falcone

Ex'd Out

Borrowed Trouble